AF410277

FALLING WITH YOU

J. COLLETTE SMITH

Published by Indie Girl Press

Paperback: 979-8-9863070-6-0

eBook: 979-8-9863070-5-3

Falling with You: An Uplifting, Second-Chance Romance

Copyright © 2025 by J. Collette Smith

All rights reserved.

No part of this book may be reproduced in any form or by any electronic or mechanical means, now known or hereinafter invented, including information storage and retrieval systems, without written permission from the author, except for the use of brief quotations in a book review.

This is a work of fiction. Names, characters, places, and incidents are a product of the author's imagination or were used fictitiously, and any resemblance to actual persons, living or dead, business establishments, events, or locales is entirely coincidental.

Cover Design by Evelyne Labelle - Carpe Librum Book Design

First printing: October 2025

To all the dreamers.
Keep reaching for the stars.

1

If Hannah Whitmore was good at one thing, it was diving headfirst into adventure. Traveling, hiking, sailing. But this? This was not an adventure. It was more like a backwards crawl into the shadows where one could disappear, and nothing sounded more appealing right now than disappearing.

Off the grid. Out of sight, out of mind, and hopefully, out of the divorce tornado she'd found herself sucked into. Falls Hollow, Texas was one such place and Hannah coasted into the sleepy little town she once called home with high hopes for a fresh start and most importantly, anonymity.

Too bad the universe didn't get the memo. Her first stop, Donnie's Pack & Fill—a convenience store on the outskirts of town that had been around since before she was born— greeted her with an array of sweet and salty snacks and a magazine rack posted at the counter filled with all the tabloids, each of which her face graced the cover in grainy horrified surprise.

WEALTHY TECH GURU, LUKE MILLER, CAUGHT WITH RISING HOLLYWOOD A-LISTER. WIFE DUMPED!

PICTURE-PERFECT MARRIAGE BLEMISHED—HANNAH LEFT WITH A BROKEN HEART.

WIFE OF MILLIONAIRE TECH GURU OUT—MISTRESS IN! DETAILS OF IMPENDING DIVORCE ON PAGE 4.

Had her life really dissolved into this? She thought of the years she'd spent building the idyllic life in picturesque northern California. Known as the supreme hostess, her love of gardening, cooking, and putting a special touch on everything she created made her home the go-to gathering place in her and Luke's circle. And it was a wide circle at that. Close friends, the who's who of the tech industry, and neighbors from the tony enclave nestled in the hills where they lived spent many weekends gathered on their silky green lawn surrounded by sweeping Wisteria and fragrant herb gardens, mingling and laughing, enjoying her whimsical dishes and fruity drinks. She loved her life. She loved her husband.

At least, she had once upon a time.

Remnants of the drift that had slithered its way into their everyday lives teetered on the periphery of her mind. An ignored detail she had yet to dissect.

Tempted to turn over each glaring trash paper, she fingered the corner of one but stopped when she noticed the young clerk watching her.

"How's it goin'?" he drawled with a lopsided grin. August, Donnie's Pack & Fill's head cashier, so said his name tag, seemed oblivious to her despair. In a way she was thankful. He didn't recognize her as the woman plastered on the covers, and that was exactly the anonymity she craved.

"Going well." She placed a bottled water on the counter and handed him her credit card.

He swiped it and kept talking. Small talk was important

in this tiny town, not that she minded. As long as no one recognized her. That was all that mattered.

"Driving through or staying a while?" he asked, then handed her card back.

"Staying a while," she responded.

"Cool. Enjoy your visit and be sure you check out Café des Amis. It's been a staple around here forever, but the new chef updated it, and the food is amazing."

Hannah remembered the cozy little café run by the Cooper family. Mrs. Cooper's cooking was the epitome of comfort food drizzled with love. She wondered who ran it now.

"Thanks for the tip. I'll check it out." She slipped her card in her wallet, picked up her water bottle, and headed out the door. Inside her car again, she took a long cleansing breath. Ready or not, it was time for a new start.

Driving through downtown Falls Hollow, Hannah caught glimpses of places she remembered from her youth. Café des Amis was indeed still standing, like August said, but it had been spruced up. There was even a pergola with outside dining, which wasn't there when she'd lived here. Belle's Blossoms, the local florist was next door, and Brady's Insurance sat on the other side, but there were a few new shops she didn't recognize: Luxe Lane, a cute boutique, Decadence, a chocolate shop—she'd have to check that one out—and a home goods store. But there was also Wonderland, the most charming bookstore in the world. That had been one of her favorite haunts as a kid.

Considering this was the first and only time she'd been back since moving away with her family seventeen years ago, it was a bit like watching a reel from her childhood play out before her eyes.

It would seem the tiny town had enjoyed a fresh polish. Old places were revived and new ones shined, yet it still effused the quaint coziness of a place hidden from the hustle and bustle of the outside world. It was the quiet she thirsted for.

She hung a left at the end of Main Street and watched historic homes slip by before the road gave way to bends and curves that eased up and down around the hills out toward the lake. It was serene out here. Clusters of live oaks spread out with their spindly limbs as if they were waving *hello*. Parts of the road wound between walls of Texas limestone as the hills rose and fell along her drive. She rolled down her window and inhaled the touch of crispness in the air. Autumn was gently making its way across the hill country.

The change of season a door inviting her to step outside.

She'd rented a small bungalow on the outskirts of town where she could hide away and figure out her next steps. The divorce papers may have been filed, but it was only the beginning of a long road ahead. Luke had filed first. Considering he had moved on with somebody new before Hannah even knew there was anything amiss, he'd had plenty of time to plan.

The day she got served she had been shopping at her favorite farmer's market, buying supplies for a small garden party she was hosting for a neighbor's birthday. A party that never happened. At least, not hosted by her.

Learning about Luke's messy affair while standing in line at the market was like taking an icy plunge in a frozen lake. Biting and sharp and ten out of ten not recommended.

Having that as the catalyst for her to take stock in her decade-long marriage was soul crushing.

She'd been shellshocked and forced into days filled with attorney calls and divorce filings and soul-sucking pitying stares by anyone she ran into. When she'd finished her countersuit, including a request to change back to her maiden name, she'd packed all her personal belongings into her shiny SUV—the one joint asset she was allowed to keep —and left. The end of a "perfect marriage" all boxed up in her car.

She'd left with one thought in mind: get as far away from her shattered life as she could. She longed for anything that kept her mind off the empty shell her life had become. Hopefully, the hush of Falls Hollow would provide it.

The decade she'd spent building a life with Luke had vanished in a blink. Her chest ached at the thought. Where had it all gone wrong? With a purse of her lips, she shoved the notion away. All she wanted to do was settle in, take a breath, and let the calm of nature in this quiet corner of the world soothe her broken heart.

To be fair, Luke had owned up to his mistake. He'd apologized, groveled for forgiveness even, but it didn't change the fact that he'd fallen for his secret girlfriend. The most embarrassing part? Hannah had met the up-and-coming star at a charity event and had invited her into their world. Dinner parties, fundraisers, any event Hannah was involved with she made sure to add the young actress's name to the guest list. If she'd had a glimpse into the future, she wouldn't have welcomed her with open arms, but fate had a way of weaving its story no matter what people did to try and change it.

Given everything that had been laid bare through their separation, would she have said yes to Luke Miller all those years ago if she'd known then what she knew now? When a resounding yes didn't fill her heart, she tucked the uneasy truth away. She wasn't ready to face it.

Hannah rounded a bend, and the turquoise waters of Lake Bonnell shimmered into view. Sunlight danced across the surface in bands of buttery gold. She had forgotten how gorgeous it was out here. Wildflowers dotted the shoulder rimming the road in purple, orange, and yellow. They were imperfectly perfect.

A timid smile broke across her face. Maybe she'd made the right choice in coming here. Inexplicably, her hometown was the first and only place that had crossed her mind when she sought to leave California, as if her subconscious knew what she needed. She'd left Falls Hollow at seventeen, the summer before her senior year in high school, when her dad had taken a job in Richmond, Virginia. At the time it'd been a devastating blow. Born and raised in the small town, it was the only home she'd ever known. She'd left friends and school and a whole life behind.

Starting over as the new girl her senior year was awkward. It had taken her a while to settle in. Teenagers weren't the most accommodating people on the planet, but the hardest part had been letting go of the relationships she'd left behind. One in particular brushed across her mind.

Callan Locke. The name evoked memories of dances and football games and weekends at the lake watching the sun breach the horizon as it melted into the crystal waters and stars took its place lighting the purpling night sky.

Her belly tumbled at the memory. Callan had been her high school boyfriend and first love. She hadn't thought of him in ages, not because she'd forgotten, but because it had taken her all of college to mend the pieces of her shattered heart. The fortress she'd built to protect the fragile remnants was forged in steel, determination, and an iron will.

Leaving him had been the hardest thing she'd ever done, but she'd had no choice. Her family had moved across the country. She'd tried to stay in touch, to hold onto what they had, but he'd ignored every call, every text, even the gut-wrenching letter she'd written had seemed to fall on deaf ears. Guess she hadn't meant as much to him as she'd thought. The acknowledgment had stabbed her in the chest.

With a shake of her head, she shooed the images out of her mind. She hadn't expected such a rush of nostalgia. Callan Locke was probably long gone from this tiny town.

Turning her focus back to the road, she continued past the lake toward the outermost edge of town. It wasn't long before her GPS alerted her to slow down and turn onto a narrow lane that ran alongside a winery.

"That's new," she said out loud.

A sign loomed into view as she drove past. *Hillcrest Vines Family Vineyards* was etched across the top, with bunches of grapes wound around a trellis painted underneath. She knew Texas Hill Country was home to quite a few vineyards, but she didn't know one had sprouted up in Falls Hollow.

The lane curved around and ended at her rental. A small house made of Texas limestone with wood trim sat several yards off the road. With a narrow front porch where she could soak up the beauty of this part of the country, it was perfect.

While it was a far cry from the eight thousand square foot Spanish style rambler she'd shared with Luke, this little hideaway, miles from the noise that had surrounded her, was just what she needed.

Within a couple of hours, Hannah had unpacked and

put her things away. She was always one to make a home out of wherever she was. Her and Luke's travels had taken them around the globe and at each stop, she'd nestled in and created a comforting space where they could kick their feet up and relax. It had once been one of the things he'd appreciated about her.

She glanced at her phone. Two missed texts from her mom popped up. She'd kept up with Hannah's four-day drive across the country, regularly checking in and making sure she was all right. Hannah knew it was more out of concern of what she was going through than tackling the long drive. As an only child, she was the center of her parents' world, which was both a blessing and a curse depending on the day.

With a quick tap, she FaceTimed her mom.

"Hi, honey," her mom, Catherine Whitmore, chirped across the line. A pediatric nurse by trade, her bubbly bedside manner was always on.

"Hey, Mom." Hannah sunk into the plush sofa in the living room. "I finally made it."

"Bet you're glad to be off the road." Mom chuckled, her smile lighting up her grass green eyes. Hannah had inherited her mom's eyes, but that was where their similarities ended. Unlike Mom's curves and petite frame, Hannah took after her dad. Long, lean, and athletic. She'd played volleyball growing up but fell out of love with it sometime during high school. Now, she relied on Pilates and jogging to keep herself in shape.

"You have no idea," Hannah said.

"How much has Falls Hollow changed?" Mom asked.

Most of Hannah's parents' friends had also moved away within a few short years of their exit. It was the reason they'd never visited. They didn't know many people who still called this little town home.

"Not that much, really. I mean, it's been well taken care of and there are a few new places in town, but it's still the cute little place I remember."

"Kind of like Pine Hills?" Hannah's parents had moved from Richmond to a quiet town nestled in the Blue Ridge mountains after her dad had started working from home. They loved the cozy ambiance of the community there.

"Yeah, kinda," she agreed.

"So, what's up first on your agenda?" Mom asked and Hannah knew that was her way of gently nudging her to not withdraw from the world. After what she'd been through, and her subsequent decision to escape to Falls Hollow, her parents worried she'd tuck away in the hills licking her wounds, afraid to put herself out there again.

Hannah knew better. She needed time and space to get her bearings, but she wouldn't hide forever. Eventually, she'd find her path.

She hoped.

"There's a winery next door. I think I'm going to walk over there and check it out."

Mom's face lit up. "That sounds fun."

"I've heard there are some great wineries over there." Dad's face popped in front of Mom's.

"Hey, Dad." Clad in a lightweight sweater and baseball cap, her dad flashed his dimpled smile. "Golfing today?" Hannah asked.

"Heading out now. It's good to see you, honey." He blew her a kiss.

"You, too, Dad." She waved at him, and he moved away revealing Mom's face once more.

"Ben, don't forget we're meeting the Harrisons for dinner at six." Mom called out to Dad. "Sorry, hon. Guess I'll let you go. Let me know how the winery is."

"I will. Bye, Mom." She waved at her mom and ended the call. Seeing her parents' faces, even if by phone, always made her feel better. She was thankful for them. Now more so than ever.

It didn't take long for her to realize who her real friends were after she and Luke separated. Sadly, only a couple rallied by her side. And now they were over seventeen hundred miles away living in a world she no longer occupied. This escape to Falls Hollow was about more than figuring out her next steps.

It was about finding who she was.

She'd spent so many years taking care of her and Luke's home, hosting parties, and volunteering for one thing or another that she'd lost touch with herself. Who was Hannah Whitmore? It was a burning question she didn't have the answer for. Yet.

She grabbed a sweater, tied it around her shoulders, and headed out the front door. Today was the first day of the rest of her life. With God's grace she'd make it a good one. Somehow.

2

Hannah ambled across the wide field toward the winery. Brief gusts of wind blew her long chestnut hair around her face, whipping it from side to side. The sun beamed overhead in the late afternoon sky, sparking bursts of warmth on her skin. It was the perfect fall day with bright skies and birds zipping and diving down to the ground, then back up again in their whimsical flights of fancy. She fluttered her eyes closed and inhaled a deep breath, taking in the fresh scents of wildflowers and grass and new possibilities.

The winery's parking lot held only a few cars. Hannah crossed the black pavement and entered the shop. As soon as she crossed the threshold, she was welcomed by the heady scent of cheese, fruit, and the earthy fragrance of lavender. Tall ceilings with arched trusses rose over her. Strands of tiny white lights wrapped around them creating a cozy ambiance. She padded across the stained concrete floor in her flats eying the displays filled with wine and gifts, cheese and crackers. This was her kind of place.

She stopped at a tasting table where two little chalkboard signs sat in the middle of a tray of cheese, crackers, and jam. Beautiful cursive writing scrolled across each, one detailing the creamy goat cheese and the other high-lighting the locally made raspberry jam. Unable to resist, she scooped up the cheese on a cracker and using a tiny silver spoon topped it with a dollop of jam. She popped the treat in her mouth and let out a hushed moan. It was delicious.

She spun around to see which pairing of wines on the shelf behind her were recommended when she bumped into a man hurrying past.

"I'm so sorry. I didn't see you there," she blurted, embarrassed.

He turned to face her and placed his hand on her arm steadying her. "No, it's my fault. I was rushing past." He gazed down at her with mocha eyes, and she glimpsed something familiar, something that went far beyond a simple glance.

He canted his head, his eyes narrowing into a question, an answer, a surprised realization.

"Hannah?" His husky voice strained.

"Callan?" Her mouth went dry. Of all the people in the world, he was the last person she expected to see. She figured he would have left Falls Hollow long ago for college and then whatever would come next. Callan had been an all-star baseball player in high school with a promising future. He could have had any pick for college. Maybe even a pro career. What was he doing here?

"What are you doing here?" They said in unison.

An uneasy laugh tumbled from her lips.

"I live here," he said as if it were the most obvious thing in the world.

A plethora of questions raced through Hannah's mind.

Too fast for her to make sense of any one to ask, so she blurted the first word that came to mind. "Still?"

"Yeah." He relaxed his hands on his hips. The gesture sent her back in time to the first conversation she ever had with him. She'd been standing in the hallway of their school, Falls Hollow High, talking to one of her friends when Callan strode by with some guys from the baseball team. They'd stopped when one of his friends started talking to hers. The homecoming dance was three weeks away and the guy had decided asking her friend to the dance in front of everyone was the safest way to get a yes. He'd been right. Her friend had accepted, giggling and blushing the whole time.

Hannah had glanced at Callan and rolled her eyes. He'd plopped his hands on his hips and lasered in on her. "Guess you already have a date?"

"No. Are you asking?" Hannah had teased. Beyond having him in her French class, a subject he was awful in, she hadn't known the newest member of the Falls Hollow High Roadrunners baseball team. They'd only been a month into their freshman year, after all.

"Maybe," he'd quipped.

She'd folded her arms across her chest feeling uncharacteristically bold with this guy. "Well, if you ask me properly, I might say yes."

He'd taken a step back, his arms spread wide to nudge his friends to the side, then dropped on one knee. "Hannah Whitmore, would you do me the honor of attending the homecoming dance with me?"

He'd known her name. Hearing it rumble from his lips had made her belly tumble and she'd said yes. By the time the dance had rolled around, they'd become inseparable. It was a connection that had lasted almost three years, until that late summer day in August when she'd said goodbye. The memory soured her stomach.

She drew herself back into the present. "I thought you would have moved away a long time ago."

"Not everyone moves away."

Four words that sliced through her sharper than a shard of glass.

Her defenses rose. "Not everyone has a choice."

His Adam's apple bobbed as he swallowed, and she couldn't help noticing the way his light blue chambray shirt lay open at the hollow of his throat. Seventeen years was a long time, but he wore it well. If anything, he'd grown into his rugged good looks well with tousled light brown hair that framed his chiseled face. The tiny cleft in his chin gave him the right amount of boyish charm. And Callan had always oozed charm.

"What brings you back to town?" He shifted from one foot to the other and buried his hands deep into the pockets of his jeans. Changing the subject was never a smooth act for him. When he was focused on a topic, Callan could talk for hours. He liked to flesh out every thought, every detail, before moving on, and right now his gaze scrutinized her from head to toe as if he could somehow delve into her mind and read her thoughts.

Hannah was glad he couldn't.

His switch to casual conversation was forced, but she could only imagine the number of images racing through his mind because she was experiencing the same. Picnics at the lake in their favorite spot, baseball games with her cheering him on from the stands, and cool fall nights spent gazing at the stars lighting up the big Texas sky. First love. High school romance. Memories of a simpler era when life unfolded one easy day at a time.

She hadn't thought of Callan in years, but seeing him here, in the flesh, initiated a wave of nostalgia to crash over her. Her lungs tightened searching for air. With a quiet, cleansing breath, she willed her nerves to settle.

"It's a long story," she said.

Where to begin?

How much did she want to share?

She hoped he wouldn't ask.

"Well, Falls Hollow hasn't changed too much."

"I noticed when I drove in, although there are a few new places."

"Yeah, I guess so."

"This place is new." She turned to glance around the shop, and he nodded at her comment on the obvious.

"So, what do you do?" She had no idea what else to say.

The awkwardness between them grew into an uncomfortable bubble.

"Oh. My. Gosh. Hannah Whitmore?" A high-pitched voice squealed.

Hannah whirled around right into the arms of a young woman who squeezed her in a tight hug. When she let go, she leaned back, and a huge grin lit up her whole face.

"How long has it been?" The young woman asked.

Wearing the same type of chambray shirt, except in a pale lavender shade, the young woman had a long ponytail of honey blonde hair pulled high that accented defined cheekbones much like Callan's.

Recognition hit Hannah like a thunderstorm.

"Lizzy?" Her eyes darted between Callan and his younger sister.

"What are you doing in town?" Lizzy asked.

"It's a long story." She and Callan said in unison, although his clipped tone bore an air of sarcasm.

She ignored him and kept her attention on Lizzy.

"I'm only in town for a while. I rented the little bungalow next door." She flipped her thumb toward the front entrance, and Lizzy let out a laugh.

"I know exactly where you're talking about. That's—"

"Don't you have a tour and tasting to host, Lizzy?" Callan interrupted.

"Actually, I need you to take it. One of my orders just arrived and part of it is missing, so I have calls to make."

Callan's jaw tightened, but he didn't argue.

"Do you work here?" Hannah asked.

"This is our family's winery. Didn't Callan tell you?" Lizzy asked.

"Um, no. He didn't mention it."

Callan slid his hands out of his pockets and folded his arms across his chest all business-like. "It didn't come up."

"You should go on the tour and tasting with the next group. It starts in five minutes, and it's the best way to see everything here," Lizzy added with a burst of enthusiasm.

"I didn't sign up or pay or anything—" Hannah tried to back out, but Lizzy wouldn't hear of it.

"It's free for old friends." She winked.

Guess she was going on a tour of the winery.

"Okay." She looked at Callan who was a pillar of stone. Unreadable eyes, rigid jaw, and a stance that said *enter at your own risk.*

"The tour meets at the back of the store." He nodded toward a narrow alcove leading to a door.

"Sounds good. I'll go wait over there." She faced Lizzy. "It was great seeing you again." She squeezed Lizzy's arm, then slipped past her eager to escape Callan's glare.

While the tour and tasting sounded delightful, the host was decidedly not, but Lizzy gave neither of them a choice.

"It's great to see you, too, Hannah. And hey, make sure Cal shows you how to check the progress of fermentation with the wine. He skips the interactive part of the tour sometimes." She angled her head toward her brother and gave him a playful shove as she hurried away.

Two years younger than Hannah, Lizzy had looked up to her when she and Callan had dated. They'd always gotten along well. It was kind of nice seeing her again after all these years.

Too bad she couldn't say the same about Callan.

3

———

Hannah huddled with the rest of the tour group at the back entrance of the winery. It wasn't a very large group. Two older couples who appeared to be on a trip together, given the pieces of conversation she overheard, and two girls, maybe college age, who were immersed in an animated discussion about one of their "insufferable" ex-boyfriends.

Callan strode up, all long legs and attitude. Hannah considered faking a phone call to bow out of the tour, but a tiny voice in her head reminded her she'd done nothing wrong. Her family had moved because of her dad's job. Leaving Callan wasn't something she'd wanted to do; she'd had no choice since they'd moved several states away to Virginia.

She'd tried to keep in touch with him, but he'd ghosted her as if she'd never existed. If he had a problem with her being here, that was on him not her.

She channeled her inner gracious hostess persona and plastered a broad smile across her face. He side-eyed her and kept walking, stopping at the head of the group.

"Hi, everyone. Welcome to Hillcrest Vines Family Vineyards. I'm Callan and I'll be taking you on today's tour and tasting. Our tours are casual, so please, feel free to ask questions."

"How long has this winery been here?" one of the older men asked.

"My family bought the land sixteen years ago and it took us five years to produce our first vintage: a sauvignon blanc that won as best debut at the Hill Country Wine Festival," Callan answered with a sense of pride.

Hannah had no idea his family had started a winery, but to be fair, she had no idea what happened to Callan after she left Falls Hollow. Their story ended seventeen years ago.

"If you're all ready, we'll head out for the tour." He opened the back door and walked out.

The group followed and Hannah waited to tag along at the end. Putting space between her and Callan was probably a good idea given the pointed glances he kept casting in her direction. She wanted to act like an adult about this unexpected run-in, but her nerves seemed to be as rattled as his. She found herself clutching the shoulder strap of her purse like a lifeline.

Normally, she would have enjoyed a wine tasting. Not today.

Callan led the group into a separate building where large steel vats were housed. He launched into his presentation of how storing and fermenting in stainless steel tanks was the preferred process with sauvignon blanc, which was the type of wine their winery produced. His knowledge was impressive and his passion for the subject reminded Hannah of how jazzed up he used to get before a game. The memory of it tickled her.

"How long does it take to make the wine?" one of the older ladies in the group asked.

"Great question," Callan responded. "Fermenting takes about two weeks. After that, the wine is moved to a steel tank where we let it age for four months before bottling. White wines age quicker than reds, which means we can go from harvest to bottle sooner."

The tour progressed out to the vineyard where rows of grapevines wrapped around trellises spread out across acres of land. With rolling hills, it made for a picturesque scene. Hannah could see how this life would appeal to someone. Creating something from scratch, tending to it, growing it, and building it into something tangible, something real, and something all your own was a massive undertaking but the reward would be so sweet knowing it was all yours.

As they ambled down a row one of the young girls stared, whispering to her friend while giving Hannah a look that spelled trouble. She knew that look. This girl recognized her.

Heat flamed up her neck into her cheeks and she casually rested her palm against her neck trying to hide the blush burning through her. The last thing she wanted was for anyone to figure out who she was. Especially in front of Callan. So far, he hadn't given any indication that he knew about her troubles and for some reason she couldn't quite pinpoint, she wanted to keep it that way.

The girl who had been whispering to her friend leaned closer. "Are you Luke Miller's wife?" Her tone was hushed but not as silent as Hannah would have liked.

"You must be mistaking me with someone else," Hannah responded a little too quickly.

She hated lying, but she did not want to have this

conversation. Not here. Not with a stranger. Not with anyone.

The girl tilted her head to the side, eyes narrowed. "You look just like her."

One of the older couples standing nearest to Hannah glanced back. Callan was deep into explaining the harvesting process and they appeared less than thrilled that she and this girl were chatting away.

Hannah flashed them an apologetic smile and they turned around giving their attention back to Callan. She faced the young girl and spoke as quietly as she could.

"I'm sorry. You're right, I was married to Luke, and now I'm trying to distance myself from all that. As you can imagine, this is a very difficult time for me, so if you'd please, please, do me a favor and not let anyone know who I am. I'd like to work through this privately."

Her emotions bled through her words and the young girl seemed to understand. Maybe she took pity on her. Who knows? At least she agreed to keep it between them.

The tour wrapped up in a barn-like building that had an overhead door on one end and French doors on the other. Both were open to let the breeze rustle through. A long rectangular table made of thick oak sat in the center with matching benches on each side. A round iron chandelier hung overhead with tapered lights made to look like candles. Paintings by local artists hung on the walls. An antique buffet sat along one wall with a beautiful vintage tea set in the center that looked like something straight from a French country estate with gold trim and a burst of roses painted around the delicate porcelain pieces.

Lizzy joined the group with a palpable energy Hannah remembered from their youth.

"Now it's time to wrap up with the best part of the tour—

the tasting," she trilled. "Grab a seat while Callan gets today's selection, and we'll get started."

She pulled glasses from a rack on the opposite side of the room from the buffet. One by one she placed them on the table in front of each guest.

Hannah watched Callan slip out of the tasting room, and the second he was gone, the young girl who recognized her took the seat next to her.

"I hope you don't mind me asking, but how are you going to hide from all the press? I mean, everyone knows who you are. You were kinda married to a kajillionaire."

Lizzy glanced their way, not close enough to overhear, but close enough to notice the girl's vested interest in Hannah. She shifted uncomfortably in her seat.

"Well, Falls Hollow is a small town. I'm hoping I can just blend in and not be bothered. I don't think people around here are all that interested in that kind of stuff. At least, that's what I'm hoping."

She tried to be as polite as possible, but she wanted this girl to leave her alone. The less attention she got the better.

"Maybe not. But Austin's close by, and people like me know who you are. This place is becoming kind of a hotspot for tourists."

"Good to know."

Please, for the love of all that's good in this world, end this conversation.

The girl's friend tipped her head forward and swiveled to face Hannah. "Is it true that Luke's girlfriend is pregnant?" she whispered in a half-hearted attempt to be discreet.

Hannah was tempted to excuse herself from the tasting, pretend she was getting a call or remember a previous appointment, but she worried her abrupt departure would raise questions. Especially with the way Lizzy was eyeing her.

"I don't know." She shook her head praying they would drop it.

Callan re-entered the room. "Here we go," he announced.

Hannah had never been so happy to see Callan Locke stride into a room.

Relieved, she crossed her legs and shifted her body to face the other end of the table where he set down three bottles. The two chatty friends behind her quieted. Maybe they finally got the hint.

Callan handed a bottle off to one of the older gentlemen seated to his left. "Please pass it around so everyone can take a look while I uncork these."

He lifted a bottle in his hand and Hannah noticed the rugged sturdiness of his grip. They'd been teenagers when she'd last laid eyes on him, and while he'd been an all-star baseball player he was still a boy. But now, Callan Locke was all grown up. Adult Callan had filled out in all the right places turning him into a striking man.

His eyes slid in her direction and when their gazes met, a riot of butterflies took flight in her stomach. She cleared her throat hoping to settle the swarm in her belly.

No such luck.

What was wrong with her?

Chatty Girl tapped her on the arm. She turned, prepared to defend another onslaught of questions. Instead, Chatty was handing her the wine bottle being passed around.

Hannah took it. "Thanks."

She ran her fingers across the label. Sepia edges gave way to a cream shade in the middle where the words *Hillcrest Vines Family Vineyards* was printed in burgundy lettering, an image of grapevines wrapped around a trellis just below. Simple but elegant. Her favorite way to pair things.

Callan popped the cork and poured a tiny amount into his glass, then he walked around the table pouring the same amount in everyone else's. When he returned to the head of the table, he picked up his.

"If everyone will pick up their glass and hold it up to the light." He waited while everyone did as he instructed.

His eyes lingered on Hannah, and a flush came over her. It would seem his focus was as rattled by her presence as hers. She raised her glass and zoned in on the contents. Liquid the color of pale golden sunlight settled, cool to the touch, and she watched as the light from the overhead chandelier played across the shimmering goblet highlighting the crystal-clear wine within.

"From this angle you can see the clarity of the wine. Look to see if there's any debris floating about or sediment settling at the bottom, which are things you don't want to see." Callan held his glass out and turned it slowly from side to side inspecting the liquid.

Hannah noticed the discerning gaze he leveled on the wine. He was truly studying the contents, making sure his creation was perfect. Something about the intensity he put into what he was doing gave her a tiny thrill. This was more than a job to him.

Luke's work had always been about being the best, launching the newest facet in technology before anyone else, and of course, the money. He liked fancy things. Not that there was anything wrong with wanting to be successful, comfortable, but their financial position became his guiding principle. It wasn't passion or a love of what he was doing, it was ambition.

He was a guru of software development and nothing

excited him more than leading the charge with the next big thing.

When she was in the thick of it, his drive to achieve more settled in the back of her mind. It was who he was, not her. But now that she was on the outside looking back in, she realized how far she'd fallen out of tune with herself. The idea unsettled her.

"Next, gently swirl your glasses. This aerates the wine and releases its aromas." Callan's voice interrupted her thoughts.

Hannah followed each step, entranced by the command he held over the room. She enjoyed the sensation of being a newcomer, a novice to the world of wine tasting, although she was far from, but Callan had a way of making it feel like her first time.

Maybe it was the huskiness of his voice that captivated her. She'd always loved the sound of it when he'd whisper in her ear. The way it would shudder down her spine.

"Now, bring it to your nose and take a deep inhale." He did as he instructed alongside everyone else. "Sometimes closing your eyes can help you process the different notes better."

He fluttered his lids closed and took another big whiff of the golden liquid.

She knew how to do it, but Callan's love for his family's wine oozed from his pores, in the way the faint lines in the corners of his eyes relaxed and disappeared, the hint of a smile curling up one side of his mouth as he breathed in the aroma.

She swirled her glass, brought it to her nose, and soaked in the cool, fresh scent. The first note that hit her was citrusy. Grapefruit, to be specific. An aroma that was crisp, tart with a hint of sweetness, and overall perfect. It was followed by the scent of fresh-cut grass. She had to admit she was impressed.

"Finally, for what you all came here to do: taste." He let out a small chuckle and the rest of the group did the same. "When you take a sip make it small and let the wine coat your palate. Notice the balance of sweetness, acidity, and other flavors. Focus on the taste, the texture, and the overall impression of the wine. When you swallow, pay attention to the lingering taste and texture, which is the finish."

Callan tilted his glass to his lips and took a small sip, demonstrating how to let the wine linger in his mouth while savoring the notes releasing before finally swallowing. His lids closed once more, fully immersed in the experience.

Everyone followed his lead, each taking a sip from their glass and holding it for a beat before swallowing. A few "mms" whispered around the room.

Hannah relished the long finish and the well-balanced flavor that lingered after she swallowed. Hillcrest Vines' selection was a surprising delight.

"So, what did you notice?" Callan glanced around the group, hopeful.

"It's really crisp. I like that," one of the older women said.

"I taste fruit, but I'm not sure what. Maybe lemon?" her husband added.

"It's citrus, so you're on the right track, but it's not lemon." Callan swiveled his head side to side waiting for someone else to jump in.

"It's grapefruit." Hannah set her glass down.

Appreciation spread across Callan's features oddly satisfying her. She wasn't interested in showing off her flavor profile skills but giving him the answer he was searching for reminded her of how well they used to read each other's minds. It had been a long time since she'd experienced that level of connection. A disconcerting revelation.

He pointed a finger at her, a grin playing across his lips. "That's it."

"Whatever's in it, it's good," Chatty Girl said as she took another full sip.

"Mm-hm," one of the older women agreed.

"Please enjoy the rest of your glass. Lizzy has some appetizers to go with it." He motioned toward his sister, who approached the table with a charcuterie board in her hands.

She placed it in the center of the table, then grabbed a stack of dishes from one of the buffet cabinets. After passing them around the table, she reached for a stack of napkins sitting on top of the buffet and handed them out.

Hannah was so engrossed in the tasting she hadn't noticed Lizzy leave or return.

"Tug on your ear if you need rescuing," Lizzy whispered to Hannah when she handed her the napkin.

Hannah's eyes rounded. Had Lizzy noticed something pass between her and Callan?

"What?" she whispered back.

Lizzy slid her gaze toward Chatty Girl, and Hannah's heart almost stopped. Had she overheard their conversation? If Lizzy found out about her life in California, then that was as good as Callan knowing, too. Lizzy and her brother were close. They didn't keep secrets from each other.

Hannah gave her an indiscreet shake of her head. If she acted like nothing was bothering her, then maybe Lizzy would assume it was all a misunderstanding.

Lizzy winked. "Don't worry. Your secret is safe with me."

Blood drained from Hannah's face leaving her clammy. Lizzy knew everything.

4

———————

Hannah stood at the register with a bottle of sauvignon blanc, a pack of goat cheese, a box of crackers, and a small jar of the raspberry jam she'd tasted. She wanted to hurry out, but she truly enjoyed everything she'd tried. Plus, it would be rude not to buy something.

While the young girl behind the counter tallied her purchase, Callan walked over, hands in his pockets.

"That was a good guess back there." He leaned back against the counter sizing her up in one glance.

"This wasn't my first wine tasting." She handed the cashier her card.

"I gathered that."

A beat hung between them and Hannah wondered what he was thinking. If what Lizzy said a few minutes ago was true, then Callan had no idea what kind of life she'd left behind. That didn't mean he wasn't curious though.

The girl handed Hannah her card.

"Thank you." Hannah tucked the card in her purse and picked up the paper bag full of the products she'd bought.

"It was good seeing you again, Callan. This place is amazing."

Something shadowed across his features, and he rose to his full height towering several inches over her. "Thanks."

He pulled his phone from his back pocket and grimaced at the screen before shoving it back in his pocket again.

She wanted to ask but decided it was best to let it go. The less she involved herself with him the better. She was hiding out, not on vacation.

"Well, I better go put all this up." She started to walk away and hadn't made it three steps when he called after her.

"Why are you here, Hannah?" His voice rumbled behind her.

She froze. Couldn't he let it go?

Turning slowly, she racked her brain for a reasonable answer. This wasn't a topic she wanted to get into, especially with Callan, but she'd never been good at lying.

"I'm going through some changes right now, um, switching career paths and stuff. I thought Falls Hollow would be the perfect place to rest and recharge while I iron out my plans."

Not a lie but not exactly the truth either.

He studied her, nodding. Whether he bought her response or not, she couldn't tell.

"What do you do?"

Her throat constricted. "Huh?" she mumbled through pressed lips.

"Your career? What is it you do?"

All those times she'd reached out to no avail, not even a whiff of acknowledgment, and now he wanted to talk. An ember flickered inside her, and not the warm and fuzzy kind.

"I was in marketing, but I didn't get as far as I'd hoped." Given that her degree was in marketing, there was a nugget of truth to that statement, however small it might have been. She had the diploma just no job to back it up.

Meeting and falling for Luke several weeks after graduation hadn't been part of her original plans. Theirs had been a whirlwind romance. Introduced at a party through a mutual friend, Luke had asked her out by the end of the night. He was whip smart and quietly charming. They'd gotten married within eighteen months when she was only twenty-three. Five years older and infinitely curious, Luke had already started his career in the tech industry where his brilliant mind pushed him leaps and bounds beyond his peers.

Hannah had been content to be his steadying force, his sense of home. She hadn't thought she'd given up a career but instead had changed course, and together they'd built a life she'd enjoyed. One that had ended with a bang.

Standing here face-to-face with Callan, the perfection of that life paled.

"So, what are you doing now?"

Hannah's mind whirred. Holding her bag tighter, an idea blossomed. "I'm working on creating a lifestyle brand."

Where are you going with this, Hannah? Stop. Abort. Quit talking!

"Oh. That sounds cool."

"Yep." She rocked on her toes. He bought it.

The lies were mounting up and she didn't like it, but she was riddled with embarrassment. Callan had found such sweet success with his family's vineyard; the last thing she wanted to share was the details of how her life had spun out from underneath her. Not to mention the public shame of having her face plastered all over social media.

Being married to somebody famous made her famous by connection. She had never done anything on her own to earn that level of recognition, but that didn't stop the paparazzi from snapping pictures of her whenever she was out and about around town. As if what she ate for lunch was newsworthy.

Given Luke's infidelity and their impending divorce, she had become a hot target as of late. Something she was desperate to have distance from.

It was one little white lie, she told herself. Besides, after today she'd stay away from the winery, and she'd never see Callan again. Problem solved.

"Well, good luck with it."

"Thanks." *Whew!*

A few more steps and she'd be out the door and away from his piercing eyes. His were easy to get lost in, and she did not need to get lost in anyone's eyes right now. Especially his.

Her time in Falls Hollow was temporary. Once all the noise over her divorce died down, she'd find a place to settle and start over. Maybe Richmond so she could be near her parents.

Leaving again meant no time for attachments. She'd been down that painful path with Callan once; she didn't want to go through that again.

She reached for the door, and Lizzy sprung up out of nowhere.

"Hannah, wait." She squeezed her in for a hug and Hannah could hardly breathe with the crush of the paper bag against her chest. "Did you tell Cal where you're staying?"

"I did." Hannah didn't know why that mattered, but Lizzy seemed to be buzzing over it. When she looked over at

Callan, he shifted his stance with his arms tight around his chest.

His jaw needled from side to side. "My family owns the bungalow where you're staying."

Hannah's ears rang. Did she hear him correctly? She was seconds from walking out the door and secluding herself safely inside the bungalow, hunkered down with enough supplies so she wouldn't have to venture out other than to take quiet nature walks where she could embrace the beauty of her surroundings. Alone.

She needed time. She needed space. She needed the swell of beating wings erupting in her belly to cease.

"Oh, I didn't know."

Of course, she didn't know. Guess the universe found humor in having her find the one perfect place for her to get away and then have it belong to the family of the guy she'd had to walk away from so many years ago. She didn't appreciate the universe's humor.

"With you back in town and staying so close by, you've got to come over for dinner at our parents' house. They'd be thrilled to see you again." Lizzy squeezed her hands together in excitement.

"That's very thoughtful of you, Lizzy, but they don't need to go to all that trouble for me."

Dinners at Callan's house when she was young had always been fun. His parents had loved popping in their favorite CD and cranking up classics from the eighties. They'd all crowd around the kitchen table together and eat, play cards, and relish every moment out loud. Their door was always open for friends and neighbors. You never knew who might be there.

"Please, you know how our parents love company. We go by there a couple times a week for family dinners, and tonight is one of those nights, so I insist. It's no trouble at all. Right Cal?" Lizzy tossed the conversation to her brother who seemed less than thrilled with his sister's invitation.

He shrugged his shoulders, arms still tightly wound around his chest. "Sure."

There was no getting out of it without being rude. But tonight?

Lizzy's inquisitive stare wouldn't let her off the hook.

"Okay, then thank you. What time should I come by?" Hannah directed her attention to Lizzy. She couldn't bear the awkwardness between her and Callan any longer.

"Six-thirty."

"Perfect. I'll see you then." When she reached for the door this time, no one stopped her.

Outside in the fresh air, away from Callan's scrutinizing gaze, she huffed out an extended breath. Curling up on the sofa and enjoying a glass of wine while she ate her weight in cheese and crackers and jam would have to wait. She was having dinner with her high school sweetheart.

TRAILING down the sidewalk along Main Street, peeking in the windows of the shops surrounding the downtown square, Hannah soaked in the last of the afternoon sun while reacquainting herself with her hometown.

It was nice to walk around out in the open without any paparazzi tailing her. Ever since the news of her and Luke's divorce broke, especially with his affair being the reason, guys with cameras seemed to lurk around every corner waiting to catch the right shot. Her frowning or with a sad look on her face were particularly popular. Trying to keep up a façade that she was okay wasn't easy, but she didn't have to do that here. This place induced a level of serenity she enjoyed.

She wanted to put together something for Callan's parents as a thank-you for having her over. A new home goods store, Hearth & Home, sat a few doors down from Café des Amis—a local favorite she'd enjoyed frequenting when she lived here. They made the best lemon lavender cupcakes.

After picking up supplies to make a basket for the Lockes, she popped into the café to grab a half dozen of those scrumptious cupcakes. When she entered, she was taken aback at how the place had been updated but still managed to ooze coziness from every corner. It was even more delightful than she remembered.

She paused near the front counter, waiting her turn. A young guy, maybe mid-twenties and wearing a baseball cap, was helping the customer in front of her. When she used to live here, the friendliest lady was the server, and she always gave Hannah an extra scoop of ice cream whenever she ordered a bowl. It was a sweet memory that hadn't crossed her mind in ages.

While she'd gone to school with the owners' granddaughter, Gemma Cooper, Gemma had been a year older and someone she'd only known as a fellow student at Falls Hollow High. With Gemma in the next grade level, they'd run in different circles. She wondered if the family still owned the adorable lunch spot.

"How ya doing?" the young guy asked when it was her turn.

"Great, thanks."

"Table for one?"

"No, I'd like an order to go please."

"Sure thing. What can I get you?"

"I'd like half a dozen lemon lavender cupcakes, if you still make those?"

"Sure do. That'll be eleven fifty-five."

She handed him her card. He swiped it, gave it back, and she tucked it into her purse.

"You're everywhere, aren't you?"

The voice came from behind her like the low rumble of a finely tuned motor coming to life.

Bracing herself, she turned to respond to the person she couldn't seem to shake.

"Hi, Callan. Long time no see." It was a lame joke, but she didn't know what else to say.

Hello high school crush who's haunting me again. Fancy meeting you here.

Or—

Oh, hi ex-boyfriend who I haven't thought about in years, but now I can't seem to get you out of my head. Or presence.

Or better yet—

Hey, my first love, my first kiss, my first vision of happily ever after. It's great running into you again. And again, and again, and again.

He smirked. For a horrified second, she wondered if she'd voiced her thoughts out loud.

"It's a small town. Running into each other more than once is inevitable."

Her chest deflated in relief. She hadn't uttered any nonsense out loud.

"True."

Hand braced against the counter, he leaned to one side and a thousand images blurred across Hannah's mind: Callan twirling her around by the lake's edge watching her as if no one else existed, scooping her up in his arms after winning a big game, stealing kisses under an inky sky after their first date. Broken pieces of memories she'd buried away, the recollection too raw to process.

His hair still lived in that in-between stage—not too short and not too long. An imperfect mop that soothed his angles. She found herself clenching her fingers together at her sides silently commanding herself not to reach out and swipe that one loose strand hovering over his eye.

"You don't have to come over tonight, if it makes you uncomfortable. I know how pushy Lizzy can be."

"It's okay. It's not like I have anything to do."

Way to be rude AND make yourself sound needy.

He twisted his lips to the side. "Suit yourself."

"Here you go." The young guy behind the counter handed her the box of cupcakes.

"Thanks." She tucked the box under her arm ready to flee this awkward conversation.

While Callan was being polite trying to give her an out from dinner, he also didn't seem enthused about her going. She didn't blame him. She wasn't exactly riveted about the idea either. Especially considering the buzz that sparked when he was near.

"Guess I'll see you later." She gave him a half-hearted smile.

"One other thing." He straightened up and she wondered if he'd had a growth spurt after high school. He appeared to have gained an inch or two on her. "I used to live in the bungalow when my parents first bought the land, and even though we rent it out as a vacation rental now I know there are still some quirks. Like the pipes groan if they haven't been used in a while. Things like that."

"I hadn't noticed anything, but thanks for letting me know." She thought the place was perfect. Cozy, clean, and far from prying eyes. She didn't care if the pipes squeaked as long as she could stow away in a cocoon of privacy. That was all that mattered.

Of course, having Callan and his whole family right next door made that difficult.

"Well, if you have any issues, let me know. I sort of manage the place for Mom and Dad." His tone was blah as if he was required to make her aware he was the acting landlord.

Naturally. It would seem the universe was determined to keep an open link between them. Maybe she should stop by the hardware store on her way back. She was capable of handling minor problems.

But Callan? He was not a minor problem.

5

Ribbon and twine spilled over the side of the small kitchen table where Hannah set up her supplies. The basket in the center was coming together with a few of the items she'd picked up in town. A cinnamon pumpkin soy candle from the home goods store, which was owned by the cutest couple who made a lot of their products themselves, sat next to a bar of oatmeal honey soap. Both smelled so good she had to buy an extra one of each for herself.

She added in the box of cupcakes, with the twine she'd tied around it, and tucked fresh flowers in earthy shades of gold and orange along with greenery inside the basket. Afterward, she wrapped ribbon in a satiny shade of ivory around the perimeter and placed an envelope on top carrying a handwritten note. She stepped back admiring her handiwork. The finished product looked like an explosion of autumn.

Creating beautiful settings always gave her such joy. Whether she was setting a table, making a basket, or decorating her home, she curated the pieces with careful consideration elevating her designs with a thoughtful touch.

Maybe in another life she could have had a lifestyle brand. She shook her head nudging the fantasy from her mind. Given her current circumstances, and what little she walked away with from her marriage, she had no business entertaining such a notion. If anything, she needed to create a resume, however sparse, and start thinking realistically about what she was going to do.

She had enough money to hold her for a while, but it wouldn't last forever. And with the divorce dragging through the court system and any part of their assets she was owed bogged down in litigation, she needed to prepare for her new future—whatever it may bring.

An hour later she was dressed and ready for dinner at the Lockes'. She'd tried on three different outfits going back and forth over which one looked casual but nice, natural yet made her look her best without being too much.

She had a very specific image in mind. It took a while to find it.

With one last glance in the mirror, she smoothed her long, straight hair to one side over the rust-colored dress she'd chosen. Made of cotton with full sleeves that banded at her elbows, a matching sash cinched around her waist, and a skirt that flowed to mid-calf and twirled when she spun, it was the perfect blend of cute, casual, and flirty. Not that she was aiming for flirty, but it suited a fun night out with friends.

The Lockes could still be considered friends, right? Maybe not exactly friends, but they weren't strangers either.

Not wanting to stress about her choice of attire any longer, she scooped up the basket she'd put together and headed out the front door. The sky was showing off with a glorious sunset. Streaks of rich orange melded into varying shades of pink as the sun dipped toward the ground.

Hannah paused to soak in the beauty of it all. Wide open skies, a hint of a chill in the air, and the scent of clean air unfettered by pollution soared over and around wrapping her up in contentment. Her heart melted in appreciation. When was the last time she'd experienced such quiet bliss?

After loading the basket into the backseat, she settled into her SUV and drove into town. The Lockes lived in one of the old homes in the historic district of the downtown area. Lovingly maintained for over thirty-five years, their home was a two-story 1920s era American Craftsman. Four tapered columns with stacked stone at the bottoms spread across the front of the house framing the porch.

Hannah remembered sitting on that porch drinking hot chocolate with Callan, thinking life was perfect. It had been for a while.

Not much had changed. Two wooden rocking chairs with a table between them sat on one end and a long bench that had once been a pew at the local church sat on the other. Callan's parents had purchased that pew when the church underwent renovations. A wreath of fall leaves hung on the front door.

Her chest swelled at the familiarity of the place. The sounds of laughter echoing on the breeze. A fresh pot of spaghetti simmering on the stovetop. Almost three years of memories lived here.

She approached the front door, basket in hand, and knocked. When she heard footsteps pattering on the other side, she sucked in a short breath. The door flung open, and she was greeted with the warmest smile she'd ever seen.

She breathed a sigh of relief.

"Hannah Whitmore, aren't you a sight for sore eyes."

Callan's mom, Connie Locke, pulled her into a snug embrace. Notes of honeysuckle danced on her skin. It was the same perfume she'd always worn, the aroma of it tickling Hannah's nose.

"Hi, Mrs. Connie." Hannah gave her a tight squeeze. She leaned back. "I brought you a little something." She handed Connie the basket.

"Oh, sweetheart, thank you. You didn't have to do that." Connie took the basket from her arms and admired the contents as if it was the nicest gift in the world.

She'd always made Hannah feel like part of the family.

"Hannah! You made it." Lizzy popped up behind her mom. "Come in."

Lizzy and Connie stepped back to make room for her. Walking inside the foyer was a little like entering a time capsule. A wooden chair painted olive green still sat next to the half oval entryway table that had graced the entrance of the Lockes' home since her time in Falls Hollow.

A few new pieces had been added: a mirror framed in gold hung over the table, a large painting of the lake with the hills in the background hung on the wall across from the table, and a basket with birch stalks sat in the corner.

The sense of joy and home still hung in the air.

"Thanks again for having me."

"Of course. Let's go to the kitchen and grab a glass of wine."

Connie led them through the living room and into the kitchen which had enjoyed a complete update. With charcoal grey cabinets, marble countertops, and gleaming stainless-steel appliances, it looked like something out of a design magazine.

"Your kitchen is beautiful." The sight made Hannah

long for her old kitchen, which was just as lovely and twice as big.

She missed it. Mainly, she missed creating her favorite dishes and sharing them with friends.

"Thank you. It was a long time coming, right hon?" Connie stroked her husband's back while he stood over a pot stirring something with a wooden spoon.

"Yeah, yeah, but it's done." Hank Locke, Callan's dad, chuckled and planted a quick kiss on his wife's forehead. When he glanced up, his eyes rounded and a grin as wide as Texas split his cheeks. "Well, look who we have here."

"Hi, Mr. Hank," Hannah said, genuinely happy to see Callan's dad.

As sweet as Connie was, Hank had always been the fun one. The jokester. The one who laughed the loudest at every gathering.

"What brings you back to town after so many years?" He lifted the spoon and inhaled the contents, then picked up a pepper grinder and added more to the pot. He was also the main cook in the Locke household.

"I can tell you what brings me here." Hannah eased over to the stovetop and took a whiff of the tangy aroma she'd noticed the second she'd walked into the kitchen. Hank was cooking up his famous spaghetti sauce. "If you bottled and sold that, you'd make a fortune."

Hank's laugh bounced off the kitchen walls. "Maybe when I retire."

He had been an insurance agent with Brady's Insurance, a local firm, when Hannah was a teenager. Now he and Mrs. Connie owned a vineyard. Strange how life worked.

"Are your parents in town, too?"

Her parents had become acquaintances with the Lockes

when she and Callan had dated, even attending some of Callan's baseball games together.

"No, sir. Just me."

He arched his brow, waiting for more details.

She could only imagine his curiosity over her return to Falls Hollow after so much time had passed. Admittedly, she wondered herself. Sometimes being drawn to a place, or a person, came without a clear understanding. Clarity came with time.

"I'm in between jobs, sort of, at the moment. I booked your bungalow for a getaway while I figure things out."

"Falls Hollow is the perfect place for that," he agreed.

"Would you like a glass of wine, dear?" Connie asked.

"That sounds great. Thank you." Hannah walked over to the narrow island in the center of the kitchen, her purse strap clutched tightly in her hand.

Lizzy must have noticed her fierce grip because she reached for it with an expression of "I got you" etched across her features.

"Let me put this up for you."

Hannah relinquished her lifeline with her phone tucked inside. There was no need to keep it out. She needed a break.

"Thanks," she said as she let go.

She hoped she could let go of her turbulent nerves, too, but when she glanced up, Callan entered the kitchen, and her knees knocked together.

Lizzy eyeballed him when she walked past with Hannah's purse. Hannah figured that was her silent warning for her brother to play nice and not rattle their guest. Unfortunately, his signature scent entered the room with him as well, dizzying Hannah's senses. Earthy cedarwood with a hint of patchouli and that raw edge of danger-meets-nice-guy.

Hannah almost had to fan herself from the fire radiating off his skin.

"What's up?'

The timbre of his voice vibrated against her ears, and she had the sudden urge to curl into his chest and nuzzle into the crook of his neck. She batted the wild thought away.

Never in a million years had she expected to see Callan again, and she most assuredly hadn't envisioned having such a reaction to his presence. It was as if someone had unlocked the vault, flooding her with the emotions of their past that she'd bottled up and tucked away long ago.

Reaching for her wine, her fingers curling around the glass, she brought it to her lips desperate to douse her jitters.

"Just chatting with your mom and dad."

She kept her glass steady in her hand. If anything, she was skilled at proper etiquette. A necessity for any good hostess or guest. She needed to draw on that resolve now and channel it into a nice evening with old friends. That was the best way to view Callan. Otherwise, her mind ran amuck with haphazard thoughts that cluttered her judgment.

"You need any help, Dad?" Callan turned his attention on his dad.

"Grab the bread while your sister sets the table." Hank raised his chin toward the island where Connie had set a loaf of French bread she'd pulled from the oven.

"I'm happy to help, too," Hannah offered.

"There's a tossed salad in the fridge if you want to get that out," Hank said.

"Sure."

She walked over to the refrigerator, a wide Sub-Zero model, and retrieved the ivory ceramic bowl with the salad.

When she set it on the table, her fingers grazed Callan's as he placed the bread next to it, and she noticed the slight jerk of his hand when he pulled away. The gesture unsettled her.

While she was combatting a wave of nostalgia threatening to disarm her, he appeared repulsed by the mere brush of her fingers on his skin. The realization stung.

A young girl around seven or eight bounded into the room wide-eyed and full of energy.

"Hey, Dad, I was supposed to help Bitty with the bread."

Her gaze was locked on Callan and understanding slowly seeped into Hannah's subconscious.

Hannah's chest tightened.

"Sorry, squirt, Pop asked me to put it out." Callan ruffled the top of her head playfully.

Her sun-streaked locks fell in gentle waves to her shoulders. Lapis eyes, flawless skin, and endless curiosity made up the rest of her petite frame.

The girl propped her hands on her hips. "Can I be the taster?"

Callan flicked his thumb at his dad. "Ask Pop."

His dad responded with a curl of his finger beckoning her to come over. Before she did, she narrowed her eyes at Hannah as if a wild animal had wandered into their midst.

"Hi." Hannah gave her a little wave.

The girl slid her hands down her sides. "Hello."

She dared a peek in Callan's direction who squatted beside her.

"This is Hannah. She's an old friend of the family." His eyes posed a silent question, and Hannah responded without hesitation.

"It's nice to meet you. What's your name?"

"Summer." She brushed one side of her hair out of her face.

"I like that name."

A pang squeezed inside Hannah. Same narrow nose, same inquisitive stare. This was Callan's daughter.

"Me, too. My dad picked it out because I was born in the summer." She whirled around and ran over to Hank, obviously okay with Hannah's presence.

Callan rose and slid his hands in his pockets. Hannah felt Lizzy and Connie's stares on her, waiting to see how she'd respond.

Seventeen years of life had passed. A lot could happen in that amount of time. Hannah had been married, and she'd wanted to start a family even though Luke kept pushing that desire further down the road. Callan had experienced a lot of life, too. She couldn't hold that against him.

She gathered herself. "She's precious, Callan."

A relieved grin spread across his face and the sight of it sent a fizzle of joy through her.

"Thanks. She's my little ride or die. She's a handful, too, but so was I at that age."

His mom nodded vigorously, which tickled Hannah. Although she hadn't met Callan until high school, his boldness had been obvious from the start. She could only imagine what he had been like as a young child.

"Mm, mm, Pop, this is yummy." Summer shimmied and handed Callan's dad her spoon.

"Then that can only mean one thing." He paused and leaned in closer to his granddaughter. "Dinner time!" they exclaimed in unison.

It didn't take long for Hannah to settle into the rhythm of enjoying an evening of food and conversation at the Lockes', much like old times. Afterward, she insisted on helping with the dishes. Connie finally handed the duty over to her and Lizzy while she put away the leftovers.

Callan was on dad duty while Hank cleaned off the island and kitchen table.

It had always been like this. Everyone pitching in to do their part.

She and Lizzy worked in tandem: Lizzy rinsed, and Hannah loaded the dishwasher. When she placed the last plate into the rack, Lizzy sidled closer.

"Why don't you catch up with Callan? I'll tuck Summer in and read her a book."

Lizzy was determined to facilitate some sort of conversation between her and Callan, but if Hannah was being honest, she was quite curious about Callan's life after she left. Mainly, she wanted to know why he had never responded to her, but that was a more difficult subject to broach. Maybe she'd save that conversation for another day.

"Okay." She tucked one side of her hair behind her ear.

Lizzy was already in motion, heading into the living room where she took her niece's hand in hers and led her upstairs for a bedtime story.

Ready or not, she and Callan were going to have a face-to-face. Whether she got any answers to her age-old questions remained to be seen. After all, interrogating him about why he'd ghosted her was probably not the best way to start a conversation with him if she wanted any chance at a friendly reunion.

If that was even possible.

6

_____

Callan's parents were in the kitchen putting the cupcakes on a plate. Their lemony aroma was delicious, but Hannah was too full, and nervous, to think about eating anything else.

She took a deep breath and walked toward Callan who was picking up a few stuffed animals around the living room and dropping them into a box by the hearth.

"So, you're a dad." She didn't know how to start the conversation, so she decided to just spit it out.

Callan chuckled. His throaty rumble sent a smattering of goosebumps up her arms. She clasped her hands in front of her pretending like she was perfectly at ease. To be certain, she was not.

"Yeah, for a little over eight years now."

"She's adorable."

"She keeps me on my toes, that's for sure."

Questions burned her tongue, but she pursed her lips holding them at bay.

Where's her mom?

Who's her mom?

They were talking, at least, but he wasn't offering a lot on his own. Maybe he shared the same awkward nerves she did.

"It's getting late. I probably should head back to the bungalow." As much as she wanted to learn more, she didn't want to push.

Maybe it was the coward's way out. This would not be a light discussion, and she didn't know how much she wanted to share about herself. To be fair, she couldn't expect him to do all the talking. He'd have questions, too.

He placed the last toy in the box, then set a timid gaze on her. "If you want to catch up a bit, we can."

It was as formal as an invitation as she'd get and a sign that he wanted to clear the air between them. She took it.

"Sure."

"Would you like a cup of tea? I've developed a habit of drinking a cup of chamomile before I go to bed every night."

"Yeah, that would be great. Thanks."

Her spirit buoyed at more time with him. Maybe she'd finally get some closure. After all, that was all she really wanted, right?

While he brewed the tea, she visited with his parents who were each enjoying a lemon lavender cupcake. They gathered around the island, laughing about old times when Hannah and Callan were younger, adding in anecdotes about Summer being a young female version of her dad with her outgoing personality and high energy.

She filled them in on her parents' life in Richmond, using that as a way to skirt around details of her own life, which she kept to a minimum. Thankfully, they didn't push for more. By the time the tea was ready, the conversation had wound down and Connie and Hank bid Hannah and Callan goodnight.

"Promise you won't be a stranger while you're in town," Connie said to Hannah as she gave her a hug.

"Promise."

Hannah wasn't sure how, but she was going to keep that promise. Seeing the Lockes again had been a balm to her aching heart with their kindness and zest for life.

Luke's parents traveled a lot. She had only met them a handful of times over the years. It was strange how their relationship with their son—their only child—mostly existed through sporadic calls and texts. Her relationship with her parents was so different.

After they left the kitchen, Callan handed her a cup of tea. Steam billowed over the porcelain cup in thin plumes.

"Let's take these outside." He didn't wait for her answer.

She followed him out the back door onto the patio. He sat down in an Adirondak chair by a small table, and she sat in the one next to it. Curious. Anxious. Unsure if she was ready for this.

The house was situated on a large lot with mature trees and a pergola near the back fence with a fire pit that hadn't been there when she'd dated Callan. Moonlight, bright as day, flitted through the branches enough that they didn't need any exterior lights on.

She took a sip of the soothing tea, then placed her cup on the table. "There's nothing quite like a Texas sky."

"Nope," he agreed with a grin. "It's even bigger at my place."

"Really?"

Her belly tumbled at him sharing a tidbit of his life with her on his own. She was glad he'd invited her to stay.

"I live on the outskirts of town, near the winery, on several acres. It's a work in progress." He took a slow sip as if pondering if he wanted to share more.

"The land the winery's on is gorgeous. I can only imagine the stunning hill country views you have."

"I can't complain."

She glanced down at his ring finger. It was bare, which she already knew from seeing him earlier at the vineyard. He caught her staring, and she darted her eyes away, not sure what to say.

He put his cup on the table next to hers and rested his arms on his chair, his hands dangling over the ends.

"I'm not married. Never have been."

When Hannah canted her head to the side, he ran his hand across the top of his head and continued.

"I met Summer's mom in college. She was from Illinois, and she came to UT on a scholarship. We started dating our senior year and continued for a few more after graduation, then an unexpected pregnancy happened, and she decided marriage and family weren't for her.

"Once Summer was born, she relinquished all parental rights to me and moved back home, and we haven't spoken since."

The news punched Hannah in the gut. She'd assumed divorce, not something as tragic as Summer's mom abandoning her. And Callan.

"Oh, Callan. I'm so sorry."

He nodded. "It was tough."

Hannah didn't know what to say. What he had gone through was pure devastation and so different from her own post-college life. She'd breezed through graduation into Luke's arms and an idyllic life most people only dreamed of. Yet in retrospect, it bordered on an emptiness she hadn't noticed before. Not until this moment, sitting here with Callan, witnessing his pain still etched in faint lines across his wide forehead.

Her experience was more like a carousel with beautiful galloping horses spinning endlessly through the same scenes, the view better than the ride.

Her divorce was awful, humiliating, but the raw pain she saw in Callan's eyes did not mirror hers. Hers held anger, resentment, but the hurt was different. Less, somehow.

"Thank goodness you were here, close to family." Hannah shifted her whole body toward him, fully aware of the tiny breach in his wall.

He was opening a door, however tiny of a sliver it might have been, and giving her a glimpse into his world.

"Yeah, they were my saving grace. Summer's, too. Lizzy and Mom pitched in from day one with feedings and diaper changes and sleepless nights. I don't know how single parents do it without help." He shook his head and took a sip of his tea, keeping the cup in his hands as if it were an anchor.

"From what I can see, you've done an amazing job with her."

Hannah longed to reach over and cup her hand around his. It was odd experiencing such a sensation. Callan was from another time, another life, a frozen memory thawing in the gentle autumn night.

Her heart ached for him. No one deserved that kind of loss and heartbreak, especially at such a young age.

"Thanks" He took another steadying sip, a bookend to the personal snippet he dared to share. "What about you? What did Hannah Whitmore get into after leaving us small-town folks behind?"

His comment stung, even though she knew he didn't mean it that way.

"You know it wasn't like that."

"I know. You were seventeen. Moving wasn't your idea."

This was a classic example of one of his uncomfortable shifts from one topic to another, but he'd shared something so private, so personal, it was his way of moving on.

A backlog of questions piled up in her mind. If he understood how out of her control the move was, why didn't he respond to any of her attempts to talk to him? It was like he'd punished her for something she didn't do.

"So, why didn't you answer any of my calls or texts?" She didn't hold back. This was her chance to finally get some answers.

He shifted uncomfortably in his chair before putting his teacup back on the table.

"We were young, Hannah. I don't know."

She opened her mouth to push for more when the back door creaked open.

"Dad, I can't sleep. Will you lay with me for a minute?" Summer poked her little head outside, eyes wide with hope.

"Of course, pumpkin."

"I should get back to the bungalow. It's getting late." Hannah picked up her cup and rose.

No matter how badly she wanted answers, she had to remind herself that his family had been nice enough to invite her over. She didn't want to overstay her welcome.

She had to accept the fact that she may never get the answers to her questions.

"Here, I'll get that." Callan took the cup from her hand and a shiver needled across her shoulders when his fingers brushed hers.

"Thanks. And thank you again for dinner. It was delicious."

"That was one hundred percent my dad." He chuckled.

"Well, thank him again for me." She turned toward Summer. "It was nice meeting you, Summer." She flashed the little girl a broad smile and Summer reciprocated with one of her own.

She glanced back at Callan. "Good night."

There was so much she wanted to say, so much she wanted to know, but that chance had slipped through her fingers in a blink. An ache bloomed in her chest.

"Night, Hannah."

Summer let her glide past, and she found her purse on the kitchen island, slung the strap over her shoulder, and saw herself out. Once inside the safety of her car, she blew a heavy breath between her lips. She hadn't gotten the answers she was searching for, and she had no idea if she'd get another chance alone with Callan. Honestly, she wasn't sure if she wanted to. Seeing him again had stirred up emotions she believed faded a long time ago. Facing that truth was a shock to her already fragile system.

SUNLIGHT STREAMED through the front window dousing the book Hannah was reading in bright light. She'd been up since five and already had breakfast, a cup of coffee, and a stretching session in lieu of her normal Pilates practice.

Usually, she went to a Pilates class three days a week and ran two or three miles every afternoon five days a week, but she didn't have a gym membership anywhere in Falls Hollow, so stretching was it. Maybe she'd do a run along one of the trails around the lake later. Right now, she was enjoying a relaxing morning.

An avid reader, she spent time each morning and each evening reading. She was halfway through a holiday romance, and the descriptions of a snowy mountain cabin had her longing for Christmas time.

Christmases as a kid growing up here with her parents were some of her most cherished memories. While Falls Hollow didn't get snow, it was still a magical place during the holidays. Main Street would come alive with the whole downtown square swathed in twinkling white lights. Storefronts were decorated with wreaths and bows, decorative snowmen and elves, and lots of Christmas cheer.

Christmases in Los Altos Hills where she'd lived the last decade were beautiful, but the generic perfection of the decorations lacked the charm of Falls Hollow. Something she hadn't considered until now.

It would seem the longer she was in this tiny town, the more she realized how she appreciated the simple things.

She tucked her bookmark in her book and placed it on the coffee table. Another favorite morning routine was a long walk. It wasn't something she did every day, but when she could squeeze one in, she did. With the sun greeting the day awake, Hannah tugged on her favorite jacket, hoodie down, and headed out to stretch her legs.

It wasn't long before she found herself nearing the winery. It was as if her feet had a mind of their own, leading her toward the vineyard behind the buildings. The view was scenic with the rows of trellises spread across the field, the hills haloed in buttery rays as the backdrop.

She paused at the start of one row admiring the plump grapes. She leaned in to get a whiff of their sweet aroma. A good wine had always been a part of her get-togethers. She missed those.

An image of her gardens back home, the fragrant herbs and colorful flowers, loomed across her mind. Maybe real contentment was found in the beauty of the things that brought one joy.

"You're up early."

Callan's voice startled her. She could hardly contain the prickle of her nerves tickling underneath her skin before she swiveled to face him, the images in her mind morphing into the vision of the vineyard splayed out behind him in a watercolor of green and gold.

"Hey. I didn't see you there."

"I was a couple rows over when I saw you walk up." Dressed in jeans that hugged his long legs just right before covering his boots, he was the perfect image of a real-life cowboy with the hat and flannel shirt to match. No plaid, but still.

The current that flowed between them was tangible. At least to her.

"I guess this type of work makes you an early riser, too." Hannah tucked her hands into the pockets of her hoodie as a way to ground herself.

"It's a dawn to dusk kind of schedule."

"I bet."

Their conversation last night, cut short before she could get the answers she desperately wanted to know, played across her mind on repeat as she stood there, inches from him. She wanted to ask but couldn't find the words.

Biting the inside of her cheek until it practically bled, she stretched her neck from side to side trying to relieve the knots twisting from her jaw to her shoulder. Talking to him had never been so hard.

"Uh, I'm sorry we got interrupted last night." His lip curled up one side.

She almost sighed out loud. His lopsided grin was always her favorite.

Relief flowed through her like a river unleashed. Maybe some synchronicity remained between them.

"No need to apologize. Dad duty comes first." She chuckled and his shoulders relaxed.

"If you want to walk with me while I check the vines, we could finish catching up."

"I'd like that."

He headed down the row and she moved in step with him.

"I believe we left off with what you did after moving away."

She knew that wasn't where they'd left off. Her last question had been about him ghosting her before Summer had stepped outside halting their conversation. He was stalling, but to be honest it wasn't an easy subject for her either. She'd get back to it, but it was only fair that she disclosed some details of her years after school. How much she wanted to share was another story.

"Well, being the new kid during senior year was challenging, but I got through it, graduated, and went to college at USC in California. One of my dad's co-workers graduated from there—his kids did, too—and I wanted to go to school out of state and experience a little adventure, you know?"

"I remember you never backing down to a challenge, so yeah, I could see you wanting that." He laughed and the tension between them softened.

It made it easier for Hannah to open up and share some of the last several years with him. Still, she was cautious about how much she wanted to divulge. She had no idea how he'd respond to her high-profile divorce and ensuing media coverage. That life had never been for him.

"College was fun. I got a degree in marketing and yadda, yadda, yadda, here I am."

Revealing that she'd never used her degree or details

about her failed marriage were hard to put into the right words.

"That's a lot to yadda over." He side-eyed her for a full three seconds.

How could she explain that she had devoted her life to creating the perfect home, hosting gatherings with neighbors and colleagues, and being a support system for her busy husband only to have it all crash and burn in a messy public way?

It was the path she'd chosen, a lifestyle she'd enjoyed until she'd stepped away and gained an ounce of perspective. Luke traveled a lot, her friends were his friends, and the days were to-do lists to be checked off. When had her life become nothing more than a calendar of events?

Ugh!

"Well, I met my husband not long after I graduated from USC and we got married a little over a year later, but . . . we're kind of going through a divorce." She was not telling this in the best manner.

"Kind of?"

"We just filed recently, and the process is going to take a while."

"Divorce is hard. I'm sorry to hear that." Understanding rimmed his chocolate eyes. He might not have gone through a divorce, but he'd experienced loss.

His words should have comforted her, but all she could think about was how he would react to her big, public life. His own life was so far removed from such spectacle.

"Thanks."

"You know, you haven't said where you live?"

She knew she was being vague. She also knew Lizzy was aware of her situation and had tried to give her a chance to tell

Callan about it last night, but they'd been interrupted. It was time to share a few details with him. If she didn't, she risked him finding out some other way and that would probably be worse.

She also didn't like Lizzy having to keep her secret. That wasn't fair to her.

"I've lived in Los Altos Hills, California for the last ten years or so, but I left after the divorce papers were filed. I, um . . . I'm not sure yet where I'll decide to stay. I'm letting the dust settle a bit first."

"You're not going back home?" His gaze roamed over her searching for clues.

"No." She spat out her response. Too quick.

He stopped walking, forcing her to do the same.

"My husband—ex-husband, whatever—he works in the tech industry and he's well-known, so our divorce is kind of the talk of the town right now."

That was a mild way to put it.

The space between his eyes pinched together. "You're moving away because people know you're getting a divorce?"

He was right. Uprooting her life because of a divorce didn't make much sense, but he had no idea the number of eyes and ears on her right now. Not to mention how alone she felt when the news broke.

Only a handful of friends reached out to check on her. Most stayed away unsure which side they should choose, not that there should have been sides if they were real friends, but she was only beginning to realize that truth since she'd left.

"It's complicated." She resigned herself to the most stock answer she could think of. When she was ready, she'd tell him everything but today was not the day.

"If you don't want to talk about it, you don't have to. But if you change your mind, I'm willing to listen."

Her heart puddled at her feet. The furrow of his brow showed he didn't understand, but he offered her grace, and time, and a waiting ear whenever she was ready.

In that instant she knew that when she was ready to talk about it, really talk about it, he was the only person she wanted to have that conversation with.

There were still a lot of unsaid words between them, but a part of her was ready to forgive, to release some of the hurt she'd carried over the way he'd ghosted her.

Step by step she was reaching for the reins of letting go.

7

———————

Hannah had just finished getting dressed when someone knocked on the front door. It had been a couple of hours since she'd run into Callan in the vineyard, and while he told her he'd lend her an ear whenever she was ready to talk, he hadn't pressed the subject any further. They'd spent the next half hour discussing innocuous things like the variety of grapes he used to make the wine and the whole winemaking process from harvest to bottle. His love for the vineyard was obvious.

Three more knocks rapped on the door.

"Coming." Hannah pulled the door open to a smiling Lizzy.

"Hey! Sorry to bother you. Are you busy?" Lizzy blurted out in her usual bubbly way.

"No, what's up?" She motioned for Lizzy to enter and closed the door behind her.

"So, our assistant manager, who's basically my right hand, also handles the creative pieces for the shop. She called in sick today, and I was wondering if you'd be willing to help out. We have a bunch of new stock that needs to be displayed."

"Me?" Hannah never minded pitching in to help someone, but she had no idea why Lizzy would ask her to fill in for something like this.

"The basket you put together for my parents was so cute. You obviously know your way around creating eye-catching pieces, and I'm clueless when it comes to that kind of stuff.

"I know the winery isn't exactly swamped with customers, but there's a lot that that goes on behind the scenes, and with your creative eye you're the perfect person to help me with this. Please?" Breathless from her rapid-fire plea, she clasped her hands together in prayer position. "I wouldn't ask if I didn't have all that stock to unload, and Roberta, the employee who's out, sounded really sick. I have a feeling she might be out for a few days."

How could Hannah say no?

"Sure."

Lizzy squealed. "Thank you!"

She had to admit Lizzy's exuberance was infectious. It felt good to be needed, and to have an opportunity to get creative. Maybe digging her hands into something would quiet her bustling thoughts, relieve some stress. Besides, she could use a distraction.

"I promise not to take up too much of your time. Three hours at the most."

"It's fine. I don't have anything planned for today anyway."

"Perfect. Let's go." Lizzy was out the door before Hannah could say anything more. Helping Lizzy out at the shop would give Hannah something to do. Plus, she'd no doubt see Callan there, too. Maybe that was the real motivator.

HANNAH HELPED Lizzy move items from the shelves to a long table set up in the stockroom where they put together displays before placing them around the shop. Chit chat flowed between them as if no time had passed.

Lizzy snorted. Her signature laugh.

"Girl, I am D.O.N.E. with dating right now. Falls Hollow isn't exactly brimming with eligible bachelors. The last guy I dated lived in Austin, which is only a whopping thirty-to-forty-minute drive from here, and he made it sound like I lived in another country." She rolled her eyes. "I stay so busy that I don't have time to get into the whole social scene in the city. And don't even mention dating apps." She raised her hand over her head. "They are the worst."

Hannah hadn't experienced the world of online match-making since she met Luke so soon out of college. To be honest, she was thankful for that. Like Lizzy, she'd heard a lot of bad tales.

"I've heard." Hannah chuckled.

"So, what about you? I read that you met your soon-to-be ex through mutual friends. Is that true?" Lizzy eyed her cautiously, appearing to test the waters before she bombarded her with questions.

"Yep. We met at my college friend's birthday dinner. She was dating a guy a few years older whose brother worked at the same company as Luke, and Luke tagged along with him."

"And?"

Lizzy wasn't one to stop with one detail. She needed the whole story.

For some reason Hannah felt at ease with Lizzy. She found herself opening up and telling her everything. She hadn't even done that with her parents. Embarrassment of the whole situation left her skittish, afraid to talk about what happened for fear of judgment or pity, or her own thoughts of self-loathing.

Luke might have walked out on their marriage, but she'd played a part, too. Understanding her role in the end of their relationship, and more importantly of herself, kept her tongue-tied. Facing harsh truths was never easy.

After walking Lizzy through the whole timeline of her and Luke, a weight lifted from her chest, however small it might have been. It was a start. A relief to talk about it in the open with someone.

Lizzy wrapped her arm around Hannah's shoulders and pulled her close in a sweet but unexpected gesture. "Don't beat yourself up, Hannah. Relationships aren't perfect, and some, well they're better off fading into the sunset than coasting in a sea of ambiguity."

Lizzy made a good point. Hannah and Luke had drifted into a routine, a weekly schedule of get-togethers with friends or charity functions, his work and her constant state of being a support system for him.

If she thought back objectively, she remembered their early days of getting to know one another. Things had moved fast. *He* had moved fast. His brain constantly whirred from one project at work to the next, always shifting and thinking and working harder, and he'd whisked their relationship up into the same level of frenzy.

He'd showered her with gifts. He'd taken her to the best restaurants. He'd laid out a vision of an exciting life together and she soaked it up like most young, impressionable girls would at that age. But had she truly fallen in love with him —his person, his heart, his soul—or had she been swept up in the lure of an amazing, adventurous life?

She recalled their first trip together. He'd booked a weekend getaway to Vail, Colorado during ski season. It was a snowy, romantic retreat. They'd skied, snowboarded, had devoured delicious food at the best restaurants and enjoyed evening strolls, hand in hand, soaking in the beauty of the mountains, the tall spruce trees that seemed to touch the sky, and mostly, each other. Luke loved to surprise her. He had always been thoughtful in that sense.

No, she'd loved Luke. Of that, she was sure. Yet, she wasn't sure if it was the take-your-breath-away once-in-a-lifetime kind of love. The acknowledgment bothered her. That was the kind of love she wanted. Maybe she'd never find it. Her heart sank.

"You really need to tell Callan though. He has no clue about the life you've lived since leaving here, and it would be better coming from you than some tabloid. He may be outgoing but he's a private person. Especially as a single dad."

"I know. I will. It might take me a minute to find the right moment though."

"I get it. But I know he'll be more understanding than you think. He's one of the good ones, even if he's my goofy brother." She elbowed Hannah's arm and flashed her a grin.

Lizzy was right. At some point, she'd have to come clean with Callan.

With a bamboo platter in front of her, Hannah tied together a bunch of dried lavender and placed it inside a small ceramic vase and moved it to one corner. In the middle was a shiny white plate in which she set a cheese ball in the center, then surrounded it with whole grain crackers and a silver cheese knife she pierced on top of the ball.

She also put out three different pairings of wine and

cheese that she placed in different spots around the shop. Each had a tiny chalkboard easel where she wrote the type of cheese and what notes it brought out in the wine.

She spruced up floral arrangements, rearranged a light strand around a shelf, and moved items around to make the bottles of wine stand out. Three hours flew by in a flash.

Her experience with food and hosting came in handy. Not to mention, she loved creating beautiful tablescapes and sharing yummy food and drinks. Mostly, she enjoyed spending time engaging people in conversation. She'd struck up several with customers as they wandered around admiring the displays.

When Lizzy had to step away to call a vendor, Hannah took over as if she were a seasoned employee of the winery. She buzzed around the shop, all smiles, and it wasn't until she noticed Callan walk in that her subconscious got the better of her, and she retreated toward the back looking for Lizzy.

Callan got sidetracked by a chatty couple who'd entered behind him, but it wasn't long before they moved along, and he headed her way.

"I didn't expect to see you here." He wiped his brow with the back of his hand, distracted.

"Lizzy needed some help." When his brow raised, she continued. "One of your employees called in sick and she needed help with the displays."

He tipped his chin upward highlighting the tiny cleft in the center. The one that aided his inherent charm.

"Oh yeah. Roberta. She's our design guru and the one who makes all this look good." He pointed around the shop. "Although, it looks a little different in here."

Hannah worried that he didn't like the changes she'd made. Lizzy had given her free rein, and she'd run with it, pulling out new items from the stockroom and putting away others while also adding more spots to highlight their wine by creating different pairings. She was pleased with how it all came out. That didn't mean he would be, too.

"We made a few changes so we could put out new stock Lizzy got in. And she kind of let me do my thing, but Roberta's done the heavy lifting. This place already looked amazing."

She meant what she said. The winery oozed that rustic old-world charm she loved.

He smirked. "It looks great, actually."

"You sound surprised."

"No, not surprised. Just unexpected, I guess."

She wasn't sure what he meant, but with Lizzy fast approaching from the stockroom she let it go.

"Sorry about that. That was our guy in Austin where we get our flowers and dried herbs. He's a talker."

Hannah swallowed a giggle. No one loved to talk more than Lizzy. That conversation was probably a very animated two-way street.

"No worries. I think we're done here anyway. What do you think?"

Lizzy waved her palm from left to right. "It looks perfect. Thank you for jumping in to help."

She hadn't exactly jumped in. It was more like Lizzy had put her on the spot, but she didn't mind. Lizzy was fun to hang out with. And the sense of relief she'd experienced after talking with her about her current situation made her lighter, happier. Something she hadn't felt recently.

"You're welcome. It was fun. I guess I'll grab my purse and head out."

Lizzy puckered her lips and scrunched her nose. "Well . . ." She drew out the word in one long syllable. "If you have a few more minutes, maybe even a little longer, I have another project I could use some help with."

Hannah canted her head, not sure if sticking around was the best idea now that Callan was here.

"We recently partnered with Decadence, the chocolate shop in town, to serve a few of their artisanal chocolates during our wine tasting tours and I need to decide which ones to use."

"So, basically you need someone to do a chocolate tasting with a wine tasting."

"Exactly."

"I'm in." Whether she had to work side by side with Callan or not, Hannah would not pass up trying out delectable chocolates.

"Perfect. Meet me out back at the picnic table in five minutes." Lizzy took off with a bounce in her step.

"You know, she'll keep you working as long as you let her." With one hand on his hip and the other cradling his phone, Callan seemed anxious. Did her presence bother him?

"It's okay. I don't mind."

His phone lit up and a pensive strain fell across his features. "I need to take care of this. If you'll excuse me."

"Sure."

He was walking away before she finished speaking. Whatever it was had him preoccupied. Maybe that was a good thing. The last thing she wanted was to ruin the progress they'd made. Overstaying her welcome would certainly do that. Plus, she was struggling to keep her emotions in check whenever he was nearby, and she was already dealing with enough.

After she finished helping Lizzy, she'd make a clean break and put some distance between them. If she stayed away from the winery and the vineyard, she could clear her head and figure out her next steps with the divorce and where she was going to live, not to mention what she was going to do. Running into Callan and his sister had thrown her off course and she'd just arrived in town yesterday. She needed to regroup, and there was no way to do that with Callan in her sight.

8

Hannah's mouth watered at the tray of chocolates Lizzy placed in the center of the picnic table. The selection ranged from dark chocolate to silky milk chocolate to creamy white, from dainty squares to plump balls baring hand painted designs worthy of a show in a fancy art gallery. Lizzy shared that one of the owners of Decadence learned chocolate-making from a long line of chocolatiers in his family. The other owner, his girlfriend, was a gifted artist who discovered chocolate was her favorite medium.

Hannah was just thankful to taste them all.

The table was behind the shop near the tasting building. It sat underneath a pergola wrapped in Edison lights and was a place for employees to enjoy lunch outside when the weather permitted. It probably didn't get much use during the summertime considering the heat of a humid Texas summer.

Before they got started, Lizzy offered Hannah half of the sandwich she'd packed for lunch. It was like high school all over again when Lizzy used to join Hannah and Callan at lunch, where she'd babble on and on about the latest student gossip. The memory brought a grin to Hannah's face.

"Eating chocolate on an empty stomach might cloud our judgment," Lizzy said.

"Good thinking." Hannah took a bite of the pimento cheese sandwich, happy to satisfy the low growl in her stomach.

Working in the shop, putting out the displays and pairings, had consumed her in the best way. She'd lost herself in the joy of making something beautiful.

They enjoyed the small break, relaxing peacefully in the gentle sunshine of early autumn. After they finished their food, they cleared away the mess and dove back into work mode.

Hannah bit into a dark chocolate ball filled with chocolate ganache and a hint of lavender.

"Mm, this one definitely needs to be showcased. It will highlight the crispness of the wine."

Lizzy typed on the laptop she'd brought outside.

"Okay, so far we have the white chocolate caramel truffle, the plain milk chocolate square, and that one." She pointed at Hannah who popped the last bite in her mouth. "I'd like to have one more."

"What about a plain square of dark chocolate, too? It's not too sweet and not too bitter, which will allow multiple notes in the wine to stand out."

"Good thinking." Lizzy added more notes onto her laptop.

"Hey, Aunt Lizzy."

Callan's daughter, Summer, ran over to the table, her backpack bouncing up and down as she ran. Hannah couldn't help noticing the resemblance she bore to Callan, the sight of which induced a longing in her she couldn't explain.

She'd wanted to start a family early on after she and Luke got married, but with the hours he was working he'd convinced her it wasn't the right time. The hours only got longer and his interest in becoming a dad waned with each passing year. Before long, Hannah had resigned herself to waiting until her thirty-fifth birthday as the final push for trying for a child. Divorce came knocking at thirty-four.

With a toss of her hair, she nudged the memory away.

"Hi, Summer." She flashed the young girl a warm smile.

"Hi." Timid curiosity etched her face, but she turned her attention back to Lizzy. "Dad said you're eating candy out here."

Lizzy laughed. "It's not exactly candy. It's artisanal chocolate."

Summer scrunched her nose. "What's that?"

"Fancy chocolate with unique tastes." Lizzy tapped her on the nose. "Would you like to try one?"

Summer looked at Hannah. "Do you like it?"

"I do. Want me to pick out a piece for you to try?"

The little girl shrugged her shoulders. "Okay."

Hannah picked up one of the plain milk chocolate squares and handed it to her. Summer turned it over in her palm, inspecting it before she took the tiniest bite. She swiveled her jaw side to side.

"Tastes like chocolate."

"Yep. Wanna try another one?" Hannah asked, amused at her reaction.

"Yes, but don't tell my dad. He only lets me eat candy as a special treat."

"Promise." Hannah eyed one of the white chocolate caramel truffles. "Do you like caramel?"

"Mm-hm." Summer's eyes rounded.

Hannah picked up one of the truffles and handed it to her. "Try this one. I think you'll like it."

Again, Summer took a small bite, then moved her mouth around while she tasted the candy. Her eyes widened as big as saucers.

"I like this one." She shoved the rest in her mouth and rubbed her belly with joy.

Her enthusiasm tickled Hannah. "I think that one is one of my favorites, too."

"You need to get on your homework, squirt." Callan walked up from behind them, surprising his daughter.

"I only had one."

Summer put her hands up in surrender, her mouth full, and glanced at Hannah who gave her a discreet nod. She'd promised to keep her secret.

Callan smirked as if he knew better. "Bitty's got some lemonade for you in the breakroom."

"Thanks, Dad," Summer called out as she took off.

After she ran inside, he gave Lizzy and Hannah a stern look. "If you get her sugared up, I'm going to send her home with one of you," he joked.

"A little chocolate never hurt anyone, Cal," Lizzy teased. "Besides, tonight she's having a sleepover at Mom and Dad's, so they can enjoy the extra energy."

Callan shook his head.

"How did you come up with Bitty for your mom's grandparent name?" Hannah asked.

She'd been curious since the first time Callan had said it.

"Dad's always telling her she's itty bitty because she's so petite, and the name kind of stuck."

Hannah chuckled. "It's perfect."

Callan started to laugh with her but clammed up when Summer darted back outside.

"I forgot I don't have any homework." She sat down on the bench next to Hannah. "Bitty said y'all are picking out chocolates. Can I help?"

"Of course," Lizzy said with a side eye toward her brother.

Hannah noticed a sudden edge to him, and she worried, again, that her being there bothered him.

"It's for work, Dad," Summer said in her most grown-up voice.

Both Hannah and Lizzy fought to contain a laugh. Callan was not amused.

"You can help Aunt Lizzy take notes, but no more tasting."

Summer's shoulders slumped. "Fine."

"I'll be in the vat room working late. Come tell me bye before you leave with Bitty and Pop."

"I will."

Before he walked away, Callan stole another wary glance at Hannah. Apprehension simmered in the clench of his jaw. It would have bothered her more if she wasn't experiencing a similar level of wobbly nerves. A few days ago, she never would have imagined sitting at a table in the back of a winery with Lizzy, Callan, and his young daughter, conversing as if it hadn't been seventeen long years since they last spoke. The curveballs life was hurling at her were enormous.

"I thought you girls could use a little refreshment." Callan's mom walked up with a tray holding a pitcher of lemonade alongside three glasses.

"Thanks, Mom." Lizzy reached for the pitcher and placed it on the table while her mom set the glasses down.

"Would you like to join us? These chocolates are delicious." Hannah waved one of the dark chocolate squares at Connie, tempting her with the delectable bite.

"I'd love to, but I'm going over the books. My weekly contribution to the business." She winked at Hannah.

Hannah loved how easy it was to be around Callan's family again after all these years. If she wasn't careful, she might grow attached. And that was a complication she couldn't entertain given the state of her messy life.

Why did life have to be so hard?

"Summer, we'll be leaving soon, so a few more minutes out here and then come grab your backpack."

"Yes, ma'am." Her dejected response matched the way she leaned her cheek on her fist where her elbow was propped up on the tabletop. She was clearly enjoying her time hanging out with Lizzy and Hannah, even if she couldn't participate with the tasting part.

Callan was right. She was eight going on thirty.

Connie tucked the empty tray under her arm. "Hannah, it was good to see you again."

She flashed Hannah a warm smile and Hannah's belly tumbled with gratefulness. Callan's parents were good people.

After more discussion about the merit of each of the different chocolates, Hannah and Lizzy finally chose four options to use on the tours. Hannah also suggested putting them out in the shop for more tasting. She was deep into explaining her thoughts on how creating a more interactive experience as soon as customers entered the winery, all the way through the tours, would make their winery stand out from others in the area. All offered guided tours and tastings, a couple even hosted weddings, but their shops were limited from what Hannah found online.

Bored with all the talk and no opportunity to eat more of the chocolates, Summer retreated back inside.

Just as Hannah was about to excuse herself for a second time, Lizzy got a call from Roberta, the employee who had called in sick. When she learned Roberta had the flu and would be out for at least several days, she practically begged Hannah to fill in during her absence.

"I know you're here for other reasons, and I don't want to intrude on your time, but this is a busy time of year for us with tours and tastings, and I could really use your help. We'll pay you. Add you on as a temporary consultant or something."

With her elbows propped up on the table, Lizzy rested her chin in her hands, hopeful.

"I understand your predicament, Lizzy. I do. But I don't know. I've got to figure out my next steps, where I'm going to live, what I'm going to do. Plus, I don't think Callan is comfortable with me being here."

"I know this whole situation is a little weird and unexpected—"

"That's an understatement," Hannah interjected.

"Talk to him. Clear the air, tell him what you're going through, all of it, and get some closure for both of you. What happened between y'all was a long time ago, and a lot of life has happened since then. You're adults now. There's no reason why you can't be friends, or at least friendly while you're in town."

She wasn't wrong, but Hannah didn't know if friendship was in the cards. Not with the jolt of electricity that rocked through her every time Callan was close to her. He was a long-ago memory brought to life again.

Maybe it was nostalgia fogging her brain. Maybe it was more. Either way, she needed time to heal from the end of her marriage and the end of the life she'd known for over a decade. No matter the distance she felt from it now, more space would give her clarity. Being around Callan every day would add to the weight she was carrying.

But Lizzy's persuasive powers were too strong. Her need for help was genuine; her desire for it to be Hannah was real, too. And Hannah never walked away from someone in need. That wasn't in her DNA.

"I'll talk to him." Hannah watched Lizzy perk up. "In my own time. And maybe getting out of my head and into my hands doing something will help clear my mind. But you're not paying me. Consider this a friend helping a friend out."

The way Lizzy beamed made Hannah smile. It had been a long time since she'd felt this rush of connection. Her friends in California were Luke's friends, too. They were couple friends, colleagues, and neighbors, yet a one-on-one friendship hadn't fully developed with any of them. Not to the level she'd experienced when she was younger. She missed that.

"Deal." Lizzy hopped up from the bench. "Meet me here tomorrow morning at ten. I'll set aside an apron for you to use, so you don't get anything on your clothes."

Hannah rose. "I'll see you tomorrow."

After gathering her purse, she headed out to make her way back to the bungalow. Three feet down the path she ran into Callan. Eyes on the phone gripped in his hand, he almost walked right into her. When he looked up, she noticed the tension etched across his face melt into something else. Surprise? Apprehension? Something more?

"Sorry, I didn't see you." He slid his phone into his back pocket.

"We've got to stop bumping into each other like this." She laughed, trying to ease the friction fizzling in the air.

"Heading out?"

"Yeah. Lizzy and I finished tasting the chocolates. I think we chose some good ones."

He nodded.

"Well, good night." She started to walk away, and he called out after her.

"It's starting to get dark. I can walk you back if you like."

Hannah hadn't given any thought to walking alone. Not here. Falls Hollow was the kind of town where people didn't even lock their front doors.

She didn't know whether Callan was using his manners—a prerequisite in a southern upbringing—or if he had something he wanted to say. Either way, she suddenly liked the idea of him joining her as she crossed the field under a big Texas sunset.

"That would be great. Thanks."

He joined her, quiet, contemplative, but it was the kind of comfortable silence two people who knew each other well enjoyed. For a long moment, Hannah savored the peacefulness of their walk, the beauty of the sun painting the sky in rich shades of gold, and the peaks of the hills surrounding them like a group of friends.

It was a refreshing breath of calm. Until Callan visibly tensed and Hannah worried what would come out of his mouth next.

9

"Thanks again for helping Lizzy today. I know she can be a handful, but she means well."

"I had fun, actually. It was nice to focus on something other than my divorce."

Hannah wrapped her sweater a little tighter around her shoulders, bracing against the falling temperature. She considered starting a fire once she made it back to the bungalow.

There was the cutest stone fireplace in the living room begging to be brought to life, and curling up in front of a crackling fire with a cup of hot tea and a good book sounded like the best way to end the night.

"Summer is a great kid, by the way." She loved the way a proud grin slid across his face at the mention of his daughter. Callan was no doubt an amazing dad.

"Thanks. She's everything to me."

"I'm looking forward to getting to know her better while I'm helping out at the winery."

Callan stopped walking. "What are you talking about?"

"Lizzy asked me to fill in for a few more days. Apparently, your employee, Roberta, is out with the flu, and Lizzy said she has a lot on her plate right now."

He worked his jaw from side to side and Hannah sensed the ease of their conversation shift like a rubber band stretched too thin. She looked up at him watching the words behind his stare form on his lips.

"Did she now? Well, if she needs the help, I get it, but um, Summer only comes to the winery after school or on the weekends sometimes. And she's young, you know. Impressionable."

"What are you saying?" She didn't like the sudden change in his demeanor, or the way he withdrew from her.

"Kids are more intelligent than what people give them credit for. Summer might not know anything about us, but she's smart enough to sense the tension. It won't take her long to figure it out, and I've spent the last eight years protecting her. She's been through enough. I don't want her getting comfortable with you hanging around and then have to clean up the mess when you leave."

Hannah's jaw hit the ground. "Callan, I didn't mean anything by what I said."

"I'm not saying you did. It's just that, you're passing through town on your way to wherever, and I don't want her to get hurt if she gets used to you being around. That's all."

Hannah sensed a lot more simmering beneath his poised exterior. Whether it had to do with anything beyond Summer she didn't know. However, she understood his concern. He and Summer had suffered an unimaginable kind of desertion. Protecting his daughter was paramount, yet the bite of his words pierced straight through her.

"I understand. You've been through a lot. Both of you. I

don't want to do anything to add to that. I'll let Lizzy know I'm happy to help by working remotely, if that's possible. If not, I can arrange to come by when Summer's not around."

She tugged her sweater tight, this time bracing from his resistance to her. She understood—she did—but that didn't ease the sting of his desire to draw a line between them.

"Tell Lizzy I'll call her in the morning. Good night, Callan." With her fingers twisted in the soft cotton of her sweater, she gave him a weak smile before turning away to continue on alone.

It would seem there was no possibility of mending bridges with him.

"Wait." The word fell quiet as a whisper from his lips.

She paused, reluctant to face him for fear his reticence would be a bullet to her heart. Instead, she saw a flurry of emotions flicker in his gaze. Hurt, trepidation, longing, hesitation all rumbled across his stormy eyes, dark clouds threatening to drench them in a turbulent sea of uncertainty.

"I didn't mean to come off like a jerk." He peered at her through a loose strand of hair shadowing his eye.

Hannah took a beat to collect herself. She knew he bore the pressures of being a single parent and having anything throw him and the life he'd built for his daughter off kilter would no doubt cause him concern. But she had no intention of disrupting his world.

Honestly, if she listened to her good common sense, she didn't want to be a part of his world. She had enough of her own problems to handle. Yet, every time she locked in on his gaze all common sense went out the window.

"I get it, Callan. And please believe me when I say I don't want to do anything to make you uncomfortable. I think

Summer is a sweet girl, but I would never insert myself into her life in such a way."

"I believe you. It's just that seeing you again, out of the blue, and with Lizzy practically hiring you at the winery, it's a lot all at once. Especially with all the other issues I'm dealing with."

The way he rubbed his chin as if realizing he'd said too much needled Hannah.

"What's going on?"

"It's nothing."

Hannah tilted her head to the side. "You offered to listen to me. I can do the same for you."

He took a short breath as if he were playing a game of mental tennis in his mind, trying to decide if he wanted to divulge anything or not. When he started walking and talking at the same time, she hurried to keep up.

"The winery is struggling," he admitted.

Hannah was surprised. From what she'd seen, the winery was doing fine. Maybe not bustling with business, but according to Lizzy, they were booked with tours and tastings.

"What's going on?" she asked.

"Well, like I mentioned during the tour, our first vintage did really well right out of the gate. It won best debut at the Hill Country Wine Festival, which helped sales, but I haven't been able to capture that same level in subsequent vintages. Our wine is good, but it needs to be better than good in order to stand out in a crowded market. Especially with us being local.

"We ship very little outside of Texas. Only to customers who've been to the winery and wanted to order more once they returned home. We're not equipped for large-scale distribution, but at the same time, we need to grow. It's a Catch-22."

The more he talked, the more his steps fell in line with the rhythm of his words. Fast at first and then slowing to a steady pace as he released his worries out into the open. To her.

"Are you trying to recreate the same flavor as your first vintage?"

"Yes and no. At first, that's what I was trying to do, but so many factors play into how a batch of wine will turn out that it's impossible to make an exact copy. What I need is something new, something fresh that's as good or better than the first."

"That makes sense. What things have you tried?"

Callan ran his hand down his face. "I've played with fermenting techniques. I've let the wine age for longer spans and shorter spans. I've tweaked several things over the years, but I haven't had a 'wow' moment."

Callan had always been a tad of a perfectionist. He demanded the best of himself when he played ball, and he encouraged others to do the same. It's why he'd made such a good team captain. Hannah imagined that trait rolled over into his work life, and from what she gathered, his life as a parent, also.

"Have you considered making a blend?"

"Yeah, but I'd prefer to perfect our sauvignon blanc first, then branch out."

"You could do both at the same time."

From the way he twisted his lips to one side she knew he was focused on getting their current wine where he wanted it.

"Anyway, that's why I snapped. I have a lot on my mind

and not enough space to juggle any more. I'm sorry. You didn't deserve that."

"No worries. It's forgotten."

"Don't cancel on Lizzy. I know she's swamped with Roberta out. Plus, she'd kill me if you bowed out because of me. Just be careful around Summer. Please."

"Deal." He was giving her the tiniest open, but it was better than nothing. She'd rather some semblance of closure between them, even if a part of her ached for more.

Hearts don't always get what they want.

"Now, what about you?"

"What about me?"

"Why did you really come all the way back here?"

"I told you why." The bungalow was close, but not close enough to avoid diving into the real reason she came here. He had shared a glimpse behind the scenes of his life. Was she ready to do the same?

"Come on. You drove across the country to a place you haven't stepped foot in over seventeen years because you're going through a divorce?"

Now, it was her turn to play mental tennis over whether she should tell him everything or not.

"My divorce is more high profile than I would like." She allowed the words to come naturally. If she shared every detail, then that meant she was ready. If not, at least he'd have some idea of what she was going through and that was better than lying to him.

"What do you mean?"

"My ex has a very successful career in the tech industry as a software developer, which is why he's well-known. That recognition has rolled over to me, too. Navigating a divorce and all the drama that goes with it has been overwhelming. I needed some space to figure things out, you know? Falls

Hollow popped into my mind out of nowhere and now, here I am."

He stopped walking and turned toward her. "How well-known?"

Hannah knotted her fingers in her sweater. "My ex is Luke Miller."

She held her breath waiting for awareness to break across his features. When nothing registered, her breath escaped in a deflated hiss. Lizzy was right. He really had no idea what kind of life she'd left behind.

"Should I know him?"

"Maybe? I don't know."

She didn't know what to say. Luke wasn't just known within the tech world, he was a public-facing person who was in the news and in magazine articles and showered at awards banquets for his achievements in the industry. He hadn't created just one massively successful software platform, he'd built three. He was also the kind of person who grew to like the lifestyle that went with fame.

Callan studied her, and she wondered what thoughts clouded his inquisitive mind. How much more did he want to know? Would he push her for answers? He already wanted to protect his daughter from her. Did she make it worse by confiding in him?

"Don't let one bad incident ruin the rest of your life. It's a hard lesson. One that took me a long time to learn. But if there's one thing I remember most about you, it's that you don't give up."

A thin line cracked down the middle of her heart. He'd extended her a kindness no one else had. Living under the bright lights as Luke Miller's wife, she'd developed a plastic-coated shell that kept her insulated, distanced from the realities of the world around her. But Callan had ripped that away to see the real Hannah underneath, and he'd extended an olive branch to say, "I see you, and you're going to be okay."

If she'd ever wondered what she had loved most about him, she knew now. Callan Locke was one of the good ones, like Lizzy had said. And that was a rarity in any world.

10

***

Hannah crossed the parking lot of the winery with a touch of renewed vigor in her steps. While romance might have only existed in the past for her and Callan, after their conversation last night, she relished knowing that at least a chance at friendship existed between them. A belief that he could be a positive force during her time in Falls Hollow.

No matter the jitters she endured whenever he was close, neither were in a place for anything more. He was a single dad raising a young daughter who'd suffered immeasurable loss. A mother abandoning a child was its own kind of death. Hannah wouldn't disrupt the life they'd built. Besides, the ink was barely dry on the divorce filings, and she had a whole new life to figure out. Anything more was a wish not ready to be granted. However difficult, however much she longed for more, she accepted that.

She breezed through the door and found Lizzy behind the front counter.

"Morning." She waved at Hannah all smiles. "I've got

something for you." She reached under the counter and pulled out a tan apron with the winery's logo emblazoned on the front in burgundy lettering.

Hannah took it from her hands. "Thanks."

While she'd agreed to help Lizzy with her workload, she also understood Callan's concerns about his daughter getting used to her being around. Sticking around Falls Hollow wasn't on her agenda. That knowledge needed to stay at the forefront of her mind so Summer wouldn't experience a sense of loss when she left.

"It'll give your clothes some protection while we clean out the tasting room and add a few displays. I figured that would be a great way to showcase some items so customers will check them out in the shop before leaving."

"That's a great idea." Hannah handed Lizzy her purse. "Do you have a place for this?"

"Of course." Lizzy took her purse. "There's a spot in Cal's office where Mom and I keep our stuff."

"Great! Thanks." Hannah slipped the apron over her head and tied the strings around her waist securing it into place. "Guess I'm ready."

She put her hands out to the sides, palms up.

"You look like a regular." Lizzy chuckled. "Let's go."

After they stowed her purse in Callan's office, Hannah followed Lizzy outside to the tasting building. The doors on either side were open allowing the whisper of a breeze to flow through carrying the promise of another beautiful fall day. Boxes of candles were stacked on the long table next to a pile of wooden plaques with sayings painted on each. Things like *Home is where the heart is* and *Find joy in the ordinary* and one Hannah particularly liked *Mindset is everything.*

She could use that reminder.

"Are all the products you carry locally made?" Hannah picked up one of the candle boxes and admired the elegant packaging.

"They're either locally made or carried by a locally owned store. We try our best to support local vendors as much as possible." Lizzy reached for one of the plaques and held it up. "These are made by the owners of Hearth & Home, the home goods store on Main Street. And they also carry those candles, which are handcrafted by someone in Fredericksburg."

"You know, that's something you can play up in marketing the vineyard. Sourcing locally is important to a lot of people," Hannah spat out as if she were some marketing guru, which she was not.

A marketing degree did not equal experience.

Lizzy grimaced. "We haven't spent as much time on marketing as we should, to be honest."

"What kind of advertising have you done?"

"We have brochures at the register, and we bought a spot on the local mailer that goes out once a month to everyone who lives here. Oh, and we're listed on the Texas Winery Registry website."

By Lizzy's dejected look, Hannah's face must have given away what she was thinking.

"That's all good." She tried to be positive.

"But not enough, I know." Lizzy leaned back against the table, arms folded across her chest. "Mom and Dad are semi-retired, so they only stop by every now and then to help out. I'm in charge of the tours and tastings, but I also handle the daily operations.

"Roberta was the first, and only, full-time employee we

hired outside of the harvesting crew, who are seasonal workers. We have Jen and Brian who work part-time—they're both college students—and then Cal who makes the wine. All that to say I've let the marketing piece fall through the cracks because I stay busy with everything else."

Hannah bit the inside of her cheek contemplating Lizzy's dilemma. She might not have any real-life experience, but she knew the basics of marketing. Enough to at least brainstorm some ideas with Lizzy. Callan couldn't fault her for trying to help, could he?

"Plus, our budget is stretched thin as it is. Adding money to a marketing bucket will be tough."

Hannah thought about Callan's admission regarding the slump the winery was experiencing. Having few marketing dollars meant she'd have to get creative. The challenge spurred a speck of excitement. She wanted to dig her hands into something to get her mind off the divorce, and this could be it.

"What if we come up with some ideas that don't cost anything?"

"I'm game for any suggestions you have." Lizzy perked up.

"Have you ever hosted anything outside your normal tours?"

"Like what?"

"I don't know. Maybe a tasting fundraiser or a festival of some kind."

"Those don't sound free." Lizzy scratched her chin, doubt evident in her eyes.

Hannah paced around to the other side of the table, her fingers tapping on her arms. "You'd be surprised at what you can put together when you partner with other business owners."

In California, she'd been known for hosting parties for friends and colleagues, but she also had spent a lot of time volunteering for different causes, even taking the lead with a few events. She might not have had any corporate experience, but she'd been involved in sales and marketing in other capacities.

"What if you reached out to a few of the business owners whose products you showcase here and see if they'd be interested in joint marketing? Again, it could involve coming together to host a fundraiser for the town, maybe, or putting together a festival or weekend market of sorts. Each of you could contribute time and products, enlist volunteers to help with building and running the booths, and then have someone—ideally someone willing to pitch in for free—to create a social media campaign. Maybe even print old-school flyers and find places in Austin willing to put them out."

Lizzy stretched her neck from side to side taking in Hannah's suggestions. "Those sound like good ideas but finding the time to actually do them is another thing."

"I'll help. You already have me here filling in for Roberta. Use me while I'm here." The itch to pitch in, to have something outside of her current problems to focus on, grew.

"I feel bad asking you to do more."

"You're not asking. I'm offering."

She knew she was walking a fine line between pitching in and becoming too involved, but she couldn't shake the desire to do something. As long as she kept it professional, Callan wouldn't mind, would he?

Lizzy pursed her lips together, then broke out into a wide smile. "Okay. Let's do it. But only if you truly don't mind."

"I promise. I don't mind at all."

"Okay, but we should probably tell Callan."

"Tell Callan what?" In a handful of long strides, Callan was across the room and next to Lizzy in seconds. He didn't look thrilled to hear what they had to say.

"Hannah has some great ideas for advertising the winery."

Before Lizzy could expound on those ideas, Callan shifted his stance from one side to the other as if bracing himself for something he wouldn't like.

"These are free, or at least cheap, suggestions of things we can try to get our name out there more. It doesn't hurt to try. We need the business. Tours and tastings aren't producing the volume of sales we need."

Lizzy watched her brother for his response, hopeful in the way she leaned closer to him.

Callan ground his jaw. "How cheap?"

Hannah knew she could do this, and do it well, but she could see the doubt written all over him.

"You already showcase products from local businesses alongside your wine, so reaching out to those owners about doing some joint marketing should be easy. I told Lizzy I'd take the lead on this—I know how busy both of you are— but I won't get in the way."

She searched his eyes, silently telling him she'd be cautious around his daughter. As desperately as she wanted something to get her mind off the divorce, she understood his concern and wouldn't do anything to jeopardize the promise she'd made.

Silence stretched out for a beat. Something in his eyes said he believed her, but that wasn't the issue.

"You still haven't answered my question. How much would this cost?"

He locked in on her and her pulse raced. He wasn't buying their ideas, and he hadn't even heard them yet.

"Mainly, your time, or mine more specifically, and products. A lot of the work can be done by volunteers. You'd be surprised at how many people are willing to pitch in, especially in a town like this, if we show them the benefits of increasing business in the area or how we can do something for the town."

"That sounds great but how does increasing the winery's sales affect people in the community?" He plopped his hands on his hips, his confidence brimming that he could poke holes in her plans.

An ember flared to life deep in the pit of her stomach, and in an instant, she wanted nothing more than to prove him wrong.

"Well, one idea I had is a fundraiser. Pull the community together to raise money for something the town needs. The exposure businesses would get by being involved is good. Another idea is hosting a festival or market of some kind. You can get creative on how to advertise in Austin and the surrounding communities, as well as online to reach a broader audience. The point for each business owner is to increase sales, which would be a boost to the local economy. That has a ripple effect."

She paused, waiting for him to say something. Anything. If he said no, then he was just being stubborn. If he said yes, he'd expect solid results for the effort. Either response would pose a precarious line for her to walk.

Maybe she'd bitten off more than she could chew. After all, she'd come here to get away from the craziness surrounding her divorce. The last thing she needed was to jump into more drama by getting in over her head.

Seconds ticked by that seemed like an eternity.

"Falls Hollow used to have a fall festival, but it kind of faded away over time. Something like that might attract more tourists."

Hannah rocked on her toes, pumped with the "yes" he was leading into.

"But it takes a lot of work and a lot of time to put one together. And I still don't see how you can advertise it for free."

Deflated but not deterred, she pushed onward.

"I'll bet there's someone you know, maybe a college student or something, who'd be willing to handle posting on social media. We can use pictures of the vineyard and displays around the shop for the graphics, which can be put together quickly. Does the winery have a social media account?"

Lizzy nodded. "Yes, but we don't post much."

"That's okay. It's a place to start."

Lizzy snapped her fingers. "Don't forget the flyers you mentioned."

"Right. We can call on local businesses all around the area to see if they'd put some of our flyers in their stores for customers to see. It'll be a grass roots effort, but you've gotta start somewhere. I believe we can do it."

Hannah looked to Lizzy for backup.

"Me, too," Lizzy agreed. "It's better to try something than to do nothing, Cal."

By the way he puckered his lips, Hannah knew he was cornered.

"If we give this a shot, it can't get in the way of our regular work. This is our busy season for tours. Plus, I'm tied up trying to improve our wine. No matter what else we do, if we don't make our vintage stand out, then nothing will turn this place around."

Hannah knew he was right. Being average wouldn't keep their sales up. While she knew nothing about making wine, she knew what she liked, but now wasn't the time to share any more ideas with Callan. He'd had his fill for the day.

11

———————

Mote-filled light streamed through the windows of the shop coating the shelf in a buttery glow, where Hannah rearranged a display. She'd spent the afternoon taking pictures all around the vineyard. Snaps of displays in the shop, ones of the rows of grapevines spread across the field, and even a few of the vat room where Callan was working.

She'd made sure to take shots around him careful not to interrupt his process so he wouldn't kick her out. He might have agreed with her idea for hosting a festival, but he'd made it clear that the winery's daily work came first.

When she'd finished with the shot of the display, she approached Jen, one of the part-time employees, at the front counter.

"Would you mind telling me what you think of these pictures I got?"

"Sure." She reached for Hannah's phone and started swiping through the images. "These are cool."

Satisfaction swelled in Hannah's chest. She had a vision in mind of how to best show off the winery. There was a lot to like with the shop and tours and stunning scenic views. Enticing people to visit with beautiful pictures was key.

Once she'd narrowed down the selection with Jen's help, Hannah moved all the pictures to an album for the winery and added notes on her phone of what she wanted to include in the social media posts and flyers. She wanted to run her ideas by Lizzy, but Lizzy had taken a group out for a tour and tasting.

Her feet started walking toward the vat room before her mind committed to where she was going. With a nudge of the door, she slipped inside. The cooler temperature of the wine room tingled across her cheeks. She pulled the sleeves of her chunky sweater down when goosebumps threatened to run up her arms.

Callan stood, back to her, scribbling notes onto a clipboard. He must have been lost deep in thought, considering he didn't turn around when she entered. For several seconds she watched him. The way he moved from one vat to the other, studying his notes, marking new ones.

Appreciation swarmed her. The boy she had known was bold, inquisitive, and committed to things one hundred percent. Her included. Those traits were still evident in his passion for his work.

The memory of their last time together in high school crushed her. He'd been distant, aloof, for a week, ever since she'd told him the news. Her dad's job transfer had come about out of the blue. One phone call from his boss, an initial phone interview with the office in Virginia, and suddenly her parents were planning a move across the country in a matter of weeks. Her whole world had shattered.

Callan didn't understand. His family had lived in Falls Hollow for generations. She'd been a relative newcomer, being only a second gen resident and all. Her extended family lived in different cities, different states. While Falls Hollow was the only home she'd known, she understood there was a whole, big world outside its city limits.

When he'd started to pull away from her, a part of her soul started to detach. Stitch by stitch she felt herself coming undone. As she'd reached up on her toes for one last kiss on that final day, he'd turned his cheek to her and pulled her in for a shaky hug instead. In a blink, he'd slipped through her fingers like smoke, disappearing into the fog of her memories.

Seventeen was a hard enough age. Throw in leaving the only home she'd ever known, her school and friends and entire life, and it became a cocktail of tears and anxiety.

What would it be like to be the new kid in school, especially as a senior?

Would she make any friends?

Would she even try?

Turns out, she'd fared better than she'd expected she would. It hadn't been easy. Not by a longshot. But as the days turned into weeks and the weeks into months, she'd settled into her new surroundings and made new friends. Life went on.

Except for her and him.

Try as she might, and she had tried to reach him over and over only to be ghosted, she'd never heard from him again. Never saw his eyes dance with mischief or heard the low register of his voice against her ears or felt the warmth of his touch on her skin. The loss of him had created a hole in her heart. One that took her years to seal off; a vault of emotions wrapped in images she hadn't allowed to surface.

Until now.

When he glanced up, a crooked smile crawled up one side of his face. "How long have you been standing there?"

Every image, every feeling she'd ever experienced with him overtook her, almost bringing her to her knees. It was too much. She needed to get a grip on herself. They were friends at best. Too many years and too much life had passed between them. Neither could handle more in their shaky lives right now. Especially her.

"Not long." She swallowed the lump rising in her throat. Callan was a part of her past, and for a brief time her present, not her future.

She wandered over to him. "You looked deep in thought, so I didn't want to interrupt."

He folded pages over on his clipboard. "Yeah, I'm trying something new with this batch. Shortening the aging process before bottling it to see if the flavor is fresher and maybe stands out more."

"Gotcha. When will you taste it?"

"I was about to do that now, actually." He placed the clipboard on a nearby table. "Want to try a taste?"

"I'd love to."

A ping of joy reverberated through her. Any connection she could have with him, any bridges they could mend, would mean a lot to her.

He pulled out the tall barstool for her to sit. She slid in and watched while he gathered two glasses from a nearby shelf. After he set them on the table he walked over to one of the vats and using a wine thief—a plastic tube inserted into the vat to remove the wine—Callan pulled out a small amount and poured it into the glasses.

"Honest feedback only." He pointed the wine thief at her before placing it on the tabletop.

"Of course."

She picked up her glass and proceeded to swirl the contents before sniffing them. The aroma tickled her nose in the most pleasant way. Grapefruit, tart and sweet, hit her like a burst of citrusy flowers. She took a small sip, swished it around her mouth and then let it settle, each note dancing across her tongue in invigorating sparks. Brisk, fresh, and inviting.

She swallowed, savoring the long, cool finish that tingled down her throat. As good as it was, nothing stood out in an obvious way that would make this wine a clear winner over other brands. She wasn't sure how to tell him.

Callan kept his hand wrapped around his glass but hadn't taken a sip yet. "So?"

"The grapefruit is stronger with this batch, which I like."

"But?"

"That's a personal thing. Some people enjoy that flavor and like to be able to taste it. Others don't."

She worried her bottom lip between her teeth, hesitant to give him the feedback he needed, yet one glance at his eager face and she knew she had to be honest. He'd want nothing less.

"But the biggest thing, and what I know you're looking for, is distinction. What makes your wine stand out over others, and I'm not sure what that is."

"That's it!" He splayed his hands out, palms up. "That's what I've been telling Lizzy and Mom and Dad, but they think our wine is fine. Our sales don't indicate fine."

While he knew what was wrong, she was relieved her response didn't upset him.

"Lizzy said you haven't spent much on marketing. That will make a difference."

"I know, but to survive in this industry, or better yet, to *thrive* in this industry, you need to separate yourself from others. Even if it's the tiniest difference, that niche can elevate a product."

He was right. Any business owner would tell you it's not about reinventing the wheel but tweaking your product or service to differentiate it from similar ones in the market.

"What all have you tried?"

He ran his fingers through his mop of hair, and Hannah had the sudden urge to do the same. She shook the notion from her mind with an imperceptible nod. Telling herself that she and Callan could be nothing more than friends was a reminder she had to put on repeat.

"I've adjusted the temperature, fermenting time, the length of aging. I don't know what else to try."

Hannah thought for a moment, contemplating the various changes he tried with the process, not sure what else she could add.

"That first year when your wine won as best debut, did you use the same process as you do now?"

"Yes, and while using the same process to keep your vintages as close as possible is recommended, there's no guarantee that your wine will taste the same from year to year. Too many factors, like weather and the harvest, play into that."

Hannah nodded, understanding how it worked.

"Maybe our first year was a fluke or maybe we won just because we had the best entry that particular year. Who knows?" He let his hand fall to the table.

"Your wine is good, Callan. Really good. I don't believe it was a fluke."

Her comment elicited a faint grin. Enough to awaken a flight of butterflies in her belly.

He picked up his glass in a toast. "Thanks for the

honesty. Our entry that year might not have been a fluke, but I still have work to do."

She raised her glass and clinked his, her eyes never leaving his as they both took a sip. She felt solid ground beneath her feet as planks came together, mending and connecting the invisible bridge between them.

It had been so long since she'd experienced that sensation of aligning with another person in such a deep, real way. How had she not noticed anything missing between her and Luke?

Hannah set her glass down. "I took a bunch of pictures of the winery I'd like to show you, so you can tell me which ones you'd like to use for the marketing pieces."

She retrieved her phone from her pocket and pulled up the pictures, ready to launch into all the ideas she had. He scooted his barstool next to her so he could get a closer look.

She stilled. Cedarwood and fire mixed with a touch of patchouli tickled her nose. It was annoying how good he smelled.

Focus, Hannah.

"I think the displays are great for showcasing your product, but the pictures of the winery and vineyard give people a glimpse into the inner workings of your business. It's about connection. Especially on social media. You want to find your audience, if you will, and then connect with them by taking them behind the scenes and showing them the beauty of this place.

"Marketing is about more than 'buy my thing', it's about building rapport and relationships."

"Hmm." Callan reached out and pointed to one of the pictures of the vineyard. "Like that?"

"Exactly." She scrolled to the ones she'd taken of the vat room, including the pictures with him in it. "This is the reality of making wine. People like to see that. They like to learn and try new things."

"You have a knack for this. Where did you work before coming here?"

"Uh, well—"

Before she could say anything more, Summer bounded into the room.

"Hey, Dad." She stopped next to him, her vibrant blue eyes bright with curiosity. "What are y'all doing?" She peered back and forth between him and Hannah.

He reached for his and Hannah's glasses and moved them to the side while simultaneously scooting his stool back away from her. "We were tasting the current batch of wine."

His movement was stiff, almost awkward.

Hannah's belly twisted. He went from engaged to detached in a blink. She knew he was nervous about anything disrupting his and Summer's daily life but realizing he considered her a disruption bothered her. A lot.

"I'll show the rest of these to Lizzy and see what she thinks." Hannah closed the pictures app on her phone.

"Good idea. She has the final say anyway since that's her domain." Callan stood and took their glasses off the table, then returned them to the shelf where he'd gotten them.

"Guess I'll see you two around."

She rose, not sure what else to say. Her phone buzzed. Out of instinct she looked at it, and when she saw that the first few words of the text were in all caps, and the fact that it was from her attorney, her hearing roared.

YOU SIGNED A POSTNUP. CALL ME!

"Is something wrong?" Callan asked.

She'd frozen in place when she'd read the impossible text glaring like a thousand spotlights on her phone screen.

Blood drained from her body. Weak-kneed and nauseous, she clenched her jaw tight praying for every ounce of strength she could summon.

"No, just a reminder of something I have to do. I'll see y'all later."

She shoved her phone in her pocket and escaped through the open door, anxious to catch her breath. In a matter of seconds, her day went from good to obliterated, and she had a sinking suspicion it was about to get worse.

12

With her phone pressed to her ear, Hannah paced back and forth in front of the fireplace in the bungalow. She had excused herself to Lizzy in a rush to leave the winery and call her attorney back. Thank goodness Lizzy didn't ask questions because Hannah was too keyed up to have a coherent conversation.

"I don't understand?" She palmed her forehead, stricken with a fresh wave of panic.

"Luke's attorney sent me a copy of the postnup today. Apparently, he'd waited at Luke's request. I guess he thought you'd sign the divorce decree as is, but now, since you've countered, he's pulling out all the stops to make sure you walk away with basically what you came into the marriage with. How did you not know you'd signed this?"

"I told you. The only thing I ever signed was paperwork to protect our assets and set up a trust when Luke's career took off. He never mentioned a postnup."

"Did you read through the document before you signed it? Or better yet, did you get an attorney to do so?"

"Luke's attorney was our attorney. We went to his office

together and I signed next to wherever Luke signed." Hannah slumped down on the sofa, head in her hand. "I trusted what he told me."

"And what exactly did he tell you?"

Hannah racked her memory of that day. Her recollection was short, but she hadn't noticed anything amiss.

"Luke told me about the meeting a couple of days beforehand. He said he'd met with our attorney to draw up the trust and to make sure all our finances were in order with his latest promotion in place. I mean, Luke was already successful when I met him, but his career kept escalating, and by a month into our marriage, he'd gotten a big promotion that put him on track to move to a C-level position that same year."

"And by year three of your marriage, he'd bought out fifty-one percent of that company pushing his net worth into the stratosphere."

"In a nutshell, yes."

Her attorney, Sheila Hopps, sighed though the phone. Hannah had retained Sheila's services when she filed her countersuit to Luke's divorce filing. Sheila worked at a firm well known for handling high-profile divorces. Plus, she spoke to Hannah in a genuine manner. Something most attorneys, at least in her experience, did not do.

"Hannah, the only paperwork Luke's attorney has is this postnup. I've checked. Unless you can prove you had a hand, a serious hand, in Luke's success, this postnup will stand. I will do everything to fight it, of course, and make sure you get your fair share, but I want to be honest about the expectations. At best, we can hope that Luke will reconsider and make you an offer. There's no guarantee. I wish I had better news for you."

Tears burned Hannah's eyes. She fought to hold it

together, not wanting to collapse into a blubbering mess. She believed Sheila would fight for her, but she had her limits. The law was the law, and Hannah was going to end up on the short end of it.

"I understand, Sheila. Please keep me posted."

"I will. Hang in there, Hannah."

"Always. Thanks Shelia."

Hannah ended the call and tossed her phone on the coffee table. What money she'd walked away with was a miniscule fraction compared to her and Luke's net worth. Well technically, *his* net worth. His postnup play made sure of that.

Guess his parting gift was a pity payout to get her out of his life so he could move on with his new girlfriend and their unborn child.

Her stomach roiled.

Hannah knew the rumors were true. Luke had admitted as much. While he and his new love hadn't made it official, it was only a matter of time before she started showing. The paparazzi followed their every move, eager to be the first to officially break the news. They fed their salacious stories to the world to make a quick buck. She didn't miss that part of her life.

BY THE TIME NIGHT FELL, Hannah had finished reading her book and made herself a big salad for dinner. She'd also started playing around with some dried lavender she'd purchased in town, mixing it with her favorite shea butter lotion and slathering her legs with it. The aroma it left behind was relaxing. Peaceful. It was the perfect scent to calm her shaky nerves.

Snuggled up in her favorite navy-blue leggings and boxy sweatshirt, she pulled her hair up in a high ponytail and took out a pot to make some hot chocolate. One of her favorite cold weather treats. She preferred making her own over store-bought brands. It was easy, quick, and utterly delicious.

Her thoughts raced over what she was going to do. When she'd confronted Luke after being served the divorce papers, he'd quickly given her a portion of their savings so she could set up her own account.

In the midst of his confession of what he'd done, he'd told her he'd be fair but finalizing everything would take a while. He'd handed her a check—it was a solid amount, but not enough to live on for long—and an apology. Then he'd turned, picked up his overnight bag, and left.

The recollection was bitter on her tongue. Had he withheld the postnup because he knew it wasn't fair? Why the change of heart? Wasn't his infidelity enough of a blow?

She blew out an exasperated breath. She didn't want to think about it anymore.

As soon as she'd poured herself a cup of the steamy cocoa and sat down on the sofa to enjoy it, the lights blinked. Once, twice, and then they went out.

She froze, waiting to see if they'd come back on. After a few seconds passed, she turned the flashlight on her phone on and set her mug on the coffee table before rising to peer outside the front window. She hadn't noticed any rain, but storms could whip up out here in a flash.

She looked from side to side, the moon shining bright enough to feature a cloudless sky.

With a shrug of her shoulders, she walked to the bathroom where she had placed the oatmeal and honey candle she'd also purchased when she'd gone shopping. After lighting it, she brought it into the living room and set it on the chunk of wood that served as a mantel for the fireplace.

She settled into the sofa once more and took a sip of her hot chocolate. It was rich and creamy perfection. It reminded her of the hot chocolate Mr. Hank, Callan's dad, used to make. The memory of it soothed her.

Minutes ticked by—two minutes, five minutes, ten minutes—and she wondered if she was the only one experiencing an outage. The winery was close enough she could see it from the front porch, so she stepped outside to check. Exterior lights shone in the distance.

She was the only one in the dark.

She wandered back inside and put her cup down. Maybe she should call Callan. After all, he was the landlord of this place. If she were staying anywhere else, that's what she would have done.

After knocking the thought around her mind for a few minutes, she picked up her phone and called him.

Ring one, her belly squeezed. Ring two, she started second guessing herself. Ring three, he picked up.

"Hello?" His voice rumbled through the line.

She pictured him in a tee shirt and jeans, kicked back in one of the chairs on the front porch of his parents' house where they used to hang out on cozy nights like this one.

"Hello?"

He spoke again making her realize she'd gotten lost in the image playing across her mind.

"Oh, hey. Sorry, my phone made a weird noise."

Not true but she didn't know what else to say to cover up her momentary lapse.

"It's Hannah."

"Hey. Is everything okay?" His voice rose an octave, and she could only imagine what he was thinking.

When was the last time she'd called him? Seventeen years suddenly seemed like a million years ago.

"I'm sorry to bother you, but the electricity went out over here. I don't know what happened."

"It's probably a fuse. Sorry about that. I can come by and check."

"Yeah, that would be great. I mean, it's not hot or anything in here considering it's fall, but I'd still like to turn on the lights." She chuckled.

"Give me a minute to call my neighbor so she can keep an eye on Summer, then I'll head over."

She hadn't thought about the fact he had a young daughter at home. At eight years old, she was too young to stay by herself.

"I'm sorry, I forgot about Summer. I mean, I didn't forget about her. I just didn't think about her being home by herself. You can wait till tomorrow. I'll be fine."

She bumbled her way through trying to let him off the hook. Being without electricity for one night, especially with the weather as beautiful as it had been, wouldn't hurt her. She'd survive.

"It's okay. It's part of my job as acting landlord. I'll see you in a few."

"Okay, thanks."

She hung up. A little rattled, she busied herself by straightening the coffee table and plumping the pillows. She wasn't sure why, but a thrum of nervous energy buzzed through her. Callan took care of this place for his parents. That's all. It wasn't like he was coming over to hang out, yet she found herself in the bathroom with her phone flashlight shining bright so she could make sure she looked presentable.

No makeup, her hair pulled up in a ponytail, dressed in

sweats, she was still young enough to pull off the natural look without much fuss. Not that it mattered. The electricity needed repairing and Callan was the one to call. She waved her hand in the air as if to push away all errant thoughts.

Back in the living room, she decided to light a few more candles. There was a big one in the center of the coffee table and two smaller ones in the kitchen, plus one in the bedroom. She grabbed the one out of the bedroom and set it on the small dining table. Once all the wicks were lit, the bungalow glowed with a homey warmth that made her smile.

It didn't take long for Callan to arrive. Yet, when he knocked on the door her heart climbed up her throat. With one deep, cleansing breath, she squared her shoulders and reminded herself this was just a house call to fix her lighting issue.

Be polite, be cordial, and get on with it she told herself.

She opened the door, and the sight of him in his jeans and stark white tee shirt knocked all of her logical thinking askew.

"Hey," she blurted out in a huff.

"Hey."

She stood there staring for a second before coming to her senses.

"Come in." She waved him in and stood back so he could cross the threshold into the living room, suddenly wishing she had at least put on some lip gloss or something.

"I'll go check the breakers and see what's going on."

With his toolbox in hand, he spun on his heels and went straight to work. To be honest, she was thankful. The less chit chat, the better.

He swiveled his head toward her. "I can show you where the breaker box is in case it goes out again. That's the first thing to check. And flipping a switch is easy if all the fuses are working. I don't have any extra at home, so if one is out, I'll have to wait until the morning to run by the hardware store."

"That's fine. I shouldn't have bothered you anyway. Like I said, the weather is cool, so I'll be perfectly comfortable with the windows open until tomorrow."

"It's no problem. I live close by and like I said, it's my job." He tilted his head toward the kitchen. "Come on."

She followed him into the kitchen where he opened the door to the narrow laundry closet that housed a stackable washer and dryer unit. The breaker box was on the right-hand wall. He pulled a flashlight from inside his toolbox that he had placed on the counter, then pulled the panel open and started flipping the switches, one after another, but nothing came on. After he finished going through both rows, he closed the panel door. He cut off his flashlight and dropped it back into the toolbox before snapping the lid shut.

"It's a fuse."

Hannah pinched her lips together and nodded.

"The wiring is original to this house, installed when it was built in the eighties. It might be time for an update."

"That sounds like a big undertaking."

She leaned against the counter across from him. In the faint light of the candles flickering in their glass votives, she noticed the way he still tilted his head when he was deep in thought. Adding a remodel to his busy to-do list would be difficult. He had his hands full with the vineyard and being a full-time dad.

"It's not a quick fix, that's for sure. But replacing the fuse will take care of everything while you're here. You won't have to bump around in the dark." He smirked and she had the sudden urge to press her fingertip against the cleft in his chin. Something she had done countless times when they'd dated.

"Good deal. I can handle one night of bumbling around in the dark."

He picked up his toolbox. "Well, I guess I'll let you get some sleep."

"Thanks again for coming out to check on it. I appreciate it."

"Of course." He took a step to make his way to the front door and words flew out of her mouth without any preconceived idea.

"Would you like some hot chocolate?"

What are you doing?

"Hot chocolate?" His confused expression melded into a curious one.

"Yeah, I made some right before I called you. It's probably more like lukewarm chocolate now, but I have plenty for another cup."

"Um, sure. I guess."

Good job, Hannah. Great way to make him feel uncomfortable.

"I mean, you came all the way over here and I hate to waste it." She struggled to come up with something to say that didn't make her look like she was trying to turn this into something more than a house call, because she wasn't. She couldn't.

She shouldn't.

"Actually, a cup of hot chocolate sounds pretty good." He grinned, and every worry, every concern she had about her questionable behavior evaporated into the night.

13

***

Hannah nestled into one side of the sofa, her legs curled underneath her, with her cup of hot chocolate cradled in her hands. Callan sat on the other side, but considering it was a small sofa his proximity dizzied her senses. He was boyishly handsome with a rugged edge. Sharp planes, teddy bear eyes, and endless charm.

"This is pretty tasty," he said after taking a long sip.

"Thanks. It's my favorite cold weather drink."

"I remember." His eyes darted at his slip, but she tucked the sentiment away without acknowledging it. Embarrassing him wasn't on the menu.

Not to mention the fact she'd made enough gaffes of her own.

Leaning over to set her mug on the coffee table, she wondered if she should dare to bring up the subject of their break-up and his subsequent ghosting of her. Since they'd been interrupted the first time she'd asked, she'd waited for another chance to get some resolution. Closure of any kind from that period would satisfy her. However, she had no idea what would satiate her in the present.

"Speaking of memories . . ." She settled back into her spot ready to dive in. "You never finished telling me why you didn't respond to me when I tried to reach out after I moved away."

"I told you. We were young."

"That's not really an answer, Callan."

Maybe she was being pushy. *It doesn't matter* she told herself. Seventeen years of life lived existed between them. That amount of time rubbed away at the rough edges dulling the sharp pain of abandonment, of loss and unanswered questions and wondering if it all had been real.

But being around him had brought it all back again, and she wanted answers.

He crossed one leg over the other, resting his foot on his knee, one arm leaning over the side of the sofa and the other hand holding his ankle, braced for her inquisition.

"What do you want me to say, Hannah? You moved. There was no way to continue dating with over a thousand miles between us."

"I realize that, but you could have at least said something."

"Again, say what? You texted me as if nothing had changed. Like we could keep talking and hanging out whenever you might come into town, which, by the way, was never."

"I might have been able to come visit, especially if you had responded in any way."

"I don't know what you're getting at. Are you saying you're mad because you wish we'd have tried some long-distance thing? We broke up. It ended. What was the point in staying in touch? We both moved on, and I'm really confused right now."

He ran his fingers through his hair obviously perplexed at her line of questioning.

To be fair, this wasn't going how she'd planned. She wanted to know why he never responded. He could have text once or twice, even if it was to say, "Good luck with the rest of your life."

But he hadn't. Nothing. Nadda. Zip.

Hannah laced her fingers in her lap. "I know we broke up. I'm not saying we could have changed anything about that. I just didn't understand why you never responded. That's all. Even if it was to say, 'Have a nice life'."

She tucked a loose strand of hair that had slipped from her ponytail behind her ear.

"It bothered me back then, and I don't know, seeing you again woke that memory up and I had to ask."

Something in his gaze softened as if a nugget of understanding hit him. "You wanted more closure."

"I guess. Yeah."

"When we talked that last day before you left, I took that as the end. Relationship over. No need to stay friends when you wouldn't even be here. Maybe I was clueless." He let out a shaky laugh. "I didn't respond because I didn't know what to say. You were gone. I was here. And let's face it, a seventeen-year-old boy is about as clued in to other people's emotions as his own. I didn't want to lose you, and I didn't know how to deal with it."

Air filled her lungs; relief at finally getting an answer. Whether she liked it or not was a different story. Time would answer that question. But at least he hadn't ghosted her because he hadn't cared.

Her lips curled into a friendly grin. "Guess I never

thought about it from your point of view. It makes sense now."

"So, we're good?"

"Yeah."

"Good, because I have some bad news."

Her eyes rounded. "Oh?"

"If my dad gets a taste of this hot chocolate, he's going to be jealous. He believes his homemade version is as famous as his spaghetti sauce." He took another sip, then held up his mug in a mock toast to her.

Thrilled that he loved her hot chocolate, she broke out into a giggle.

"I'll keep it a secret." She mimed ticking a lock across her lips.

After placing his empty mug on the coffee table, he scooted to the edge of the sofa. "I need to get home. Are you sure you'll be fine till tomorrow without electricity?"

"Absolutely. I'm going to crawl into bed and get a good night's sleep."

He rose. "Cool. I'll pick up the fuse in the morning and come out tomorrow afternoon after work to replace it."

"Great! I'll be at the winery helping Lizzy so no rush."

She walked him to the door and pulled it open to let him out. After stepping outside onto the porch, he turned to face her.

"I'm glad we cleared everything up. It feels good to close the door on all that high school stuff."

"Me, too. Good night, Callan."

"Good night." He pivoted and she watched as his long legs carried him to his truck in a few strides.

The truck engine turned, and she closed the door, her back leaning against it. While she was relieved to hear his side, something felt wrong about closing the door on Callan Locke.

OVERNIGHT STORMS LEFT the ground soaked. While the sun was shining big and bright this morning, Hannah had to dodge numerous mud puddles on her way over to the winery. She made a mental note to add rubber boots to her shopping list. This morning, she had to settle for her favorite pair of sneakers. At least they were washable.

Today, with Jen's help, Hannah put together several social media post ideas to show Lizzy. Jen was good at creating content. Something Hannah shared with Lizzy. With so much on her plate, it would help Lizzy to delegate a few duties, and Hannah thought Jen would be perfect as their social media manager. She only needed a couple extra hours per week to handle creating and posting, which Lizzy managed to squeeze into the budget.

With that off her list, Hannah could focus on making the displays in the shop stand out from the moment a customer entered. She was also eager to play around with a few new ideas that had blossomed. Although she didn't have a reason to host a get-together, much less a place to have one or anyone to invite, she yearned to get back to experimenting in the kitchen and crafting little welcome baskets and gardening. While the latter was off the list until she found a permanent place, she could cook anywhere.

As far as putting together essentials for the perfect evening at home, she had purchased candles and bath salt she could indulge in for herself. But what she was really craving was creating something of her own. It was as if the little white lie she'd told about working on her own lifestyle brand had planted a seed, and now, it had taken root, consuming her with ideas for recipes and mixtures, of cute little wicker baskets filled with wondrous things. Thoughts of what paired well together danced across her mind, from food to drinks, to lotions, scents, and touches of cozy luxury people could surround themselves with.

Could she create something of her own? Becoming an entrepreneur seemed preposterous, yet a part of her wondered if the possibility was tangible, possible. Maybe even pursuable.

In truth, she had to do something. Thanks to the post-nuptial agreement she'd signed, there was the chance she'd walk away from her marriage with what she'd arrived in Falls Hollow with. She was the only person she could count on looking out for herself, and that included figuring out how to support herself.

Finding a place to live was one thing, paying for it was another. Figuring out where she was going to live was a whole other animal. Her funds were limited, so even without a hard timeframe in front of her she needed to start putting things into action.

Lost in a daydream, she barely registered someone calling her name.

"Miss Hannah?"

She turned around and saw Summer standing behind her, head tilted to one side as she stared at her.

"Oh, hey Summer. I didn't see you there."

"That's because I just walked up."

"Right."

"What are you doing?" She scrunched her nose, and Hannah followed her gaze to the shelf where she'd been rearranging bottles of wine placing three different vintage years in a row.

"Helping your Aunt Lizzy with the displays. What are you up to?"

"I'm bored."

Hannah bit back a laugh. It was the weekend, and Summer was spending her day at the winery. For an eight-year-old, that must have felt like some sort of punishment.

"Would you like to help me with something?"

The little girl's eyes lit up. "Sure."

She knew she needed to proceed carefully. Spending time with Summer was fine, yet spending too much would encroach on Callan's concerns. She needed to keep it simple and short, act like she was just another employee temporarily helping out, which she was. She would respect his wishes.

"Okay. I want to put together something like a spa basket."

"A spa basket?" Summer narrowed her eyes. Being only eight, she probably wasn't familiar with things like spending the day at a spa.

"Have you ever heard of a spa?"

"I think so."

"It's a place people go to relax. They get massages and meditate and usually enjoy a delicious and healthy lunch."

"Oh." Summer shrugged her shoulders, unimpressed.

Hannah chuckled. "It's a grownup thing."

"Can I still help?"

"Of course." She curled her finger at the little girl, encouraging her to follow.

Zigzagging through the shop, she picked up a bottle of wine and a candle, a wheel of Brie that she handed to Summer to hold, and a jar of raspberry preserves. They ran into Hank, Callan's dad, at the back of the store where he was walking through the back entrance.

"Hi, Mr. Hank," she said with a slight wave.

Hi, Hannah." He glanced down. "Hi, squirt. What are you two up to?"

He shrugged off his jacket and folded it over his arm. He wasn't quite as tall as Callan, but he had the same shade of brown hair, although his was mixed with streaks of grey. With one slight dimple, he exuded a playfulness that matched his boisterous personality.

Hannah loved how Callan's whole family worked together. Building a family business, each playing a part. It was appealing.

"Summer's helping me put a basket together."

As if on cue, Summer held up the wheel of Brie and the jar of preserves. "It's a *spa* basket."

The way she emphasized *spa* was adorable.

Hank's chuckle seemed to voice his agreement. "Well, you two have fun. I'm going to help your dad with a few things, and then I'm going to take Bitty out to dinner." He ruffled Summer's hair. "It's good seeing you again, Hannah. You've been a welcome relief for Lizzy since Roberta's been out."

"I'm happy to help."

She appreciated how welcome Callan's parents made her feel. Their kindness made her smile.

With Hank on his way to assist Callan, Summer followed her into the storeroom.

After setting their items on the worktable, Hannah peered at the various stock items filling the shelves. Not seeing what she wanted, she headed back toward the door to exit the storage area.

"Come on. I have an idea."

She encouraged Summer to follow along and the two of them made their way to the tasting room.

Once inside, Hannah made a beeline to the buffet table. She pulled the center cabinet doors open, glanced inside, then closed the doors. Not giving up, she opened one of the side cabinets and grinned.

"Here we go." She grabbed a basket sitting within and held it up. "I think this will work perfectly. What do you think?"

She handed the basket to Summer.

Cradling the wicker basket in her small hands, Summer turned it from side to side as if she were inspecting the quality of how it was made, if it was indeed perfect like Hannah had claimed.

"I think it'll work."

"Me too." She winked at Summer before taking the basket from her. "Let's go put everything together."

When they reentered the storeroom, Hannah noticed Callan sitting at the worktable scribbling on his clipboard.

"Hey, Dad." Summer bounded over to him. "Whatcha doing?"

He put his pen down and wrapped his arm around his daughter, squeezing her in for a quick side hug. "I'm working. What are you doing?"

"I'm helping Miss Hannah make a spa basket."

"Oh really?" He slid his eyes toward Hannah.

She watched his jaw tighten. If she didn't say something quickly, he'd think she was disregarding all his concerns about spending time around his daughter.

"I had an idea. Hear me out."

He answered with an arch of his brow.

"We can put together a basket of items people can use at home to create their own spa day highlighting your wine as the main focal point. We'll include your most recent vintage with some yummy snacks and a luxurious candle, maybe a soft face towel or bath salt or something like that, which we can find locally made or sold. Then you could put it at the front counter and present it as a giveaway. I can have Jen post about it on social media, you and Lizzy can tell customers about it at the end of tours. It's a great way to create some buzz."

"Buzz?" If it were even possible, he arched his brow higher.

"Yeah."

Helping out around the winery had proven to be more fun than she'd expected. Busying herself with the displays took her mind off the divorce, and it also stirred up her creativity, her enthusiasm for crafting the perfect pairing or putting together a unique treat to dazzle someone special.

"Is this the kind of marketing you did wherever you worked?"

His question was reasonable, but she didn't have a good answer. Mainly because she never worked anywhere. But at least he seemed okay with Summer assisting her.

"I've hosted a lot of parties and guests love special treats. Gift baskets like this were always a hit."

It was a good save although the niggling in her belly made her uncomfortable.

"Sounds like an expensive party favor," he grunted.

At his core, Callan was a simple, down-to-earth guy. He wouldn't understand the life she'd led, much less like it, yet eventually, she needed to tell him the truth. And by eventually, she meant now.

"Well, it's the only real experience—"

His phone rang stopping her confession mid-sentence.

"Sorry, I need to grab this." He put his phone to his ear and stepped a few feet away to engage with whomever was on the other end.

Guess she'd have to wait a little longer to come clean, not that that upset her. Sharing details with Callan about her life with Luke made her nervous. It had been great until it wasn't.

The life she'd lived had been interesting and exciting and full of experiences she savored, yet the questions plaguing her had nothing to do with that. They were about Luke. Specifically, the connection they'd shared, the love between them that in hindsight seemed less than she'd believed.

Callan might not have been the kind of person who held much interest in such a big, public life, but he'd wonder how she'd ended up so far removed from the girl he used to know. The one who had big plans for college and her life beyond. The one who'd shifted into a whole other world. How could she explain that? And why did it bother her what he thought?

"Miss Hannah?"

"Hmm?" She snapped back to the present where Summer was holding the basket up.

"How do we fit everything in here?"

Hannah took the basket from her hands and placed it on the table next to the stash of items they'd gathered. "One at a time. I'll show you."

They added the items to the basket with the bottle of wine in the center. Each took turns shifting things around, looking at the collection from different angles. She encouraged Summer to play around with how everything was set up. With a dash of enthusiasm, the little girl pitched in, trying different arrangements much to Hannah's satisfaction. She liked spending time with Summer.

She caught Callan watching them out the corner of his eyes with an amused grin. Maybe things were all right between them. Following her own advice to Summer about placing items in the basket one at a time, maybe opening up to Callan one conversation at a time would ease the lingering discomfort and open the door to a new stage in their relationship as friends.

She might not have cared about such a thing with Luke, but Callan was different. Like Lizzy had said, he was one of the good ones. Something she was beginning to realize was important to her.

Fate had a way of intervening when you least expected it, putting the right people in your path at the right time. Seeing Callan Locke again was not on her Bingo card, but in this moment it sure felt right.

14

———

With sunset fast approaching, Hannah grabbed the lighter she'd left on the kitchen counter and proceeded to light several candles. Callan would arrive soon to replace the fuse, and she didn't want him to have to fumble around in the dark.

It didn't take long for the minty scent of lavender to fill the tiny bungalow. She inhaled the soothing aroma letting it wash over her in a breath of calm, willing it to settle her anxious nerves. Callan stopping by to fix the electricity was no big deal. It was being alone with him again, after hours, away from the winery, that induced her jitters.

If they were going to be friends, she needed to find a way to move past the images of a young Callan and Hannah experiencing the first inklings of love. Those memories were best kept tucked away.

Three knocks rapped against the front door. She grabbed her phone off the countertop and tried to get a glance of herself in the screen. It was too dark, even with the candlelight, to make out anything more than her outline, so she put the phone down and squared her shoulders as if prepping to meet someone for the first time. Maybe in a way she was. Friend-Callan was different from Ex-Boyfriend-Callan.

She could do this.

Channeling her inner hostess, she opened the door with ease, a welcoming smile spread across her face.

"Hey! Come in." She stepped back to give him room to walk inside. A whiff of melted cheese and tangy salsa followed him. "What's that smell?"

He held up a bag. "My mom found out about your electrical issues, and she insisted I bring you food. Summer wanted tacos, so I picked up an extra order to go."

He handed her the bag, and her belly tumbled at the gesture. Whether his mom played a part didn't matter. He'd agreed.

"Thanks. I haven't had good Tex Mex in ages." She took the bag into the kitchen and placed it on the counter. He followed her and set his toolbox by her food, then pulled out his flashlight and a small package containing a fuse.

"This won't take long." He ambled over to the laundry closet where the breaker box was located.

"Need some help?" She hated just standing there while he did all the work.

"I got it. Eat your tacos before they get cold. I already reheated them once since I picked them up from Los Amigos."

Los Amigos in Austin had been one of their favorites for Mexican food.

Given the hollowness in the pit of her stomach, she didn't argue. While she leaned against the counter devouring a taco, Callan worked steadily, quiet as he went. The silence burned her ears. Maybe now was the time to tell him the truth about the marketing job she never held.

"So earlier, when we were talking about the basket Summer and I were putting together, you asked about my previous experience." She wiped her hands on a napkin, then bunched it up and tossed it in the bag.

She had no idea how she wanted to launch into this admission. In a way it was embarrassing. One little white lie to save her from the stab of humiliation had turned into something much bigger. Maybe she was protecting herself more than anything. Too many truths had come to light in recent weeks, and facing her own failings had created a level of doubt and reckoning she was ill-prepared to handle.

"Mm, hmm." He pressed the flashlight between his lips as he worked on replacing the old fuse.

His focus calmed her. She welcomed the relief it gave her. Before she knew it, she'd hopped up on the counter, sitting with one leg crossed over the other, the second taco in one hand as the words sprang forth like a river.

"The truth is, I never got a job after college."

With a slight turn of his head, his eyes slid in her direction. Waiting.

She blew out a heavy breath. "I met Luke a few weeks after graduation. He's a few years older than me, so he was already into his career in the tech industry. He's wicked smart, and ambitious, and with that combo, he moved up the proverbial ladder quickly.

"At first, we did the long-distance thing while I was sending out resumes and scheduling interviews in L.A. and he was working in Northern California, but our relationship progressed pretty fast and within weeks he'd convinced me to move in with him. We went from dating to engaged to married in less than a year and a half."

Callan flipped a switch on the breaker box and the lights

blinked on in the living room. The brightness felt too revealing. Hannah smiled anyway.

"Thank you."

Callan held up a finger and disappeared into the living room. When the lights went out again, Hannah wondered if she'd spend the rest of her time here with open windows and candlelight.

"The electricity didn't go out again," he said, obviously noticing her worried look. "I just thought you might want to share the rest of your story, and tacos, by candlelight."

A feather could have knocked her over. She'd forgotten how well he listened to people. It didn't matter who, he made everyone feel like what they had to say held a level of importance that should be respected.

He leaned against the counter opposite her, hands propped behind him grasping the edge.

"You were saying?"

She put her half-eaten taco down, suddenly more interested in talking than eating.

"It was all a blur. Like I said, we went from meeting to married in a blink, but that's how Luke operates. With work, with his personal life, with everything. And with his career taking off, I shifted into a different life, I guess. Maybe lifestyle is a better word.

"We certainly didn't need the money, so my career aspirations fizzled. I don't know why. I never envisioned not working, but I guess in a way I made our life my job. From managing the house to hosting regular get-togethers at our home to volunteering with different organizations, it all kind of consumed me."

"So, you were never in marketing?" He stroked his chin, running his thumb over the slim cleft in the center.

She shook her head. "No. I got a degree in marketing,

but it sat in a frame at the bottom of a box in our attic, gathering dust instead of landing me a job.”

He folded his arms across his chest, head cocked to one side. “And the lifestyle company you said you were working on?”

“About that.” She hopped off the counter, her back braced against it as if it were holding her up. “I might have embellished a bit.”

She pinched her forefinger and thumb close together for effect.

“No lifestyle company either?”

“No. Maybe? I don’t know.”

Now it was her turn to wrap her arms around her chest.

“Why are you here then? I mean, not that it’s a bad thing, I just don’t understand why you’d come all the way here when you’ve lived in California since college. Did you need that much space between you and your ex?”

If he only knew. She bit her bottom lip while she searched for the words that would explain the magnitude of her very public divorce. One glance at his calloused hands, his blue jeans and boots, and her courage withered. How could she convey the details of such a life in a way he’d understand? More importantly, how could she do so in a way that wouldn’t scare him off?

He valued simplicity and real connections with people. Learning she spent her time with a wide circle of people she no longer called friends, or a husband she had to schedule time with on a calendar would baffle him.

“I came here for the peace and quiet so I could figure things out. Falls Hollow hasn’t been on my radar in ages, yet somehow, I found myself heading this way as if the hill country was calling to me, luring me here to start over.”

It was the truth. Raw and open and honest, even if it didn't fully explain her situation.

"My divorce its complicated, and the truth is I need to figure out what I'm going to do next." She shrugged her shoulders, defeated.

"Well, this little town might not come close to whatever you had in California, but what it's lacking in opportunities is made up by the people and the space. Give yourself some time, Hannah. You'll figure it out."

Warmth pooled through her. Seventeen years and he still knew the right thing to say.

"Thanks." A timid smile tugged at her cheeks.

Callan put his flashlight back in his toolbox and closed the lid before picking it up by the handle. "For what it's worth, pitching in at the winery has helped Lizzy and your displays look great."

Satisfaction swelled in her chest.

"Maybe creating your own brand isn't such a far-fetched idea."

"We'll see. I've gotta make money somehow." She chuckled.

"You should be all good now." He flicked his thumb toward the laundry closet.

"Thanks again for taking care of it."

"It's my job." He reminded her.

"Yeah, along with running a vineyard and raising a daughter."

"You know what they say about idle hands."

"You've never been idle, Callan."

He smirked and the image of the boy she knew rushed over her. Standing before him was like stepping back in time, but she didn't mind. Sometimes you had to take a step back in order to move forward again. And sometimes that step allowed you to right some wrongs.

She might not have shared every detail about her life with Luke, but she'd shared enough for him to understand her need for space, for clarity.

"I'll walk you out."

Standing on the porch, she watched as he climbed into his truck and closed the door, window down. He gave her a slight wave before starting the engine. As soon as he shifted gears and pressed on the gas, his back tire spun. The overnight storms had left the ground drenched, and he'd parked right in the middle of a puddle.

He leaned his head against the headrest and let out a sigh, then tried moving forward again. No luck.

"You're pretty stuck," she shouted to him.

She watched him throw the gearshift into park and get out. He bent down next to the sunken tire. "I'm gonna need your help."

"My help?" She couldn't imagine what she could do to get him unstuck.

He rose, his hands propped on his hips. "You drive while I push."

"Oh." She skittered down the steps and got into the truck. "Tell me when to go," she called out to him.

With a peek in the rearview mirror, she watched him brace his hands against the back left of the truck where the tire was stuck.

"Okay. Give it a little gas."

She put it in drive and revved the engine while he strained against the back corner of the tailgate.

"A little more," he shouted.

Her foot slammed on the pedal harder than she intended. Mud flew as the truck lurched forward, yanking the tire out of the puddle and dousing Callan in wet, sloppy muck. She hit the brake once the truck was free.

"Oh, my gosh! I'm so sorry."

She stuck her head out the window to get a full view of Callan covered in mud. Restraining the laugh rolling up her throat wasn't an option. Her shoulders shook as she let it out.

Callan flung mud from his hands before wiping them down the sides of his jeans. "Glad I could entertain you." He laughed and Hannah welcomed the rumble of it.

"I think I pressed on the gas too hard."

"You think?" With the back of his hand, he tried to wipe away splotches of muck covering his face, but he only smeared it more. "I think I need a shower."

Hannah got out of the truck, leaving it running for him. "You might need to hose off before you walk inside."

He stretched out his mud-soaked arms and twisted them from one side to the other, studying them.

"You're probably right." He dropped his arms to the side. "Or I could just rub some of this off on you."

Her stomach lurched when he took a step forward. She flung her hands up. "It was an accident, Callan. I promise."

She started backing up and he matched her step for step, then he lunged forward, and she covered her eyes with her palms as she screamed.

His laughter filled the space between them, and she peeked through her fingertips to see he'd stopped right before getting to her.

With a playful slap on his arm, she shook her head. "That wasn't nice."

Rapid clicks echoed behind her, and she whirled around to see a guy with a camera, its long lens protruding out like Pinocchio's nose, leaning around a nearby tree trunk snapping pictures of them. Her mouth went dry.

Callan slipped around in front of her taking a protective stance.

"What are you doing?" he barked at the intruder.

"I think the question is, what are *you guys* doing?" He snorted a sleazy laugh, then proceeded to take more pictures.

Before she could register what he was doing, Callan took off toward the guy. She leapt after him and grabbed his arm.

"Ignore him. Let's go inside."

"Ignore him? Some dude's hiding behind a tree taking our pictures. For what I don't know."

"I can explain. Come on." She tugged on his arm while the guy boldly started walking toward them clicking away with his obnoxious camera.

"Man, this is private property. You better leave or I'll call the cops," Callan snarled.

The guy smirked and Hannah felt the muscles in Callan's arm tense. If she didn't get him inside, she knew he would take matters into his own hands and restrain this guy until the cops arrived.

"No worries, man. I got what I needed."

Camera Guy put his camera down, letting it hang from the strap around his neck. He threw up a peace sign and hurried away to a car parked down the road near the winery. One Hannah hadn't noticed until that very second.

After he hopped in, turned the car around and drove off, Callan faced Hannah with a mountain of questions firing from his narrowed eyes.

"What was that?"

She swallowed. Stalling. This was a detail about her life she'd wanted to ease into when explaining it to Callan, but his piercing gaze went straight through her like a knife to the chest.

"Paparazzi." Her voice came out barely above a whisper.

"Why in the world would someone come way out here to take pictures of us?"

He really had no idea who Luke was or the life she'd led. Guess it was time to shed her armor and give him the full story. Tabloids and all.

"It's not you, it's me they're after. Well, me and anyone I'm with."

He propped his hands on his hips, grounding himself. "I'm gonna need more than that."

"My life with Luke was a very public one. He's well known, not just in the tech industry but across the world. As part owner of a major tech firm, he's all over and subsequently, so was I. And Luke was never one to shy away from the camera, which is how he met his new girlfriend. She's a famous up-and-coming actress that he cheated on me with."

There, she'd said it. No more lies. No more half-truths. Everything she'd left behind in California was out in the open.

It was a relief and a burden. Carrying around baggage required heavy lifting, whether the details were hung out for the world to see or not, because while the act of holding secrets in weighed a person down, revealing them could open the door for a whole new set of problems.

She had no idea how Callan would react, yet the way he clenched his jaw gave her a glimpse at the answer.

He ran his dirty fingers through his hair, composing himself. "You're telling me you're famous?"

"Kinda. I guess." She didn't realize how tightly she'd been grasping her fingers until the numbness started tingling up her wrists.

"That's a lot, Hannah. I, um, hmm . . . I don't know what to say."

"I don't live that life anymore, Callan. I left it all behind when I came here to figure out what I'm going to do next."

"Someone followed you here to sneak around and get pictures of you. I don't think you left it all behind."

"The tabloids are just trying to stir up trouble and make a fast buck since the divorce hit the news."

"The news?"

His gaze was incredulous. She didn't bother to answer. She didn't know what to say. She could feel him slipping away, their newly burgeoning friendship falling to the wayside before it even got started.

"The paparazzi started following me around as soon as our divorce went public, especially since Luke left me for someone else. I didn't think they'd follow me all the way out here."

"I'm sorry you're having to deal with this, Hannah, but I can't wrap my head around it. I have a daughter to raise, a vineyard to turn around. This is too much. We live vastly different lives, and all that," he motioned toward the tree where Camera Guy had been hiding, "is not me."

He climbed into his truck and closed the door. She watched him take a visible breath before turning to face her.

"If that guy comes back, let me know. I may not understand your world, but I want you to be safe."

He flashed her a half-hearted smile, then drove away, taking any fizzle of joy she'd experienced this evening with him.

15

———

Sleep did not come easy for Hannah. She tossed and turned, reliving the horrifying moment Camera Guy had interrupted a sweet moment between her and Callan with the clicks of his camera firing off one after another. The look on Callan's face when she'd told him the truth about her life with Luke imprinted on her brain. She wanted to burn the image away.

When she finally got up, before the sun had dared to rise no less, she'd made a full pot of coffee. A dose of caffeine was the only thing that would stop her sluggish eyelids from shutting. She was supposed to meet Lizzy at the winery for ten, which gave her plenty of time to knock out her usual morning stretching routine, but she had no desire, no energy to commit. By nine-thirty, she walked through the front door of the winery, a to-go mug of coffee in her hand.

A tour and tasting were scheduled for ten-thirty and Lizzy had invited Hannah to join her. It would be a great way for Hannah to see the flow and determine how best to introduce the raffle as well as generate other ideas to get people on the tour excited about purchasing bottles to bring home. If they fell in love with the wine, they'd want to buy more. That would drive up revenue, but not enough on its own.

Distribution was key. Right now, the winery was limited to local deliveries, with a few exceptions, and Hannah wasn't sure how to ramp it up.

Maybe Callan was right. The wine needed to stand out.

Callan walked inside from the back entrance jolting Hannah from her thoughts. He slowed when he saw her. His hesitation to approach her wasn't shocking, yet it bothered her. She hated how they had taken a step forward only to fall back several more all because of the stupid paparazzi.

Would she ever get out from underneath that dark cloud?

"Hey." She waved at him.

He nodded at her. "Hey."

"I'm waiting on Lizzy. She has a tour at ten-thirty and I'm going to join her."

"Gotcha."

Tension hung between them like a thunderstorm about to break. She wished she could convince him that she wasn't the same person she'd been in California. Not anymore.

While she'd loved the life she'd created, there were parts she didn't enjoy. Being in the public eye for one. Luke didn't mind it, he loved it actually, but she didn't. However, she'd accepted it. She'd realized it was a part of the world they lived in. A world she no longer relished. Something inside her had changed. Spending time tucked away in this tiny town had shown her that.

The idea of standing on her own two feet, creating something of her own sounded so appealing. And while starting her own lifestyle brand would be amazing, it was a daunting task that would take a lot of work and an equal amount of capital. Money she didn't have. How could she launch a business in her current position?

She needed to figure out what she was going to do. Soon.

"I've gotta grab something from my office and head back to the vat room," Callan blurted out an excuse to get away. She couldn't blame him.

"Of course. See you around."

Lizzy zipped around the corner from the storeroom. "Cal, just the person I was looking for."

"What's up?"

"That new bistro I signed up that's opening next year needs a rush order for a preview dinner they're hosting out by the lake and Brian's out on a delivery in Georgetown, and he won't be back for a while, and I have a tour starting soon. Can you go?"

She laced her fingers together pleading with puppy-dog eyes.

Callan blew out an exaggerated huff. "Yeah. Guess I'll have to."

Lizzy threw her fists in the air. "Yes! Thank you."

"You owe me one," he quipped.

"We'll help you load the truck." She grabbed Hannah by the hand and tugged her away.

"It's gonna take more than that," he called out after them.

Callan closed the tailgate of his truck, his keys dangling from his hand.

Lizzy glanced at a group of women getting out of their car in the parking lot. "Tour's here." She turned back toward Callan. "Thanks, Cal. I'll pay you back."

"You can pay me back with babysitting duty while I work on the house."

"Done."

"Do you need Hannah for this tour?" he asked.

Lizzy cast a cautious side-eye toward Hannah and Hannah wondered where he was going with his line of questioning. She lowered her chin, prepared to respond, but Lizzy answered him first.

"No, but she was tagging along to see the flow and give me suggestions on how to incorporate the raffle and other ways to encourage customers to buy our wine."

He set his steely glare on Hannah. The intensity in his eyes made her squirm.

"Could you go on a different tour with Lizzy and ride with me to make this delivery?"

When Lizzy swiveled in her direction, she sensed two pairs of eyes on her. Afraid he wanted to draw a hard line between them, maybe even ask her to stop helping Lizzy out, she almost said no. But a part of her brimmed with curiosity.

"Sure, if you're okay with that, Lizzy?"

"Yeah, I'll catch up with you later." She flashed Hannah a wink as if to encourage her before she walked away.

"So, what's up?"

There was no need to skirt around why he wanted her to tag along. In a minute, she'd find out anyway.

He nodded his head toward the truck, and she followed him to the passenger side where he opened the door, and she climbed inside. A tiny stuffed animal sat on his dashboard above the center console. She picked up the little black kitten stuffie and waved it at him.

"Summer's or yours?" she teased.

Shoving the key into the ignition, he turned the engine on with a smirk. "I'm more of a dog person."

"Do you have one?" She put the stuffie back in its spot.

"Don't have time."

"Aw, I bet Summer would love a pet."

His smirk grew into a grin. "Are you pitching one for her?"

"I just know most kids love having a pet." Her childhood pet—a grey and white stray kitten she'd found outside the school gym when she was ten—became her best friend and favorite companion as a young child. When she'd left for college, she'd left her behind with her parents. It'd been like leaving behind a part of herself. Fortunately, Patches had lived a long happy life with her parents.

"Maybe when she gets older. For now, I'm too busy with work to take on an animal."

He turned the truck off the narrow lane leading to the winery and onto the main road that circled the lake. They rode in silence for several minutes. No talking, no music, just the blur of trees, a few with leaves turning shades of gold and red, as they drove past.

"Are you going to tell me why you wanted me to ride along with you?" She shifted in her seat to face him.

He ran his thumb across his forehead before placing his hand back on the steering wheel.

"I owe you an apology."

Not the answer she was expecting. "Oh?"

"What happened yesterday with that guy wasn't your fault. I overreacted."

Relief stirred in her chest. While she didn't blame him for his reaction to being stalked by the paparazzi, the sting of his rejection had burned long after he left.

"I appreciate you saying that. Dealing with people following you around, snapping pictures, is hard to digest, but I'd grown accustomed to the nuisance. Having it thrust on you when never having experienced it is another story.

For that, I'm sorry. I should have told you the real reason I left after my divorce."

"I'll admit, I did a little research last night. I had no idea how famous your ex is. I can't imagine that life."

Her breath hitched. She wondered what pictures he'd seen. Was she in them, too? That would probably weird him out to see her in that light.

"It wasn't always like that, even though Luke's career progressed pretty rapidly. I think it was more his affinity for being in the public eye, you know? There are plenty of successful people in the tech industry that you'd never know of, but Luke liked the recognition and fancy fundraising galas, which were for good causes, but you can be charitable without posting about it. Luke's too much of a people person to be anonymous though."

"What about you?"

"What about me?"

She gazed ahead, watching as the turquoise waters of the lake shimmered into view. Lake Bonnell was known for its pristine waters. Views of it as you descended a hill were breathtaking.

"I never would have pegged you for the famous type."

"I'm not famous. Luke is."

He slowed down as he approached the entrance to the parking lot of what was going to become the newest restaurant to grace Falls Hollow. Renovations were underway on a lakeside estate that would house the bistro. Hannah loved the Mediterranean charm of the copper tiled rooftop and creamy stucco mixed in with faded brick. It looked like the perfect place to enjoy a meal with a view.

After Callan parked, he picked up his phone, swiped his finger across the screen searching, then stopped and held up his phone to her.

Hannah glimpsed the image of her face plastered across a tabloid, her eyes shielded by her hand. The picture unsettled her stomach.

"I found quite a few pictures like this one. Luke might enjoy the fame, but you're well-known, too." He flicked the image off his screen and put his phone down.

She put her head down and sighed.

"I'm not bashing you, Hannah. I think it stinks that you're going through this. But you can't hide from it forever. If you want to move on like you said you do, then you need to face it and come to grips with it before you can let it go."

Solid advice but unexpected. Had he asked her along to give her a pep talk? That seemed unlikely.

"I'm not hiding."

He hung his head to the side, eyes wide.

"Okay, maybe I'm hiding out a little, but it's just until the bulk of this blows over and then I can move on."

"I don't think your ex is going to stay out of the news, which means until the dust settles *after* your divorce is finalized, you'll be dragged through the media. This is the kind of stuff they feed on."

"I'm aware."

"So, face them head-on and tell them you've moved on and you're happy that Luke is doing the same. Whether it's true or not, it'll de-sensationalize the whole thing if you're showing the world you're not bothered."

He had a point. Yet, she also knew that high profile divorces sell papers, and no amount of platitudes would stave off the paparazzi for good.

"You're not entirely wrong, but the media needs stories that sell so they won't give up that easily. I'm thinking more of an out-of-sight out-of-mind approach is my best bet. The best thing that could happen would be if a bigger story were to come along. Not that I'm wishing that on anybody."

"Maybe. I just know pretending something isn't happening doesn't make it go away. It only prolongs the inevitable."

Wistfulness glimmered in his eyes, and she knew he was thinking about his ex walking away from him and Summer.

"You're right, but it's overwhelming. Some space from it all will help." She gave him a half-hearted smile.

His silence was his way of letting the discussion go. He'd always been bold, but he never pushed anyone around.

"You can wait here while I unload the wine." He unbuckled his seatbelt and pulled the handle on his door.

"I can help." She wriggled free of her seatbelt and opened her door before he could refuse her.

He'd shown her a level of kindness and understanding she didn't realize she needed. The least she could do was help him carry in a couple of boxes.

After settling back in the truck, Callan's phone rang. One of the subcontractors working on his house came across an issue he needed to show Callan before proceeding any further. When Callan ended the call, he started his truck and turned toward Hannah.

"Mind if we stop by my house on the way back to the winery?"

"Not at all."

To be honest, she was curious to see where he lived. All she knew was that he'd purchased an older home that he was renovating. Given their newfound common ground, learning more about his life now intrigued her. Hopefully their new truce would open him up to sharing more because she wanted to know all about the boy she'd left behind.

16

As they pulled down the long driveway to Callan's house, familiarity settled over her in a haze, but she couldn't put her finger on why.

"This will only take a minute. You're welcome to wait here or go with. It's up to you."

"I'd like to see the rest of it, if that's okay with you?"

Even mid-renovation, what stood before her was magnificent. An old farmhouse with a wraparound porch built for lazy days and wondrous views, the main structure was intact but scaffolding along the sides hinted at big plans.

"Sure, but excuse the mess. I'm adding on while renovating the upstairs."

She followed him up the wide steps and through the front door into a large foyer that led to the living room. Soaring ceilings and tall slider doors that ran across the back of the house let in tons of natural light where the view of Lake Bonnell rippling along the edge of the backyard was breathtaking.

Déjà vu hit her like a clap of thunder.

She held her hand up to the glass. "Is this where we used to picnic in high school?"

A faint memory of the old, abandoned house crossed her mind. Obscured by years of overgrowth back then, the home was a distant backdrop to where she and Callan would cast out a blanket near the water's edge to spend a long afternoon eating sandwiches and homemade chocolate chip cookies, drinking a pitcher of lemonade, and watching the occasional boat pass by.

A sheepish grin curled his lips. "It was part of an estate sale when the original owners' heirs decided to finally unload it. I even got a few cool antique pieces left behind."

The idea that he'd purchased the property where their special place used to be filled her with a sense of wonder of what might have been had she never left Falls Hollow. Not that she thought that was the reason he'd bought it. No doubt it was a good deal. And considering this was where he'd chosen to spend his life, it made sense.

Then she wondered if he'd bought this place when he'd first learned of the pregnancy, before his girlfriend had left. Had he dreamed of a life in this old home, with kids and grandkids and all the milestones through the years as a family? A hollow pang tugged inside her.

"My parents thought I was crazy when I first bought the place considering Summer was only two and all the work that needed to be done. We'd been living in the bungalow, which was fine at first, but she was getting bigger, and I knew she needed her own space.

"Bit by bit we made it through the downstairs. I've done a lot of the work myself with the help of subcontractors to save on costs. It hasn't been the fastest reno, six years in the making to be exact, but Summer loves it out here and it's a proper home for her."

She didn't know if he added the last details because he sensed the conflicting emotions rising in her. Callan had always been good at reading people.

On one hand, this property wasn't just beautiful, it held meaning. At least it did once upon a time. However, on the other, if this was simply too good of a deal for him to pass up, regardless of its past, then that would have been harder for her to digest. It would have trivialized their spot and that notion sank like a stone in the pit of her stomach.

A drill buzzed somewhere upstairs alongside heavy hammering.

"I need to check in with my sub. After that I'll give you the nickel tour."

He left her by the large slider and jogged up the staircase separating the living room from the kitchen. The drilling and hammering ceased, overtaken by the voices of Callan and his crew, but even that faded into white noise as she stared out the big glass door picturing young Callan and herself sprawled across the blanket soaking in the rays from the late afternoon sun.

There were too many memories in this town. Too many of *him*. How was she supposed to clear her head and figure out her future with faded images of young Callan mixing in with real-life adult Callan?

While she was glad he had cleared the air between them, being friends with someone who had at one time meant so much more was confusing. She'd believed a friendly relationship was the right compromise.

She was wrong.

Seeing him descend the stairs, walking toward her with his perfect-for-him bed head, his long legs and sinewy forearms, a real-life Texas cowboy/winemaker—if that was even a thing— melted her heart into a pool of want at her feet.

"Ready for that tour?" He angled his head toward the kitchen. "Follow me."

All she could do was smile. A dopey, trance-like grin that held the swarm of butterflies at bay. If she spoke, they'd flutter out in a burst of giddiness.

She was at a loss at how to contain these feelings, but she knew she had to try. With one slow and steady breath at a time, she quietly willed herself under some semblance of control.

His kitchen was something straight out of a design magazine. Quartz countertops that resembled marble, grey subway backsplash in a herringbone design, stainless-steel appliances, and a large center island anyone would drool over.

"Wow!" One word but it conveyed her awe well. "This is stunning."

She ran her hand across the island countertop as she looked up at the iron lantern pendants hanging over it.

"Thanks. Lizzy helped with some of the design choices because that part is not exactly my forte."

"From the looks of it you guys tag-teamed well."

"I can show you the rest of the downstairs if you want, but upstairs is a construction zone, so that tour will have to wait."

He said it as if she'd be around long enough to see the final reveal. To be honest, the thought of missing it bothered her.

Friends, Hannah. Just friends.

"Lead the way."

She followed him from room to room, oohing and aahing as each one showcased the timeless beauty of a farmhouse brought into the modern era. Her and Luke's home back in Los Altos Hills was a rambling Spanish style stunner. With over eight thousand square feet of cozy elegance, it was beautiful on a whole other level, yet Callan's farmhouse called to her in a way that she felt at her core.

So much of what she knew about herself seemed to be shifting as if turning from one page of a book to the next. Maybe her next chapter was unfolding right before her eyes. If she sat still long enough, she could hear her inner voice whispering.

Slow down, Hannah.

Let go of the things holding you back.

Take it one day at a time and the path before you will reveal itself.

She didn't expect it to be that easy, but she needed to move forward all the same.

He paused outside one door that was closed. "This one is off limits." He flicked his thumb at the door. "It's my room and it's a mess."

She chuckled. "Guess some things never change."

She'd seen his room at his parents' house when they'd dated and it could be described as a typical teenage boy room with a mix of clean and dirty clothes scattered about, his cleats and baseball mitt adding to the clutter on his desk.

He shrugged his shoulders. "Guess not."

They ended the tour outside on the back patio where flagstone covered the whole floor. A table and chairs were housed under a pergola rimmed with tiny white lights and Morning Glory climbed up one side. It was beautiful.

Hannah pulled the sleeves of her sweater down to her wrists warding off the cooler air.

"Your home is amazing, Callan. And this view is the piece de resistance."

She waved her hand, palm up, toward the lake. The hills

across the way served as a picturesque backdrop, with the dappled rays of the afternoon sun shining across the trees.

"I can't complain." Standing alongside her, he shoved his hands into the pockets of his jeans, casual, confident.

She turned to face him. "Did you get everything settled?" She pointed to the house's second story.

"Yeah, just needed to shift some beams."

"Thanks for the tour. Maybe I'll get to see the rest one day."

She was planting a seed. Of what, she didn't know. Falls Hollow was a pit stop on the way to whatever came next. Yet, she sensed one foot digging in, holding onto the possibility of making this visit one of the first of others to come.

"Yeah?" He angled toward her seeming to lean in a little closer.

"Yeah. I don't think this will be my last time in Falls Hollow."

The weight of his stare pulled her in as if his mocha eyes were the center of gravity.

Tiny bolts of electricity burst between them. Her breathing grew shallower; her chest rising and falling with each anxious breath. As if seventeen years had never separated them, he took a tiny step forward, one hand reaching for her waist. Every cell in her body was on high alert, waving him in like a plane making an emergency landing. Landing gear was down, the nose of the plane inching toward her, his fingers grazed the side of her sweater, and she saw stars.

They were on a trajectory to the inexplicable when his phone buzzed breaking the spell.

His hand dropped from her waist, and he pulled his phone from his pocket as he glanced at the screen.

"It's Summer's school." His brow crinkled with concern.

"Go ahead." Her body tremored from the cold crawling across her skin after he let go. Her stomach was in knots; her breathing grew labored.

They'd almost *kissed* for crying out loud. She curled her fingers tight, her nails digging into her palms. Anything to calm the release of endorphins engulfing her.

He answered and two seconds later he palmed his forehead. "I'm so sorry, Ms. O'Connell. I completely forgot about our conference. Can we reschedule for later today?" He plopped his hand on his hip and raised his head to the sky. "Thank you. Thank you so much. I'll be there at four."

Clutching his phone in his hand, he gave Hannah an apologetic look. "I missed my parent-teacher conference with Summer's teacher." He shook his head.

"Uh oh! Is someone getting detention this afternoon?" She joked trying to jumpstart a smile back on his face, but the connection they'd experienced a moment before seemed to have dropped much like the corners of his mouth.

"We need to go." He held out his arm waving her forward.

The butterflies once flitting about her belly in glee fell still, deep in slumber.

"Of course." She hurried back inside, cutting through the living room to the front door at a quickened pace.

Back inside the cab of the truck, she fastened her seatbelt and braced herself for a quiet ride back to the winery. At least, she hoped for it. She needed the silence to settle her trembling nerves. Unfortunately, the silence didn't last long.

"I'm sorry, Hannah. I don't know what happened back there. It's me. It's my fault. I'm busy all the time. I haven't dated since Kelly, my ex, left, and I was giving you mixed signals when I shouldn't have. I can't do this. I'm so sorry."

He ran his hand over the top of his hair, stress emanating from every pore in his body.

Hannah was frozen in her seat, at a loss for words. Her hands trembled in her lap, her stomach twisted, but try as she might, she couldn't shake the pinch of hurt rattling through her bones.

She'd had no business letting her guard down. What she had with Callan was a long time ago. It had been high school. Young love—nothing more. Her time here was temporary and focused on healing, making plans for the next phase of her life, not falling again for someone she dated years ago.

So why didn't her heart understand that?

"It's okay, Callan. I'm just as guilty for whatever that was." She flicked her fingers in the air as if shooing away any idea of something brewing between them. The gesture stung.

He barely looked her in the eye and to be honest, that hurt even worse. This constant teetering back and forth was muddying her already foggy brain.

If they could keep things simple, friendly, it would be so easy to enjoy her time here. Instead, she had days in front of her of working alongside Callan at the winery with both of them on edge.

"Stop the truck," she demanded in a rush.

"What?" He glimpsed at her as if she'd lost her mind.

"Pull over."

She leaned forward in her seat, one hand on the dash. Her heart climbed up her chest threatening to burst through and run away, but she didn't relent. It was the only way to squelch this nonsense.

He did as she asked and pulled off to the side and threw the gear into park while the engine idled.

"Are you okay?"

"Kiss me."

His eyes rounded with a thousand rivers of doubt running across his brow. "Wh—"

She reached over and placed a hand on each of his cheeks, then leaned in and kissed him as if tomorrow would never come. When she finally pulled back, her breath depleted, she gazed into his eyes believing that she'd feel nothing. Any lingering doubt, any what-ifs bubbling between them, would vanish in a blink.

Instead, whatever current strung them together flooded her every sense. His musky Patchouli scent tingled her nose, his lips tasted like peppermint ChapStick, and the heat turning his cheeks red mirrored the flush along her skin.

His labored breathing matched her own and she wondered if she had just made the biggest mistake of her life. How could they forge any kind of friendship after such a move? If anything, she might have given him a reason to cut her out of his life for good.

17

"What was that for?" Callan asked.

Hannah massaged her temples, trying to figure out how to explain why she'd just forced herself on him. What was wrong with her? She thought it would prove all the tension tangling between them was nothing more than leftover pieces of nostalgia from their time together.

Instead, kissing him was like coming home to the best part of her world.

The doors to the vault surrounding her heart burst open, and there was no easy way to close them again. But she had to. He had no room in his life for her. Maybe no desire either.

"I'm sorry. I thought if I kissed you, we'd both realize there's nothing between us other than the sweet memories of first love. My actions were inappropriate and rash and I'm so, so embarrassed."

She kept her head down unable to look him in the eyes.

He blew out an exaggerated breath. "I've got Summer and the winery and . . . I'm not ready."

A serrated knife to the heart would have been less painful. Callan wasn't just busy, he wasn't interested.

"No, I get it. I'm in no place to be doing this either." She flicked her finger between them.

"So, are you okay? There are no lingering feelings?"

She sensed the heat of his stare on her. When she finally peered up, she had to muster every ounce of strength she had to let him go. "No, we're good."

He pursed his lips and with a nod of his head he reached for the gearshift. "Good."

With a shove, he threw the truck into drive and pulled back onto the road.

Mortified over her actions, Hannah sat back in silence, her hands clutched firmly in her lap. Callan had the good sense not to strike up an awkward conversation. That would have made matters worse.

She didn't know whether to be relieved she'd learned his true feelings or not. To be honest, she was a little of both. With several days of work at the winery still in front of her, it was best to clear the air between them, but the end result wasn't what she wanted.

In an inexplicable twist of fate, she'd fallen for Callan Locke all over again and there was nothing she could do about it. She had to let it drop.

After they got back to the winery, she joined Lizzy on an afternoon tour. The distraction helped. Thankfully Lizzy didn't sense anything amiss, so Hannah didn't have to fend off a laundry list of questions. With Callan off to his parent-teacher conference at Summer's school, she didn't have to see him for the rest of the day, which eased the mounting tension in her chest.

By the time she made it back to the bungalow, all she wanted to do was pour herself a glass of wine and take a long, hot bath. When her phone rang, her shoulders slumped in defeat. Glancing at the screen, she saw it was her mom Face Timing her. She hesitated for a split second, then grabbed her wine and answered as she made her way to the front door.

"Hey, Mom," she chirped as if everything was great. "Hang on while I open the door."

She slid her wineglass between her arm and her chest so she could open the door and step outside. After putting her glass on the small table between the chairs on the porch, she sat down.

"What's new with you?"

"Well, your dad threw his back out playing golf." Mom rolled her eyes.

"Oh no! Is he okay?"

"Yeah, he's fine. He's taking Ibuprofen and resting. What's new with you?"

When she didn't readily respond, Mom tilted her head, chin down, and gave her that concerned mom look.

"What's going on? Did something happen with the divorce?"

Hannah leaned her head against the back of the chair. With all that happened between her and Callan earlier, she'd forgotten all about the latest development in the divorce proceedings. The recent revelation that she likely signed a postnuptial agreement, thus relinquishing her rights to everything she and Luke had built together, loomed back into sharp focus.

Her bottom lip quivered, and she bit it in an attempt to stop the burn rising in her throat. The last thing she wanted to do was worry her mom.

"It's nothing. My attorney is going through the documents making sure we have everything in order."

"Hannah, I know you." She waved her index finger at the screen. "Something's bothering you."

Her seams were starting to unravel bit by bit. And with Mom's super parental sense, she knew she couldn't hide much from her. She took a sip of her wine, letting the tartness of the grapefruit settle on her tongue before swallowing. Hillcrest Vines Family Vineyards really did make a delicious sauvignon blanc.

"I've been spending a lot of time at the winery. Actually, I'm kind of working there."

"You got a job at the winery?" Mom folded her one free hand across her waist while she held the phone with her other. She was settling in for a long conversation.

"Not really a job. You remember Callan Locke?"

"That's a name I haven't heard in a while." Mom chuckled.

"Well, long story short, his family owns the vineyard. I ran into him and his sister Lizzy. You remember his sister?"

"Of course. She was so cute, always following you and Callan around."

"She invited me to dinner at her parents' house the first day I ran into her and Callan, and then I met Callan's daughter—he's a single dad but that's another story—and then Lizzy loved the little hostess gift I brought to her parents, so she asked me to help out at the winery while one of their employees is out sick, and now I'm having feelings for Callan, and everything is a mess."

If spitting out highlights without taking a breath was an Olympic sport, she'd win a gold medal.

Mom's jaw dropped. "You have a lot of blanks to fill in, honey."

With a deep breath and another sip of her wine, Hannah shared all the juicy details of the last few days. By the time she finished, she had to admit she experienced a sense of relief. Whether she was any closer to knowing what she wanted to do with her life, it was good to untangle her thoughts and hear someone else's perspective.

"So much for your time in Falls Hollow being relaxing." Mom had propped her phone up next to the fruit bowl on the kitchen island while she made a cup of tea.

"I've been thinking about how I got here." Hannah rose and walked over to the railing, leaning her elbows on top.

"To Falls Hollow?" Mom asked.

"No, my life. I met Luke so soon after graduation and you know how quickly our relationship moved, but what I can't figure out is why I gave up starting my career. I mean, I'd taken all the necessary steps with getting my degree, and then with crafting the perfect resume and sending out applications. And then poof!" She spread her fingers wide.

"Just because what you wanted at that time is different to what you want now doesn't mean it was a bad choice. I don't see it so much as you gave something up as you shifted onto the path that interested you."

"I guess."

"You don't sound convinced."

"I worked really hard to get my degree and then I didn't do anything with it." Hannah twisted her long hair to one side letting if fall loose over her shoulder.

"Again, just because you didn't go out and get a job in marketing doesn't mean you never used anything you learned. All those events you organized and parties you hosted took planning and reaching out to let people know and putting together all the pieces. Having a background in marketing or sales or business can help with anything you do because all learning broadens our knowledge and ability."

"Maybe you should go into marketing because you're good at pitching what I want to hear right now."

Mom laughed. "It's the truth. Honey, we all experience change throughout our lives. Right now, you have a golden opportunity to forge a new path of your choosing. I'm not downplaying the divorce and everything you're going through, but if you look for the positive you'll find it, even in the hardest times."

Hannah turned and leaned her back against the railing. "Thanks Mom. I know you're right. It's just hard looking back and wondering why I made some of the choices I did."

"While we have free will to make the choices we want, trust there's a plan and purpose for you. You'll figure it out."

"Love you, Mom."

"Love you, too."

"Tell Dad to take it easy."

"I will. Bye, honey."

"Bye." Hannah ended the call soothed by her mom's encouragement, even if she was less forgiving of herself. Grace was a hard thing to give oneself.

Rays from the late afternoon sun painted the clouds in rich shades of orange and purple. Hannah stayed on the porch watching the sunset until the sun touched the horizon in a big gold ball of buttery light. To say it was stunning was an understatement. While she'd enjoyed amazing views from her home in California, nothing quite compared to the raw beauty of an open Texas sky. The quiet gave her comfort. Something she hoped she could carry over the coming days.

THE NEXT DAY FLEW BY. Hannah spent most of her time helping Jen set up the winery's social media posts for the next couple of weeks. They sorted through the pictures Hannah took, brainstormed about content, and even added a second platform to their socials.

Once Jen was off and running, Hannah joined Lizzy for the one tour scheduled for the afternoon. As they made their way through the vat room, she noticed Callan huddled over his ever-present clipboard near one of the vats, his shoulders hunched and brow furrowed deep in thought.

After the tour ended, she made her way back to the vat room. Although she was struggling with her lingering feelings for Callan, and the fact that he apparently had none for her, she couldn't ignore his distress.

She entered and found him rooted to the same spot he'd been in when the tour came through. He ended a call right as she walked in.

"Is everything okay?"

Startled, he glanced up, the lines rippling across his forehead softened. "Not really."

"Want to talk about it?" She stopped a few feet from him, careful to keep enough space between them so she wouldn't be overwhelmed by his proximity.

"That was our accountant. No matter how we look at it, and believe me we've run the numbers a dozen times, our sales have been slowly declining over the last few years. Covid hurt us like it did everybody, but we made it through, yet our sales aren't where they need to be. Having a good wine isn't enough. We need to stand out."

He put the clipboard on the nearby table and shoved his hands in his pockets.

"Have you reached out to any of your local vendors to see about putting a small festival or something together? I know that won't change your wine, but it could boost sales in the interim while you figure it out."

"Yeah, a few are interested, but it might be a while before we're all ready to do it."

"At least it's a start."

"I guess. Figuring out how to make our vintage stand out is my main focus though."

"What about making something completely different, like a pinot grigio or chardonnay instead?"

"The grape varietals we grow are specific for sauvignon blanc. Pinot grigio and chardonnay use different grapes."

"That's true." Her phone buzzed and she peered at the screen. "Lizzy needs my help with something."

"Guess I better get back to it, too." He grabbed his clipboard off the table and sauntered back over to one of the vats lost in thought.

She wanted to say something more, something to ease his worries, but she had no idea how to fix the problem. With one last lingering look, she let the moment slip through her fingers.

Back inside the winery, Hannah found Lizzy by the front counter.

"Jen was showing me the posts y'all planned and they look great! Thank you so much for doing that."

Lizzy beamed, making Hannah happy that she'd agreed to help while Roberta was out.

"Anytime. Is there anything else you need me to do today?"

"Nope. I'm getting ready to head home for the day."

"I'll walk out with you, but then I want to get a few more pictures with the late afternoon sun over the vineyard."

After Lizzy grabbed her purse, she and Hannah crossed the parking lot to her car. "In case you haven't noticed, my brother doesn't exactly have a good work/life balance."

"I know he's worried about the dip in sales. It seems like he kind of takes it personally though." Hannah stopped next to Lizzy when they reached her car.

"You know Callan. He's a perfectionist. He takes his role very seriously, but he's also gifted when it comes to cultivating the grapes and making wine."

"I remember when he played baseball he committed full force, and he was really good, too. Whatever happened with that? I would have thought he'd have pursued college ball."

"Long story short, he injured his arm pitching his senior year. It was enough to prevent him from playing at the college level, but oddly enough he wasn't devastated by it. He was going through a hard time though."

The way Lizzy's lips turned downward, Hannah knew what she meant.

She folded her arms across her chest squeezing in the ache from the chasm opening inside her. "We haven't fully caught up yet, so I didn't know."

"At least y'all are talking." She flashed Hannah an encouraging smile.

"I guess the winery became the next obvious career choice?"

"After college, Callan started working here full time, running the business alongside my parents for about five years, and when they shifted to working less hours, he made it his own with their blessing. That was six years ago. He still goes to Dad for advice, but for the most part he shoulders all the responsibility himself.

"I, on the other hand, love managing the day-to-day operations as well as hosting the tours and tastings, but I also love being able to clock in and out each day. I'm all about balance."

Lizzy lifted her palms up and down like a scale.

Hannah chuckled. "You're smart."

Lizzy laughed. "And maybe a little selfish. I enjoy my free time."

"Callan was never very good at relaxing. He was always focused on something."

Lizzy put a finger to her nose and pointed another at Hannah. "Ding, ding, ding."

They both giggled.

"I better go get those pictures before the sun sets. See you tomorrow."

"Ten o'clock," Lizzy said as she opened the door and slid inside her car.

After Hannah watched her drive away, she turned back toward the shop but before she knew it, she was walking toward the vat room at the back determined to bridge the gap between her and Callan.

18

———

Back inside the vat room, Hannah found Callan sitting on one of the barstools at the table, studying notes on his clipboard. His broad shoulders gave way to lean forearms that he rested on the table. Even from this angle she could see how focused he was.

A part of her ached over his struggles. The winery was stunning, with so much potential, but it would take more than a beautiful setting to turn the numbers around. She hoped her input was helping. Nothing would make her happier than seeing his one-hundred watt smile again.

He glanced up as she approached. "I figured you were gone for the day."

"Lizzy just left, but I wanted to get a few more late afternoon shots of the vineyard for Jen."

"How's that going?" He flipped the pages back on his clipboard and nudged it away.

"Good. She's perfect for the role."

"I'm sure she was happy for the extra hours."

Hannah pulled up the stool next to him. "May I?"

"Of course."

She settled into the seat, one leg crossed over the other. Caution enveloped her. While she and Callan were in a decent place, she didn't trust her ability to fight the growing ache in her heart when it came to him. But she wanted to help. If anything, she longed to see his family's winery enjoy the success it deserved.

"I'm curious. How did your parents end up starting a vineyard? I mean, your dad was in insurance and your mom was a stay-at-home mom."

"It was kind of one of those random, out of the blue moments." He grinned.

"That's a big moment." She laughed.

"My parents visited a winery near Fredericksburg one weekend with some friends, and my mom fell in love with the whole concept. She started doing research and had my dad visiting other wineries with her on the weekends. They realized they wanted a change. Dad was growing bored with his job, and with Mom egging him on, they decided they wanted to build something together, and now here we are."

"That's amazing! I can only imagine the leap of faith they had to take to do something like that."

"Once they made the decision, we had a "family meeting." He held up air quotes. "They told Lizzy and I what they were going to do and that they wanted it to be a family business. Since we were both still in high school, I was a senior, we could only work part time. But it sounded cool to us, so we were all in."

"And now, here you are."

"Yep. Don't get me wrong. It took a lot of hard work, but I liked it. Lizzy and I both kept working through college and then went full time after graduation. When Mom and Dad started cutting back on their hours a few years ago, they handed the reins over to Lizzy and me.

"I learned a lot from them and turns out I have a knack for winemaking. Well, until now." He rolled his eyes.

"Don't be so hard on yourself. Your wine is good."

Out of instinct she reached over and placed her hand on his forearm. One touch and lightning erupted between them. She slid her hand back, her heart in her throat.

His rounded eyes slowly went back to normal. Neither acknowledged their chemistry and she wondered if she was the only one who was struggling to fight it.

"Good only gets you so far," he reminded her.

"I know, I know. You need to stand out."

He pointed a finger at her with a cheeky grin. "If you have any suggestions for that, I'm all ears."

Hannah propped her elbow on the table, her chin cradled in her hand. If she'd had an idea, she would have shared it by now. Outside of hosting parties and organizing fundraisers, or the few marketing suggestions she'd already shared, she was at a loss. Too bad a beautiful basket of goodies wasn't the answer. If that were it, she would have solved his problem by now.

Wait . . . could that be it?

"Have you ever thought about infusing your wine with other flavors?"

"No, like what?"

Hannah rose and started pacing the way she did sometimes when she was trying to figure out the solution to a problem. It was a soothing routine that helped her think.

"I've had wines infused with herbs like lavender, mint, and whatnot, and they were refreshing and different. What if you try adding something like that to a batch and then offer it as a special selection, or a limited selection, or something like that?"

Callan sat deep in thought. Hannah watched and waited

for his response. She hoped he would at least give it a try. It might not be the answer he was searching for, but it was something to try, and she knew firsthand how taking that first step was the most important.

"That's not a bad idea. I've never tasted one of those wines, but I've heard others say they liked them."

His shoulders relaxed a fraction as if her idea gave him a splash of relief.

Hannah's spirit soared. Easing the tension he carried ignited a spark of joy deep within her. Their time might have passed, but he still held a special place in her heart, and that was enough to drive her to do whatever she could to put a genuine smile back on his face.

"I've read about the process, which isn't hard, but we'll need fresh herbs." He glanced at his phone. "It's late, so why don't you meet me here tomorrow after you finish helping Lizzy?"

"Deal. What kind of herbs do you need?"

"We can try lavender and mint, and maybe one other."

"How about I pick up the herbs we need and bring them with me tomorrow?"

"Sounds good." He rose and placed his clipboard back on the hook by one of the vats.

"Good night, Callan."

She headed for the door, a renewed bounce in her steps.

"Night. And Hannah?" He called after her.

She stopped, her hand on the doorknob. "Yeah?"

"Thanks for the suggestion."

He flashed her a lopsided grin and for a split second she saw the boy she once knew. The boy she'd loved with her whole heart. She prayed they'd find a way to navigate a new friendship, even if her heart kept whispering *I want more.*

AFTER A SLOW DAY at the winery where Hannah joined Lizzy on one small tour and tasting, she meandered toward the vat room to meet up with Callan. Her mind wandered with an array of thoughts.

With not much activity at the winery and no new displays to put together, Hannah had slipped out at lunchtime to pick up the ingredients needed for her and Callan to infuse the latest batch of wine. Walking through the downtown square, she'd taken her time, peeking in the storefronts of places old and new.

When she came across Decadence, the chocolate shop, she peered at the array of chocolates displayed on the shelves in the front window. Her mouth watered at all the concoctions: dark chocolate ganache balls, white chocolate caramel truffles, milk chocolate hearts with pretty designs. The chocolate looked more like art than food.

She stepped inside and strolled around the perimeter taking in every inch of chocolatey goodness. It was probably a mistake. It would take the strength of a herd of longhorns to not walk out with one of everything. After much discernment, she chose half a dozen pieces to purchase while promising herself she'd stretch out the enjoyment over a week.

As she exited the store, she heard the familiar *click, click, click* of a camera going off. Her gaze shot up to see Camera Guy several yards away snapping pictures of her. Heat burned her cheeks. All she wanted was to be left alone. No strange people following her. No awkward pictures gracing questionable magazines creating a narrative that didn't exist.

She was healing. She was moving on. The last thing she wanted was for that part of her life to continue here.

Before she knew what she was doing, she was strutting toward him ready to confront this nuisance.

"Why are you following me?" She'd stopped two feet from him, all fear gone.

He lowered his camera, eyes wide in shock at her boldness. "Luke Miller dumped you for the latest megastar and you're over here in some tiny, forgotten town hanging out with a new guy like nothing happened. That makes for interesting headlines." His nose wrinkled as he sneered, and it took everything she had not to lose her cool.

She remembered what Callan had told her. If she blew him off like it was no big deal, the tabloids would lose interest. No pictures, no money.

"You know, you're welcome to take as many pictures as you like. I have nothing to hide because there's nothing going on. I did buy these yummy chocolates, though." She held up the little lavender bag, cradled it next to her cheek, and flashed him a big, juicy grin.

By the way his lips turned downward, she knew she'd struck a chord. He wasn't getting any shots worth a dime today.

He gave her one last withering look before he brushed past her and disappeared around the corner.

With a deep breath, she let the moment go. Maybe she'd actually proven her point.

She wrapped up at the farmer's market where she bought lavender, mint, and even dried chamomile flowers. Given Callan's penchant for a cup of chamomile tea at night, she thought he might like trying it in the wine.

Pleased with her purchases, she drove back to the winery with her windows rolled down. Inhaling the fresh, clean air filled her lungs with hope. Something she hadn't experienced in a while. Maybe the tides were turning, nudging her in the direction of what she needed to do next.

Even with the faraway dream of creating her own lifestyle brand not quite within reach, she had to start somewhere and do something, and for the first time since arriving in Falls Hollow, she felt like she was moving in the right direction.

With her hands full, she knocked on the door to the vat room with her foot, tapping the toe of her favorite camel-colored boots against the wood. With her favorite season in full swing, she loved pairing different boots with her jeans and a chunky sweater. It was her go-to casual outfit.

Callan opened the door. "Hey! Let me get that." He took the bags from her hands. "How many herbs did you buy?"

She chuckled. "It's not all herbs. I did a little shopping while I was in town."

He dangled the little lavender bag of chocolates. "Power snacks?"

"Absolutely! We have a lot of work to do. You'll thank me later." She winked.

Although she hadn't planned on sharing her chocolates with anyone, he was worth it.

They set the ingredients up on the table in separate piles. Callan grabbed his clipboard and pulled up a barstool.

"Grab a seat," he said to Hannah.

She eased the stool out next to him and sat down.

"So, exactly how do we do this?" She'd tasted flavored wines but had no clue how they were made. However, playing Callan's assistant would be fun.

"We're going to start with a small amount to add to the current batch and mark each vat with the herb we're using. The whole process can take a few days to a few weeks, depending on the taste and what we like. We'll start tasting in twenty-four hours to see how it's coming along. That'll tell us if we want to add more or if the taste is already close to where we want it or whatever. It'll be trial and error, so don't be disappointed if the first taste doesn't yield much."

"That makes sense."

She loved how he used *we* as he described the process. They were becoming a team.

"Okay, let's start with the lavender. We want to add the whole bud without chopping it because that will preserve the aromatics which will make the infusion better."

"For someone who's never even tasted wine infused with herbs, you sure know a lot about the process."

"I've been making wine a long time. I've learned a lot along the way, including processes I haven't used. All of it is interesting to me."

"That's so cool, the way you found your niche."

If she were being honest, she was a bit disappointed she hadn't found hers. She'd loved aspects of her life, she was certain of it, but what had she accomplished?

When an answer didn't immediately pop in her mind, she wilted.

"Is something wrong?"

Clearly, he detected her change in demeanor. She tried to pull herself back together, but it was too late. He leveled a gaze on her that held her in place.

"I was thinking about all the years I wasted not doing anything with my degree." She plopped her hands in her lap. "Don't get me wrong. I've had some amazing experiences, traveled the world, met lots of people. It just feels like I lost a piece of myself somewhere along the way."

"I think you're being too hard on yourself."

She shrugged her shoulders, deflated.

"Hannah, just because you didn't go out and get some big corporate job doesn't mean you've wasted your life. Are you going to tell me you regret traveling and living in California and digging your hands into all the creative things you enjoy?"

She waggled her head side to side, pondering his perspective. "When you put it like that, no, I don't regret those things."

He had a point she hadn't considered. Her time with Luke had taught her a lot about herself. What she liked, what she was good at.

Maybe Callan and her mom were right. The path she'd chosen after college was the one she'd needed to travel to get to where she was now. Whatever changes she yearned for were pushing her in a new direction, and that was good, too. After all, life was never a straight line.

"Guess I'm going through an early mid-life crisis."

"Change is hard, I know. But things happen for a reason. Even when we don't understand or like it, we usually can look back at some point with more clarity and see how the dots connect."

He was smart on a different level than Luke, but his real-world take resonated with her.

"You're right." She sat up straighter. "Enough deep talk, let's make some wine."

He laughed and the sound of his throaty rumble made her insides quiver. She loved this side of him.

"Now you're talking." He stood up and handed her his trusty clipboard. "I'll add the lavender buds to the tank, and you write down the notes I call out. Got it?"

She hopped off her stool. "Got it."

It didn't take long to add the herbs to the separate vats. With the lavender, Callan added the full buds into the tank.

For the chamomile infusion, he placed the whole flowers in. With the mint option, he lightly crushed the leaves in his hands to release the oils before dropping them into the tank.

Working side by side, she jotted down the notes he called out for each experiment. Conversation between them was easy. There was something comforting in bringing these creations to life with him. She was glad she'd brought up the idea.

Callan stepped back after adding the last of the mint in its vat.

"I think we're done."

"I can't wait to taste them." She hugged the clipboard to her chest. Not only was she enjoying this process, getting to do it with Callan made it even sweeter.

"This time tomorrow, we'll take the first sip."

She handed him the clipboard. "Guess I'll meet you here tomorrow at the same time?"

"Yep. Same time, same place." He hung up the clipboard by the vat housing the mint infusion. "I'll help you carry your bags to your car."

He scooped up her purchases before she got her keys out of her purse. After loading the bags into the backseat, she lingered by the open door to the driver's side. She wanted to say something to reiterate how much she enjoyed working on the infusions with him, but the right words didn't come to her.

When they'd dated, neither were ever at a loss for words. Their time together was so easy, so natural. She marveled at the simplicity of first love. If only all of life were that easy.

"Thanks for carrying out my packages."

"No problem." He stuffed his hands into the front pockets of his jeans.

As he leaned casually on one foot, Hannah couldn't help

noticing the handsome man he'd grown into, the way the little cleft in his chin softened his angles and how his teddy bear eyes focused all their attention on her. Callan had improved with age, just like a fine wine. Guess being a winemaker suited him better than she'd realized.

"Thank you for helping with the infusions, and for coming up with the idea in the first place. In case you haven't noticed, I've been in kind of a rut."

"Sometimes you have to take a step back in order to move forward."

Her mom had told her that when they'd first moved to Virginia and Hannah was struggling to fit in. As a senior, she'd thought she'd jump in right where she'd left off at Falls Hollow High, but attending a new school and not knowing anybody had shaken her usual resolve. Being the new kid in school meant starting over.

"That's good advice. Not always easy to follow, but good advice." He chuckled.

She slid into her seat and Callan put his hand on the door. "See you tomorrow."

He closed her door.

She started the engine, then rolled down her window. "See you tomorrow."

She flashed him a huge smile before driving off.

Contentment settled in her bones at the idea of spending more time working side by side with him. Even with the great unknown looming before her, she knew her days in Falls Hollow, however many there would be, were medicine for her soul. And Callan was the cherry on top.

19

———

The next morning, Hannah breezed into the winery full of energy. She'd gotten up early, taken a three-mile run, and enjoyed breakfast while reading on the front porch. It had been the perfect start to her day.

"Good morning," she practically sang at Jen as she walked past the front counter toward the back of the shop.

"Morning!" Jen waved when Hannah strode by.

Hurrying down the corridor toward Callan's office to stow her purse, she turned into the open doorway not expecting to see him sitting at his desk. When she came to an abrupt stop, he peered up.

"Morning." He picked up a mug and took a sip. It was burnt orange with a Longhorns logo emblazoned on it. His alma mater she'd learned.

"Good morning. I didn't think you'd be in here."

"Well, it is my office," he joked.

"I know, but you're usually in the vat room from dawn till dusk."

She laid her purse on the narrow shelf on the side wall where Lizzy had told her she could put her things during the day. It was filled with books on winemaking and culti-vating the perfect grape. Callan took his profession seriously.

"I'll be heading back out there in a minute. I got a call from one of the local vendors I'd reached out to about the festival. He's interested but we both agreed it's something that will have to wait until next year. There's no way we can put something like that together in a month, and considering it's already October, we'd have to host it by next month at the latest since it's a fall festival."

"Guess you're right. That's a lot to pull together in a few weeks."

"But it'll be fun to bring it back."

Hannah remembered attending the festival every year when she was growing up. There were games and hayrides and a baked goods contest. That part was her favorite. Most years Mrs. Cooper, who owned Café des Amis with her husband, won. Her desserts were legendary.

The memory of it reminded Hannah she needed to pop into the café and try their updated menu now that Mrs. Cooper's granddaughter ran the place, which she'd learned from Lizzy. She had gushed about Gemma Cooper's culinary skills.

"It'll be worth a trip back here next year so you can go." The way he glanced up, peering at her through the strand of hair hanging over one eye, his gaze a timid question.

A tingle of hope burgeoned within her. Was he inviting her back for a visit next year?

"I'll definitely have to come back for that."

As soon as the words left her lips, she knew she was lying. Not because she didn't want to come back, but because she didn't want to leave.

The idea that she could stay in Falls Hollow and make it

her home again was a foreign concept she'd never have considered a few weeks ago. Yet, she'd returned to this tiny town for a respite from her troubles. A place to regroup, recharge, and find her way in the world again. She'd felt welcomed, relaxed—two things she desperately craved alongside the quiet, the anonymity, the rush of walking out in the open, living her life without the daily rush and expectations and a filled-to-the-brim calendar.

The realization scared her. Could she really settle here?

One look at Callan and she knew she'd never be able to handle living this close to him without him being a permanent part of her life. Friendship was only possible if she wasn't staying.

Her mind whirred. Hopes and worries tangled in knots, leaving her more uncertain than when she'd first arrived.

"Hello? Earth to Hannah." Callan waved his hand in front of her, and she jolted back into the moment.

"Sorry. I got lost daydreaming about the festival."

Not entirely true, but how could she tell him what she was really thinking? He'd made himself clear. There was no room in his life for her right now. Maybe ever.

Friendship was the choice she had to accept.

"I can't blame you. Those were good times." He sat back in his chair with a wide smile on his face.

"I better get out front and find Lizzy. See you later to check the wine?"

"Yep." He rose indicating the conversation was over.

When they reentered the shop, she went one way, and he went another. Much like their relationship, past and present.

TODAY HAD BEEN A BUSIER ONE, which made Hannah happy. Anything to keep her mind off Callan. There had been two tours, several more entries to the raffle, and Jen had shared that they were getting more engagement on social media. All in all, it had been a good day.

When she made her way to the vat room late in the afternoon, she used the short walk to calm her breathing and fill her lungs with fresh air. She hadn't seen Callan since this morning and her thoughts after that conversation still rattled her.

Was she really considering staying in Falls Hollow? And more importantly, could she stop herself from falling for Callan all over again?

The answer to her first question was murky. The answer to her second was loud and glaring. She had zero control over her feelings.

She found Callan setting up glasses on the table. He lined up eight total—three wine glasses and one glass of water in front of each barstool.

"Is it time?" she asked when she entered.

"Yep. Are you ready?"

She rubbed her hands together. "I think so. It's kind of nerve racking though."

"I'm a little nervous, too. Since I've never infused wine before, I don't know what to expect." He picked up a wine thief. "There's only one way to find out."

Anxious, she took a seat and waited while he extracted wine from the first vat with the lavender infusion. He filled a glass for each of them with a sample tasting, then thoroughly rinsed out the wine thief before moving onto the vat filled with the chamomile infusion. Last, he took a sampling from the vat with mint and released it in their glasses.

He handed her three notecards and a pen. "Write down

your thoughts after you taste the wine. Include what notes stand out or how the infusion melds with the flavor. Also, pay attention to the texture and the finish. All the pieces have to be right before we can say the batch is ready."

"Got it." She clicked her pen ready to jot down the information.

"Don't forget to drink water after each one to cleanse your palette."

He pointed at the tall glass of water next to her glasses of wine.

She picked up the glass with the lavender infusion. "To trying new things."

She reached out her glass for a toast.

He raised his glass. "And for making old things new again."

He clinked her glass and curiosity wrapped in a warm, fuzzy blanket embraced her. Could he mean more than the wine?

She bit the inside of her cheeks trying to restrain herself from breaking out into a goofy, lovestruck grin. The last thing she wanted was to ruin the moment by turning his words into something they weren't.

With the glass raised to the light, she studied the clarity. It was clear, as it should be. She swirled the glass then brought it to her nose and inhaled the aroma. A citrusy bath of grapefruit and lavender, subtle and smooth in their weight, soothed her with a sweet calm.

Feeling good about the selection so far, she took a hopeful sip and let the cool liquid sit on her tongue while she closed her eyes and paid attention to each note, each morsel of flavor that tingled in her mouth before swallowing. While the finish was smooth, it could have been longer.

Writing down her thoughts while they were fresh in her mind, she noticed Callan scribbling fast and furiously.

"That's a lot of notes." She pointed out.

"This batch is good, but I have ideas on what to tweak for the next one. Mainly for the finish."

She perked up in her seat. "I was thinking the same thing. Everything was perfect, but I wish the finish was longer."

"Exactly." He pointed his finger at her in sync with her appraisal. "It's an easy fix, more about timing than anything."

He put his pen down.

"Onto the next one." She took a large sip of her water and waited several seconds before picking up the glass with the mint concoction. After doing the same routine with both the mint and chamomile infusions, she filled her cards with her notes and sat back ready to discuss.

"So, what do you think?" Callan asked.

"I think they all have possibility, but you need to choose one in order to make it a special selection, in my opinion."

"I agree, and I know which one I prefer."

"Me, too." With a roll of her shoulders, she straightened in her chair convinced they were on the same page.

"On the count of three, say it out loud. One, two, three." He called out.

"Chamomile," she blurted right as he said "mint".

Shocked he hadn't picked the same as her, her mouth hung open. "No way! I thought for sure you'd like the chamomile best, too, considering you drink it every night in your tea."

"I love it in my tea, but I'm not sure how much I like it in my wine." He proceeded to arrange his glasses in a row.

"Mint is my top choice, followed by the lavender and then chamomile."

She moved her glasses around, which showed a completely different configuration.

"Chamomile, mint, lavender."

"Huh." He scratched his head.

"Maybe we need a second opinion." She chuckled, but then an idea popped into her head. "What if you host a special tasting and let customers decide? You could make a fun little event out of it."

"That's not a bad idea. Think you and Lizzy can add it to your to-do list?"

"Sure. I've hosted a lot of get-togethers. It's my area of expertise." She wiggled in her seat exhilarated at the chance to get creative and plan such an event. "Do you have a list of regular customers and VIP's you'd want to include?"

"I can put one together."

"Perfect! Bring it with you tomorrow so Lizzy and I can get started."

Rising from her stool with a burst of energy coursing through her veins, she couldn't wait to get back to the bungalow and breeze through pictures of parties she'd kept on her phone from various get-togethers and fundraisers she'd hosted over the years.

Callan rose and picked up the two water glasses.

"Sounds good, and thanks again, Hannah. You've been a big help to Lizzy and me."

His gaze soaked her in, and she couldn't break from his stare if she tried. Something about him still got under her skin in the best possible way.

"See you tomorrow, Callan."

She forced herself to walk away and leave before she said something she might regret. He'd opened the door to a new friendship, and she needed to be thankful for the small piece of himself he was willing to share.

After a long night of planning the tasting, Hannah awoke with a renewed sense of herself. She loved creating things. Whether it was cooking or mixing a homemade bath salt or infusing wine with Callan, the process of seeing her ideas through from concept to reality invigorated her.

She also loved sharing the fruits of her labor with others. The more she mulled over the idea of creating her own lifestyle brand, the more something awoke deep inside her.

Maybe it wasn't such a far-fetched dream. Expensive, yes. But she'd never been one to back down from a challenge.

With plans to host the tasting in a week, she nudged her daydreams away. For now. Her time in Falls Hollow didn't have a set expiration date. She could stay as long as she liked to carve out her business plan.

Lizzy was easy to get on board with the tasting. It seemed like whatever Hannah mentioned lined up with Lizzy's desires to help her family's vineyard grow. While Callan was in charge of cultivating the grapes and making the wine, Lizzy ran the day-to-day and she was well aware that their sales were not where they should be.

"You know, I've talked to Cal about expanding distribution, but he's worried about what an undertaking that would be. Mainly the cost."

"Do you only offer delivery to Austin and the surrounding area?"

"We're set up with a few local retailers in Houston and Dallas, too. Local stores are the only places that carry our wine. We're not equipped to handle large-scale distribution."

"I get that, but if some of these things we're trying take off you might need to go beyond your current routes."

"I guess that would be a good problem to have." She laughed. "Maybe you should talk to Cal."

Lizzy dipped her chin low and stared at Hannah as if she'd stated the most obvious thing.

"Me? I don't think Callan wants business advice from me."

She fidgeted with a nearby display, moving the bottles around several times.

"He listened to you about trying the infusions, and he's cool with us hosting a tasting to choose one. I think he listens to you more than you realize."

Heat burned Hannah's neck. Subtlety wasn't Lizzy's strong suit.

"Callan and I may have been able to let go of some of our past, but that's a far cry from me becoming a trusted source for him. Besides, he's been doing this for a long time, and he has a daughter to consider. He's lived a whole life since we knew each other."

"So have you." Lizzy took the bottles from Hannah's hands and put them back in place.

Unsure what to do with her anxious energy, Hannah folded her arms across her chest to steady herself.

"True, but he's made it clear that all we can ever be is friends. And mixing friends with business isn't the best idea."

Lizzy glanced at her phone. "Are you hungry?"

"Kind of, yeah."

"Let's grab lunch." Lizzy shoved her phone in her back pocket.

"Did you bring pimento cheese sandwiches again?"

Hannah had to admit she'd thoroughly enjoyed sharing such a simple lunch with great company when she and Lizzy had spent the afternoon tasting different chocolates to pair with the wine.

"Have you been to Café des Amis since you've been back?" Lizzy asked.

"Once, to pick up the lemon lavender cupcakes I brought to your parents' house."

"Gemma, Mrs. Cooper's granddaughter—you remember Gemma from high school, right?"

"She was a year older, so I didn't really know her, but I remember her. Why?"

"You know how I told you she took over the café since the passing of Mrs. Cooper?" Lizzy framed her words with her hands as if she was filling Hannah in on vital information.

"Yeah."

"Well, she's updated the menu with some amazing dishes. She makes a grilled balsamic chicken sandwich that will make you see stars." Lizzy blew a chef's kiss in the air.

"Mm, that sounds good."

"Get your taste buds ready for a treat."

"Okay, now I'm starving." Hannah chuckled.

Hanging out with Lizzy as adults was so much fun. She'd forgotten what it was like to have a close friend to confide in and share laughs with. Most of her time in California was spent with large groups of people. Acquaintance-level friendships became her norm.

Falls Hollow was sprinkling its small-town magic all over her and she relished every second of it. Leaving again seemed to move further and further out of her mind. And she was fine with that.

20

———————

Café des Amis was bustling with the lunch crowd by the time Hannah and Lizzy arrived. Given the way Lizzy had chattered on about Gemma's culinary skills, Hannah couldn't wait to try one of her signature dishes.

The café's cozy atmosphere delighted Hannah. Modern farmhouse chic blended with old world charm. She especially liked the antique mirrored wall where the booths sat. The crackled glass was stunning.

They slid into opposite sides of a booth and within a minute they were greeted by a young server.

"Hi, I'm Cassie and I'll be taking care of you today. What would you like to drink?"

"Water with lemon for me," Hannah said as she opened the menu Cassie handed her.

"I'll have sweet tea, thanks," Lizzy said.

"Got it. Be back with your drinks in a sec."

Cassie hurried off, pausing at a couple of different tables before finally making her way through the swinging door to the kitchen in the back corner.

"It looks amazing in here. A bit different from what I remember." Hannah glanced around at the iron chandeliers hanging overhead before casting her gaze to the black and white photos along the wall near the front counter. "I do remember those pictures though." She pointed at the photos and Lizzy swiveled in her seat to take a peek.

"Yeah, when they renovated the place, they kept some of the old to mix in with the new. Kind of like the menu." She folded hers and placed it at the edge of the table. "I already know what I want."

"That chicken sandwich you were gushing about?" Hannah teased.

"Yes, ma'am." Lizzy shimmied in her seat.

"I can't decide between the grilled chicken sandwich or the veggie one."

"Both are delicious."

"How about I get the veggie sandwich, and then we can share?"

"Mm, now you're talking." Lizzy flashed her a happy smile.

Hannah noticed a woman about their age walking around with a tray of desserts, stopping by a table to chat with customers.

"That's Gemma, right?" She pointed toward the woman, who had placed the tray on the table as she pointed to a piece of chocolate cake that looked divine.

Lizzy peered over her shoulder. "Yeah, that's her. She makes seasonal desserts to mix in with her regular offering. Dee-licious!"

"Guess I better save room." Hannah teased.

Cassie returned with their drinks and took their orders, leaving them to chat. By the tight line of Lizzy's lips, Hannah knew she had something on her mind.

"You look like you're bursting at the seams. What is it?"

She took a sip of her water, preparing herself for whatever Lizzy threw at her. Considering how Lizzy had been slowly nudging her toward Callan since she first ran into them at the winery, Hannah knew she'd try every tactic before giving up.

It was kind of sweet, really, knowing that Lizzy hung onto some semblance of happily ever after for her and Callan. She'd always looked up to them when they were dating.

"You know, I haven't seen Callan like this in a long time." Lizzy folded her hands on top of the table.

"Like what?"

Closed off? Skittish when it came to relationships? Determined to live alone for the rest of his life?

If Lizzy thought there was a chance between them, Hannah hadn't seen it. Maybe a shred of something lingered, but not enough to act on. Hannah figured that out when she'd thrown herself on him.

Wow! Did I really do that?

The memory of that moment lived rent-free in her mind. She shook the ugly image from her brain.

"Since Kelly left, Callan has solely focused on Summer and work. Not that he shouldn't give his time to his daughter, but he left zero room for anything else outside those two things. In some ways, he's become a bit of a recluse."

"I can't imagine your brother ever being a recluse."

"Not the old Callan. The one now, though?" She shrugged her shoulders. "That is until you showed up."

She cupped her hands around her glass of tea.

Hannah's heart squeezed. The mere mention of *anything* with Callan sent a smattering of goosebumps up her arms.

"I don't think he's over his ex-girlfriend. What he went

through with Kelly was a lot, and I think his heart still belongs to her in a way. He made it clear he's not ready for anything with anyone. Including me."

"Callan loved Kelly, of course. He wouldn't have considered marrying her if he didn't. Just like you and Luke. You loved him, right?"

"Of course."

"And you loved my brother."

"Yes."

"We're all capable of loving more than one person in our lives, but there's only enough room in our hearts for one true love."

Hannah giggled. "You sound like a fairy tale."

"I happen to believe in happily ever after." Lizzy placed her hand over her heart, a playful scoff teasing in her voice.

"Maybe." It was easy to get sucked into Lizzy's fantasies, but Callan had told her firsthand that he didn't have time for a relationship. For her specifically. Yet, she couldn't deny the longing for him nagging inside her.

"What we had was a long time ago, Lizzy. It was high school, young love and all that. Your first love isn't necessarily your forever love."

Even as she uttered the words, she didn't believe them. The more time she spent around Callan, the more she couldn't deny how he was the only man who had ever truly captured her heart. While she'd sealed the door shut many years ago, it was creaking open with a reminder of a past she'd never truly let go.

"Kelly wasn't his forever love, Hannah."

"What do you mean?"

"I think their relationship was kind of convenient." Lizzy leaned forward, her elbows resting on the table.

"How so?" Hannah asked.

"They were in a lot of the same classes at UT, so naturally they were around each other often. I think it was just easy. She was the first person Cal dated after you. Then when she got pregnant, things got real, you know?

"There was love there, but not the kind you build a marriage on. And while I can't imagine making the choice Kelly did, I don't think she's an evil person. I believe in some weird, twisted way she thought she was doing the right thing because she didn't want to be a mom or a wife."

"I can't fathom what that must have been like. For either of them." Hannah stirred her straw around her glass of water, trying to imagine walking away from Callan and Summer. She couldn't picture it.

"It was rough, but I think somewhere deep inside Cal there was a nugget of relief. About not getting married, not Kelly walking away from their child. He never spoke of it, but I sensed it. I think it was because his heart was already with someone else."

The way Lizzy emphasized *else* sent her belly tumbling. Callan Locke loved *her*. A bevy of images circled on a carousel through her mind. Snapshots of a life with Callan she never lived: wedding, honeymoon, holidays, kids, home. In essence, joy.

Dare she think she had another chance with the boy she loved long ago?

"If you're referring to me, I tried to keep in touch when I moved away, but Callan never responded. If I had known he still loved me—"

"You broke his heart, Hannah. The only way he could move on was to let go."

Lizzy's words rushed through her, their echo bouncing in the hollow of her aching chest. Callan had loved her. A real, heart-deep imprint that had left him bruised and broken.

But what about her? The way he'd ghosted her, not one response to a text or call, had shattered her young heart.

It had taken her a long time to get over him. Luke was the first guy she'd given a real chance after her breakup with Callan. To be fair, he'd been easy to fall for. Intelligent, laser-focused, with a smile as wide as the ocean. Their relationship had been a whirlwind.

Unlike her time with Callan. They had taken their sweet time getting to know each other, slowly falling into a deep connection where they knew what each other was thinking, what each other was feeling, without words.

Luke may have captured a piece of her heart, but Callan held her soul. That kind of love never truly disappeared.

Hannah had willed it out of her mind, hidden it behind a door, but that door had blown open the second she'd laid eyes on him that day at the winery. It was as if her soul had awakened from a deep sleep and there was nothing she could do to stop it.

Cassie approached with their food interrupting their conversation. Hannah was glad for the reprieve. She needed a moment to process all that Lizzy was saying.

"Here you go." Cassie placed their dishes in front of them. "If there's anything else you need, let me know."

With a wink, she whirled around and moved on to the next booth.

"Oh. My. Gosh. This looks delicious." Hannah picked up her grilled veggie sandwich and took a whiff. "Mm, I smell balsamic vinegar and goat cheese and look at these portabella mushroom caps. Yum."

She sank her teeth into the sandwich. The taste sent her over the moon. A sweet and tangy balsamic glaze, melted goat cheese, green leaf lettuce, vine-ripened tomatoes, avocado slices, shredded carrots, and the mushroom caps all came together between two slices of a fresh ciabatta roll for a tasty, sensory overload.

Lizzy was right. Gemma's culinary skills were on point.

"Told you." Lizzy wiped the corners of her mouth with a napkin. "But don't think we're leaving here without dessert."

"Never!" Hannah laughed.

The two of them enjoyed their lunch with little talking going on in between bites other than the latest town gossip. Lizzy was well-versed in what everyone in Falls Hollow was up to. She also shared the list of customers Callan had put together for the infusion tasting. Both were happy to see him onboard with the idea.

When Cassie returned, Gemma was trailing behind her with a tray of desserts. She swiveled it down in front of them and Hannah's taste buds popped at the array of mouthwatering treats in front of her.

"Can I tempt you with dessert before you go?" Gemma waved her hand across the top of the tray.

"Consider me tempted. I'll take that one." Hannah pointed at the decadent chocolate cake, which she had already decided to try. Gemma lifted the plate and placed it in front of her.

"I'll have the crème brûlée, please." Lizzy practically danced in her seat when Gemma placed the creamy concoction in front of her, the crust flamed to perfection with fresh berries sprinkled on top.

"Enjoy," Gemma said as she headed back toward the kitchen.

Of course, Hannah and Lizzy shared bites.

"Whew!" Hannah exhaled as she nudged the dessert

plate away. "That was amazing, but I'm going to have to add five miles to my run tomorrow morning."

"It was so worth it." Lizzy wiped her mouth. "So, back to you and my brother."

Hannah hung her head. Lizzy wasn't going to let it go.

"Just hear me out." She flashed her palm outward. "I understand it's been a long seventeen years with a lot of life lived in between. But . . ."

She took a deep breath.

"Don't write him off. If you still have any feelings for him, be open to whatever happens while you're here. It's been my experience that life is full of twisty, unexpected turns, and the fact that we've all reconnected tells me the universe might have more in store."

She glanced toward the heavens before giving Hannah a wink.

"Got it."

That was all she added. Two words but they let Lizzy know she wasn't brushing her off. Plus, Hannah knew someone greater than her was in full control. Having an open mind and an open heart was the best way to take each day. One step at a time.

LIZZY AND HANNAH spent the rest of the afternoon mapping out the details for the special wine tasting, and with Jen's help they sent out a batch of email invitations to their best customers. By the end of the day, they'd received eight *yeses* and two others that were thrilled with the invite but would be out of town.

Summer raced up to the front counter where Hannah

and Lizzy were talking to Jen, her backpack bouncing up and down as she ran.

"Hi, Aunt Lizzy. What are y'all doing?" She swiped a blonde tendril out of her eye.

"Hey, squirt. We're working. What are you doing?"

"I just finished piano practice with Ms. Miller." She narrowed her eyes at Lizzy as if the answer was obvious.

"Ms. Miller is pairing her up with someone for a duet at their recital next spring." Connie, Callan's mom, added as she walked up behind the little girl. "And she's going to play two solos."

Summer beamed. "Only three of us are getting to play two solos."

She stuck two fingers in the air with pride.

"That's awesome! High five." Lizzy tapped Summer's hand, and the little girl bounced with giddiness.

Hannah couldn't help chuckling at Summer's excitement. It was written all over her face.

"Congratulations, Summer. You should be proud." Hannah ruffled the top of Summer's head.

"Can I help y'all work now?" Summer stripped off her backpack from her shoulders and tossed it behind the front counter.

"Not behind the counter, little one. Put your backpack in your dad's office." Connie chided her with a smirk.

"Yes, ma'am." Summer picked up her bag. "I'll be right back," she said to Hannah and Lizzy before taking off toward the back of the shop.

"I love how eager she is to help," Hannah said. "Do we have anything we can have her do?"

Summer's childlike enthusiasm touched Hannah in an unexpected way. She hadn't spent a lot of time around children when she was married to Luke, other than the occasional birthday party for a friend's child. Considering how she and Luke weren't parents themselves, they weren't an active part of that circle.

Being around Summer awakened something in her. Maybe it was because she was approaching that magical thirty-fifth birthday—the one she'd pinpointed as her last year to try for a child with Luke.

With Luke and a child out the window, she wondered if she'd ever enjoy a family of her own. The thought gutted her.

"I'd love it if you'd make another basket like the one you made for Hank and me. My book club is hosting a potluck at Wonderland to celebrate our first full year together, and we'd like to give Poppy, the owner of the bookstore, a little thank-you gift for letting us use her store for our meetings each month."

Callan's mom had always been a voracious reader and Hannah loved seeing how active she still was in the community. She and Hannah's mom had become friends when Hannah and Callan had dated.

"That's a great idea," Lizzy chimed in.

Hannah perked up at the chance to craft another gift basket. Having Summer help her was a bonus.

"I'd be happy to. Summer loved putting the raffle basket together."

"You're really gifted at that kind of thing. Maybe creating your own lifestyle brand is what you should be doing." Lizzy plopped her hands on her hips, a know-it-all smirk gracing her lips.

Hannah had shared her idea for such a business with Lizzy, who had egged her on as if starting her own brand would be easy peasy. If only it were.

"We'll see." Hannah smirked back at her.

By the time Summer returned, Hannah had started picking out items for the basket.

"Bitty needs us to make a gift basket. What do you think we should add?"

Hannah showed her a box of chocolates from Decadence and a bottle of their latest vintage she'd already gathered.

Summer scratched her cheek. "Maybe some tea? My dad loves tea."

Hannah chuckled. "He told me that, and I think that's a great thing to add. Will you pick one out for me?"

"Okay."

Summer whirled around and zigzagged through the shop before stopping at a shelf with little silver cannisters of tea.

Hannah grabbed a shopping tote and followed her.

"How about this one?" Summer picked up a can of ginger tea.

"I think that's an excellent choice." Hannah took the can from a pleased Summer and dropped it into the tote. "Can you think of anything else we should add?"

"My dad eats cookies with his tea sometimes. He doesn't think I know, but I've seen him sneaking them out of the cabinet when he doesn't know I'm watching. I bet other people eat cookies with their tea, too."

Hannah bit her bottom lip trying desperately not to break down in laughter. Summer was as precocious as she was adorable.

"Cookies would be perfect. Maybe some shortbread?" She picked up a nearby package of cookies from Sugar Rush, the local bakery.

"That's perfect." Summer leaned to the side, one hand clasping her hip.

Callan must have had his hands full raising such an outspoken little girl. Hannah imagined it would be a mix of joy and *Omigosh! How do I handle this?* moments. The image of it tickled her.

"Great! Let's go put everything together."

Hannah led Summer to the storeroom area where they spent the next half hour arranging and rearranging the basket until they were both satisfied with it.

As Hannah was about to leave for the day, Summer wrapped her arms around Hannah's waist and squeezed.

"Thanks for letting me help. See ya tomorrow."

She skipped away leaving a startled Hannah to collect herself.

The gesture was quick, sweet, and completely unexpected which mirrored the turntable of emotions spinning through Hannah. Callan wasn't the only one who'd stolen her heart.

21

———————

Walking across the open field that skirted the edge of the vineyard, Hannah took her time heading back to the bungalow. Today had been perfect. From lunch with Lizzy to working side by side with Summer putting a basket together for Callan's mom, she'd welcomed a relaxed stride and enjoyed chatting with Lizzy like two old friends catching up.

The day had flown by without seeing Callan, who spent most of the morning holed up in the vat room as usual before jumping in to help with a few deliveries when Brian, one of their part-time employees, got backed up. Even though their paths didn't cross, she felt his presence while spending the afternoon with Summer. She was so much like the young Callan Hannah knew. Outspoken, energetic, and kind. He'd done an amazing job raising his daughter.

Her phone buzzed the second she entered the bungalow. Figuring it was her mom, she swiped to answer without checking the screen.

"Hey, Mom." She laid her purse on the coffee table and sank down on the sofa.

"It's Sheila. Your attorney."

Hannah sat up straight at the sound of her voice. "Oh, sorry. I thought you were my mom. Any good news?"

"Unfortunately, no. I've reviewed all the documents and the postnuptial agreement you signed is ironclad."

Hannah sank back into the cushions. "How ironclad?"

"It precludes you from receiving any of Luke's earnings as well as assets acquired from the date of the agreement forward, which means you're entitled to half of any assets acquired together prior to the agreement—plus all of your personal belongings, of course."

Of course. She pictured her SUV loaded to the brim with all her things boxed and bagged. Over a decade of her life only filled one car.

Her stomach roiled.

"What about our home?" She knew the answer but asked anyway.

"That was purchased after the agreement was signed."

Hannah fought the tightness in her throat threatening to choke her. How could this be happening?

"Basically, you're walking away with half of your and Luke's net worth prior to the agreement, which was decent, but it's a fraction of what you built up over your entire marriage. I'm sorry I don't have better news, Hannah."

"No, it's not your fault. I trusted him. I signed that document without reading it. I'm here because of me."

She knew she was smarter than that, but they were still in the honeymoon phase when she'd signed the agreement. He'd never led her wrong before, so why would she have questioned anything?

How could she have been so careless? She could kick her younger self for being so caught up in the big, exciting life she was living that she didn't take the time to pause and read through the details.

"I've still filed a motion for spousal support, but what that will be remains unseen. It can take months, sometimes longer, to come to an agreement on an amount."

Hannah pinched her lips together, nodding. "Thanks, Sheila. I know you're doing everything you can. Keep me posted."

"I will. Hang in there, Hannah. We'll talk soon."

They ended the call, and Hannah buried her face in the crook of her arm. What a mess! She'd spent over a decade building a life with Luke and it all disappeared in a blink.

Even though she was starting to realize how much they'd grown apart over the years, she never would have imagined him pulling such a stunt as having her sign a postnup without her understanding first.

Honestly, both were to blame. He'd been vague and she'd thought nothing of it. Lesson learned.

She needed a hot bath. Maybe a glass of wine. Definitely an inexcusable amount of chocolate.

After filling the tub with warm water bubbling from the bath salt mixture she'd put together, she slid in and closed her eyes, letting the warmth of the silky water soothe her fraying nerves. If only a luxurious soak would cure everything.

She allowed her mind to wander. Away from thoughts of Luke and their failed marriage. Away from worries over what she was going to do with her life. Away from anything that troubled her. It wasn't easy to do, given her brain's proclivity to thoughts racing out of control, but with focus, she was able to let go and relax. The glass of wine probably helped, too.

As she drifted, she thought about the wine and how

she'd love to taste the grapefruit notes more. While that was her own personal preference, she wondered if maybe focusing on bringing that out in the wine might be the niche Callan was searching for.

It wasn't a huge change, but finding your sweet spot didn't mean reinventing the wheel. Plus, with a push toward more marketing, that would get Hillcrest Vines Family Vineyards' name out there. Repetition was key with marketing. That much she had learned during her college years.

After a long night of uninterrupted sleep, Hannah awoke less stressed and ready for another day at the winery. She was getting used to puttering around the cozy shop.

She'd never met Roberta, the employee she was filling in for, but she owed her a huge thank-you. Not for being sick, that would be awful, but for creating such an inviting storefront that Lizzy was nervous to be without her for any amount of time. That was the whole reason Hannah was there. To fill in during her absence. Without that time, she never would have had the chance for closure with Callan, or their new relationship, whatever that was.

Yes, Roberta was due for a big thank-you.

The shop was busy this morning. Customers were milling about, checking out the wine and other goodies set out on the shelves. The sight made Hannah happy. She'd had hand in each and every display, not to mention the marketing rollout with Jen. She imagined Callan would delight in seeing an uptick in business. That sent a ripple of contentment through her belly.

"Morning," he called out when she entered his office to put away her purse.

"Good morning."

She laid her purse on the bookshelf where she left it

every day, then noticed three wine bottles sitting on his desk.

"It's a little early for a glass of wine, don't you think?" she teased.

He turned each bottle around. One had *Lav* marked across the label, while another had *Mint* written on it and the last had *Cham,* each scripted in a corresponding color.

"These are for the upcoming tasting. I tasted the batches this morning and they're ready."

"That's great! How's the finish?"

"Long and smooth."

"Perfect." Hannah clapped her hands together. "Lizzy and I used the list you made to send out invitations and eight people accepted."

"That's a good number for a sampling."

"Unless there's a tie." She chuckled.

It would be just their luck the tasting ended without a clear-cut winner.

"If that happens, we'll get my mom to make the final choice. When she and Dad were running the show, she was really good at determining the best tastes and when a batch was ready."

"It seems like they're enjoying their part-time retirement."

Hannah placed her hand on the back of the chair across from Callan, enjoying this early morning conversation with him. Talking had always flowed easily between them.

"They're busier now than when they were working full-time given all the hobbies they're into and groups they belong to. I can't keep track."

Callan grinned.

She loved seeing his mega-watt smile light up his face. It was something she was noticing more and more since she'd arrived. Not that she believed she had anything to do with it, but maybe he was becoming relaxed around her. That was enough.

"Good for them." Her phone buzzed. "Excuse me."

She pulled it out of the front pocket of her jeans. She was growing accustomed to her new uniform of jeans, boots, and a Hillcrest Vines Family Vineyards' apron worn over her top, which was currently a long sleeve silky blouse in a muted gold tone.

When she saw it was a text from Mom asking her to call her later so they could catch up, she knew her mom had read the long, rambling text she'd sent her last night about the latest development with the divorce. Namely, the ugly postnuptial debacle. She was too tired, and too frustrated, to talk, but it was time to fill her parents in on all the details.

She fired off a quick *Ok* with a hug emoji and slid her phone back into her pocket.

When she looked up, Callan was staring.

"Everything all right?"

Seventeen years hadn't changed his ability to read her mind.

"Not really. But I won't bore you with the details."

"Lucky for you I'm good at boring talk." He put his pen down and flashed her an encouraging smile. "I was about to head out to the vineyard and check the grapes. Want to join me?"

She'd never been good at telling him no and today wasn't any different.

"Sure. Let me tell Lizzy where I'll be first and then I'll meet you outside."

"Okay, see you out there."

She left his office knowing full well that Lizzy wasn't going to have a problem with her walking the rows with

Callan. She'd probably tell her to take the whole day if she needed. A tiny bit of that pushy younger sister mentality still brewed beneath the surface.

Not that Hannah was complaining. She kind of liked how Lizzy championed a relationship between Callan and her, whatever it might be. It was sweet.

Within minutes she was outside in the fresh air enjoying the cool breeze tickling her skin. She found Callan near the first row, a straw cowboy hat in hand.

"Here." He handed her the hat.

"What's this for?" She took it from him and turned it over and back, inspecting the weave of the light-colored straw and black band around the center.

"For you. I remember you used to burn if you didn't wear sunscreen. This will keep the sun off your face."

He pointed to the hat in her hands.

She'd only worn a cowboy hat a few times growing up. It was never her style. Yet, today it seemed like the perfect complement to her outfit. She placed it on her head and adjusted it front and back until she got it how she wanted.

With her hands out to each side, she struck a pose. "What do you think?"

"I think it suits you."

She beamed and tipped the hat with her finger.

"Thank you, sir," she drawled.

He laughed. "You'll need to stay a while longer to get the right accent back. Coastal California is a bit different from Texas."

"Northern California to be exact. And it took me years to refine my speech, but most people told me I still had a bit of a drawl when I pronounced certain words."

"You can take the girl out of Texas—"

"But you can't take Texas out of the girl." She finished his sentence for him.

They both laughed and joy rushed through her. Spending time with Callan was becoming easier to do, even if it was hard on her fragile heart. She should be grateful for any speck of friendship with the man she'd left behind all those years ago, but the ache in her chest hadn't dulled since she'd kissed him.

She never should have tested that theory.

"Let's walk."

They headed down the row side by side and he pointed out different attributes of a good grape, from their balanced acidity to sugar levels and ripe skins and seeds. She knew he was stalling until she was ready to talk. She appreciated his patience.

"I never knew how much detail went into making wine. It's interesting."

"And you thought I wasn't good at boring talk." He nudged her shoulder playfully.

That was her opening. With a slow inhale and exhale, she gathered her thoughts, unsure how much she wanted to divulge. He'd told her he'd be happy to listen whenever she was ready to talk. Guess it was now or never.

"There's been a hiccup with my divorce."

"Oh?" He glanced at her, curiosity brimming in his mocha eyes. Beautiful, trusting, open and honest eyes she wanted to lean into.

"Apparently, I signed a postnuptial agreement not long after Luke and I were married without knowing that's what I was signing. It states I'm only entitled to half of what we'd acquired up to that point, which was right before Luke's career went nuclear."

"He didn't tell you what you were signing?"

"He'd said our attorney, which is really his attorney, had drawn up a document to make sure all our finances were in order. I didn't think anything of it. His career was taking off and we were starting to look at houses, so I thought the attorney was just making sure we had everything together. I didn't read it, which was my fault, and now I'm paying the price.

"I mean, we were fine before he became super successful, but I spent over ten years of my life supporting him and taking care of our home and managing our life, and now, I'm being asked to walk away with half of what we had over ten years ago, which is a fraction of what we built up over the years. And I'm scared about how long that will hold me over until I figure out what I'm going to do."

A tiny sob caught in her throat, and she covered her mouth trying to contain it, but it was no use. Tears trickled down her cheeks betraying her.

"Hey, it's going to be okay."

He wrapped a sturdy, calloused hand around hers while wiping away her tears with the back of his other one. A simple, intimate gesture that instantly soothed her. She leaned into his chest without thinking and he let her, his muscular arms embracing her and holding her close.

Allowing her pent-up tears to fall was cathartic. Freeing in a way. He held her while she cried, gently stroking her back as she got it out of her system. When her tears finally slowed, she pulled back, peering up at him while she wiped the salty mess from her cheeks. She could only imagine the streaks they left behind.

His arms gently released her, giving her space to collect herself.

"I must look a mess." She chuckled picturing racoon eyes with little black rivers staining her face.

"Nah, I mean, a little extra black around the eyes probably fits right into one of the latest makeup trends."

His smirk made her laugh. "Thanks. I think."

"Here." He untucked his flannel work shirt and with the hem he proceeded to wipe her cheeks and under her eyes.

"It's clean. I promise," he said as he swiped with a gentle touch.

"There." He stood back and tucked his shirt back into his jeans. "All better."

She inhaled a long breath, trying to compose herself. Falling apart had not been on her to-do list today.

"Thank you. For all of it." She waved her hand in the air.

"What your ex did to you wasn't cool, but you're going to be fine, Hannah. Give yourself some room to breathe and trust your gut. You'll find your way."

His encouragement gave her hope. Callan never said things he didn't mean, nor did he ever fill people with false promises. If he believed she was going to be fine, then she would be. That was how much trust she still had in him.

Who would have thought the boy she'd loved so long ago would be back in her life propping her up and gracing her with a level of kindness she hadn't experienced since leaving this small town?

"I'm going to hold you to that," she teased.

"Good. Now let's finish walking these rows, and later, you can taste the three infusions."

"Works for me." She tipped her hat at him. "After you."

He grinned and headed down the row with her close on his heels. Conversation remained steady between them, for which she was thankful. Easy banter alongside a spectacular autumn morning churned her energy into an exhilarated force ready to tackle the world. Or at least the dream of starting her own business.

Maybe Callan was right. The gaggle of butterflies awaking in her belly promised her the venture was worth checking into. Like she'd already told herself—she had to do something. Why not make it her own thing? Her time at the winery had reminded her of what she was capable of, her strengths and creativity and passion for sharing joyful things.

By the end of the day, she'd jotted down several notes on her phone for the kind of products she wanted to make. Lizzy had contributed a few ideas herself once Hannah had shared that she was leaning toward starting her own lifestyle brand. Even Callan's mom thought it was a great idea.

When she went to grab her purse out of Callan's office to leave for the day, she didn't expect to find him at his desk. Normally at this time, he'd be hunkered down in the vat room.

"Hey!" She breezed over to the bookshelf and picked up her purse, then slung the strap over her shoulder. "Are you going to actually cut out early today?"

"Aren't you forgetting something?" He cocked his head to the side.

Hannah thought for a minute wondering what she could have forgotten. When he pointed to the three bottles sitting on his desk, she palmed her forehead.

"Oh, my gosh! The infusions. I completely forgot about tasting them." She slid the strap of her purse off her shoulder and laid her handbag on his desk.

He held up a finger. "I have a better idea. Are you hungry?"

"Yeah, kinda. Why?"

Her insides jittered at where this conversation was going.

"Drinking wine on an empty stomach is never a good idea. Why don't you come over and I'll cook us dinner?"

Her heart dropped to her toes. Was he asking her out?

"You can cook?" Stunned, she didn't know how to reply.

"Yes, but don't get too excited. I only have about five dishes I cook on rotation." He chuckled.

"Um, yeah, sure." Her heart prattled in her chest like a metronome stuck on vibrato.

Please don't hyperventilate. Fainting in front of him would be mortifying.

"Summer's spending the night at my parents', and I figured you probably haven't had a homecooked meal since you came over to Mom and Dad's. Plus, I'd like to thank you for all your help."

The way he rambled showed that his own nerves were getting the better of him. He might have been simply extending a friendly invitation, but the prospect of an evening alone with Callan, enjoying a fresh-cooked meal with a delicious glass of wine, sent a ripple of gooseflesh up her arms.

"That sounds great." She retrieved her purse from his desk and slipped the strap back over her shoulder.

"Cool. I can pick you up after I wrap up here, so you don't have to drive back to the bungalow afterward. Say about thirty minutes?"

"Perfect. That'll give me time to freshen up."

"You look great as you are."

The way he caught himself after the words tumbled out of his mouth, his jaw tightening with unease, touched Hannah. It was a reflexive response, but it made her feel good all the same.

She pointed to her face where faint lines from her tear-streaked cheeks still graced her appearance.

"My face would disagree," she joked lightening the mood.

"Racoon eyes. I forgot." He flashed her a flirtatious grin and she gripped the strap of her purse tighter to keep herself from teetering at the sight of his perfect, infectious smile.

"See you in a bit."

She turned and headed out of his office noticeably lighter, floating on a cloud of nostalgia and what ifs. She sensed a turn in their newfound friendship, however slight.

Dinner with Callan, at his place, with him cooking, was the very definition of a date night, but she restrained herself from jumping ahead. It was dinner with a friend. A thank-you gesture.

Somehow, she didn't believe her own thoughts.

22

———

Callan had arrived at the bungalow exactly thirty minutes after Hannah left his office. In that time, she'd washed her mottled-looking face, applied a light layer of makeup, and tried on everything she owned before settling on jeans tucked into a cute pair of brown leather knee-high boots she'd purchased right before leaving California and had yet to wear, with a forest green cable knit turtleneck sweater to top it off.

Her outfit struck the right balance between casual and cute. Considering Callan lived in jeans and his cowboy boots, she knew he wouldn't expect her to dress up. In fact, overdressing would have made him uncomfortable. His style carried zero airs.

She loved his rugged style.

Given that he was wearing a different shirt than from earlier—an untucked grey button-down—she realized he must have gone home first to change. The idea he'd wanted to clean up before their dinner together tickled her.

The drive to his place was slow and lazy along the narrow road that wound around Lake Bonnell. With the sun dipping low, it stretched the last tentacles of its rays across the fading sky in streaks of sun-soaked clouds colored in every shade of orange, from fiery flames to dying embers to golden twilight. A big, bold Texas sunset that took her breath away.

"Sunsets were gorgeous in California where I lived, but they don't compare to this." She waved her hand at the front windshield.

"You know what they say."

"Everything's bigger in Texas," they stated in unison.

She laughed, a light, joyous sound that shuddered all the way to the marrow in her bones. Such contentment filled her to the brim. She missed the simple things.

He pulled into the driveway leading up to his farm-house, and with the backdrop of the setting sun behind it, the placid waters of the lake glistening in its wake made her gasp.

"We should eat outside." She remembered the pergola on his patio strung with lights and a table and chairs underneath. Perfect for such a meal.

"You read my mind." He parked the truck, and they both got out.

The sun dipped lower, falling into the horizon, awaking lightning bugs in the distance.

"Look!" She pointed when she noticed a few light up near the edge of water.

He grinned. "Summer's convinced they're faeries who live in the woods and come out at night when they think no one is watching."

Pride gleamed across his features, tickling Hannah. Callan was a great dad.

She followed him into his expansive kitchen, daydreaming about cooking up all kinds of delicious meals. It had been so long since she'd enjoyed an afternoon of cooking and tasting and jotting down ideas of all the things she wanted to make. She longed for her own space again.

"Hope you like pasta," Callan said as he reached for a pot from a cabinet.

He placed it on the stove near the pot filler at the back of the stovetop, but he didn't add any water before he turned on the burner.

"Who doesn't like pasta?" She left her purse on the large island and walked over to the refrigerator where she pulled the door open and peered inside. "Where's the wine?"

"See that door over there?" He nodded toward a narrow door on the opposite side from where he stood, and she followed his line of sight. "Go through there."

When she entered, she found a narrow L-shaped space with low light. Stone walls were filled with rows of wine bottles tucked into wooden niches. Two wine fridges sat side by side on the back wall. She grabbed the three bottles of infused wine from one of the fridges and headed back into the kitchen.

"I should have known you'd have a wine room. That's the perfect little nook for it."

"When I renovated down here, I took my time and made sure each piece was exactly like I wanted it. This is a forever kind of home."

From what she could see, no detail was spared in the updated home. The way he incorporated the old with the new, saving parts of the old home, refurbishing certain areas while adding new ones, created the warmest and most inviting space. It was the perfect forever home.

"It's beautiful, Callan." She rummaged through a couple of drawers looking for a corkscrew.

"It's by the sink," he offered, clearly figuring out what she was searching for.

After she opened the bottles, she found his stemware in an upper cabinet with a glass front. She poured two glasses of each infusion, replaced the corks in the bottles, and set them in front of their respective glasses.

"Ready?"

He wiped his hands on a dish towel hung over his shoulder. "Yes, ma'am."

They each picked up a glass of the lavender infusion, studied the contents, then swirled the pale-yellow liquid before taking a whiff of the aroma. Satisfied, they each took a sip.

"Mm, I think you're right. This has the perfect balance of your wine and the lavender. The grapefruit pairs well with the soothing sensation of the lavender. It's refreshing."

"I agree." He glanced at his glass one more time before setting it down and picking up the mint infusion. "Now, for my favorite."

After they tasted the mint, Hannah agreed that it was ready. The same held true for the chamomile infusion, which she liked even more this time.

"I know you prefer the mint, but this chamomile blend is delicious." She took another sip, letting the crisp, cool liquid slide down her throat, relaxing her muscles in the process.

"Anything I can do to help?" she asked. Hanging out with Callan in the kitchen, cooking and sipping wine, felt like the most natural thing in the world.

She could get used to this.

Careful, Hannah. Friends only, remember?

She nudged the reminder away. Her brain was well aware of the line drawn between them. Eventually, her heart would get the message.

"You can help me chop."

He grabbed a large cutting board from a cabinet underneath the island and put it on top of the counter. After grabbing a red onion, garlic, fresh basil, and a container of cherry tomatoes in various colors, he placed the ingredients on the quartz countertop and grabbed two chef knives from a wooden block next to the wide stainless-steel range.

"Here you go." He handed her a knife and the container of tomatoes while he picked up the onion for himself.

"These tomatoes are gorgeous. Did you grow them yourself?"

Admiring one of the little bites of orange sweetness, she turned it from side to side giving it her stamp of approval. She loved cooking with a medley of tomatoes.

"No, I got it from the farmer's market. Gardening sounds great, but I don't have the time. Maybe one year."

"Once you get your initial garden laid out, seasonal planting doesn't take up that much time. And nothing is better than fresh produce from your own garden."

She sliced the tomatoes in half one at a time while she talked, slipping into an easy and familiar rhythm.

"Sounds like you have experience."

"I grew several things in my backyard. It took a lot of trial and error when I first started, trust me. But eventually I got the hang of it. It's kind of relaxing, I think."

"Well, whenever I get around to planting one, you can teach me what to do."

He scooped his sliced onions to the side and picked up a clove of garlic, smashed it, then proceeded to peel off the skin before chopping it into a fine mince.

An image bloomed in her mind of the two of them working side by side around a raised garden bed filled with rich, tilled soil. Several other beds circled them, creating what would be a dream garden space.

He turned toward the stovetop, waking her out of her fantasy, reached for a nearby bottle of olive oil, and proceeded to drizzle oil into the pot.

"When you finish chopping the tomatoes, you can add them to the pot."

Shaking her head slightly, she did as he told her and he followed suit, adding the onions and garlic to the pot also. Within minutes the aroma wafting from the range filled the kitchen with a delectable, heady scent.

"Mm, that smells so good." Hannah took a whiff of the air.

"It tastes even better."

Once he appeared to be satisfied with how the vegetables were coming along, he added a cup of water followed by spaghetti pasta and covered the pot.

"It won't take long, then we can add the basil and shred some parmigiano Reggiano cheese on top."

Her mouth watered.

With the perfect refreshing meal ready to eat, they set up outside at the table under the pergola. Callan lit the nearby firepit and coaxed the flames to life with a stick. Cozy and inviting for a crisp fall night. Hannah grabbed the bottles of the mint and chamomile infusions and put them on the table for refills.

It was a starry moonlit night. A gentle breeze, brisk with autumn scents of woodsmoke and changing leaves, wafted all around them. The lights surrounding the pergola glowed, creating a dreamy ambiance.

Conversation flowed as effortlessly as the wine. Hannah couldn't remember the last time she'd enjoyed such a nice evening.

Callan laughed as he recalled trying to teach Summer how to swim when she turned four.

"You'd think we were in the ocean with no land in sight, the way she fought me. I finally gave in and took her to swim classes instead. By the end of the summer, she was diving into the deep end and doing handstands underwater like she'd been swimming all her life. Sometimes parents aren't the best teachers."

"Or maybe she's too much like you."

Hannah raised her eyebrows, eyeing him over the rim of her glass as she took a sip.

"You sound like Lizzy and my mom. They're convinced she's a young female version of me."

Hannah remembered his mom commenting such a thing when she'd had dinner with his family after first arriving in Falls Hollow. That night seemed long ago now.

"Let's see . . . she's sharp, stubborn, not afraid to speak her mind." She counted off the traits on her fingers to an amused Callan.

"Whoa, whoa, whoa. I seem to remember you being pretty bold yourself," he teased.

She giggled. "I was nowhere near as bold as you."

"And who asked who to the Homecoming dance?"

"Uh, as I recall *you* asked *me*." She put her glass down, confidence blazing at the memory.

"*After* you dared me to."

"Ah!" she yelped as she tossed her napkin playfully on the table. "I didn't dare you. I just didn't back down when you started teasing me about having a date."

"Tomatoes, to*mah*toes," he quipped.

She twisted her lips to the side, trying to think of a comeback, but all she could do was silently swoon at his lopsided grin.

"I think your memory is a little fuzzy." She took a sip of her wine enjoying the slight buzz it gave her.

It was her second glass, and she always stopped at two. No matter how delicious, she'd never been a big drinker.

By the length of time it took Callan to finish his first glass, neither was he.

"However it went down, I'm glad it did." His steely gaze locked on her and she squirmed in her seat, acutely aware of the warmth flushing along her neck.

No matter how maddening it was to her, she'd never been able to control her blushing.

Even under a night sky, he must have noticed her rosy cheeks, considering the smirk gracing his lips. Soft, plump lips.

"Me, too."

Energy buzzed between them, pulling them into each other's orbit, tethering them with an invisible rope. She found herself leaning forward, propped up with one elbow on the table, lost in his chocolate eyes.

"We should do this again," he said, his eyes still holding hers in their grasp.

"We should," she agreed, but to be fair she would have agreed to most anything he asked in that moment.

A phone buzzed and they both jolted back. Hannah glanced around and realized she'd left her phone inside her purse, which was in the house.

"It's not me."

He waved his phone in the air right before answering. "Hey, Mom. Everything okay?"

Hannah watched as he listened, a small grin spreading across his face.

"Hi, squirt. About to go to bed?" He peered up at

Hannah and she motioned that she was going to clear the table while he finished his conversation.

After two trips, she'd brought all the dishes and their glasses inside. She handwashed the wine glasses and put them away before rinsing the dishes and loading them into the dishwasher. Right as she placed the last dish inside and closed the door, Callan walked in.

"Sorry about that. Summer wanted to tell me that she and my parents went to the bookstore before dinner, and she found out there's going to be a book club for kids during the holidays. She's ecstatic." He chuckled.

"That's awesome! Reading is such a good habit."

Reading had always been her favorite pastime. Curled up in a corner somewhere, getting lost in a good book, was the best escape.

"Do you still read a lot?"

The fact that he remembered that about her sent a fizzle of joy through her.

"Yes, I always carry one with me. Or two or three." Truth be told, she usually read two books at a time, albeit in different genres, so the stories didn't roll into one.

"I remember you reading those mushy love stories," he teased.

"They aren't mushy. They're swoony."

He canted his head to the side, brow slanted. "Is there a difference?"

"I like happy endings."

"I can't argue with that."

Hannah was surprised the lights didn't go out with the amount of electricity sizzling in the room. Gathering herself, she tucked her hair behind her ears. "Is there anything else I can help clean up?"

"You didn't have to do all that, by the way. Thank you."

"You did the heavy lifting with the cooking, which, by the way, was delicious."

His chest puffed out. "Thanks. That dish is in my top three."

"What are the other two?" If he rated anything better than the sumptuous meal they just enjoyed, she needed to know what it was.

"Hamburgers and tacos are Summer's and my favorite. Nothing beats a good burger or taco."

She should have known he'd prefer something more basic, and meatier.

"You can't go wrong with tacos," she agreed. Although she imagined his stuffed to the rim with ground beef whereas she preferred fish tacos. "I make a mean taco myself. Maybe I can cook for you and Summer one evening."

The words tumbled out of her mouth faster than she could register what she was saying. When he didn't balk at the suggestion, her shoulders relaxed.

With a nod and a grin, he agreed.

"I might take you up on that."

"Great!" Had she just asked Callan out? And had he said yes?

OMG!

She glanced at the clock on the microwave and noticed it was approaching 10:00. The evening had flown by. "I should head home. It's getting late."

"Yeah, I have a lot on my plate tomorrow. I decided to enter the Fredericksburg Wine Festival with whichever infusion wins the tasting."

A hint of excitement danced in his wide eyes.

"Really? That's great, Callan."

She was thrilled to see him putting himself back out there. Struggling to regain their vineyard's initial success had put an obvious strain on him. These infusions had put a bounce back in his step.

"Again, thanks to you."

"You're the expert winemaker, not me. I just had an idea."

"An idea that could point our winery in a new direction. Not that we'll stop making our regular sauvignon blanc, but an infusion could help us stand out."

Now, it was her turn to buzz with excitement. "Well, I think amazing things are in store for Hillcrest Vines Family Vineyards."

"Me, too. Ready for your carriage ride home, m'lady?"

He tipped his head into a slight bow.

She blushed. Again. "Yes, sir, I am."

She dipped into a curtsy, and he put his arm out. After tugging her purse strap over her shoulder, she placed a delicate hand on his forearm, his lean muscles rippling underneath. For the briefest of seconds, she imagined those arms wrapped around her in a tender embrace. Her entire body tingled at the image.

She wondered if Callan envisioned the same given the way he took his time escorting her to the front door. That made her insides shudder even more.

Leaving at the height of a great evening was perfect timing, even though she could have laughed and talked with Callan all night long. They'd come too far. The last thing she wanted was for anything to ruin the tiny sliver of a connection they'd recaptured.

At least, she thought so as they made their way down the front porch steps and paused by his truck. But when she tried to let go of his arm, he didn't let her. He wrapped his hand around hers and pulled her close, and all thoughts of walking away fled.

23

———

The heat of his breath on her forehead made her dizzy, but when she peered up into his eyes her entire world steadied. She was grounded in his strength, his kindness, and a long-ago promise between two young teens.

"I know I said I wasn't ready, but being friends with you is the hardest thing I've ever done. You'll always be more than a friend to me, Hannah."

He nudged a loose tendril from her cheek and tucked it behind her ear. His touch gentle and warm and intoxicating.

Her lips parted. "Kiss me," she whispered.

This time, it wasn't a demand nor a warning. It was a request, and he answered with a soft stroke of his plump lips on hers. Her head tilted back, welcoming his touch.

Emotions tangled into a lilting melody: happiness, desire, joy, and a love so sweet she could taste it. When they finally parted, his chest heaved in time with hers. He pressed his forehead against hers and wrapped his arms around her pulling her closer.

"I never thought I'd see you again, much less hold you in my arms. Tell me this isn't a mirage."

"It's not a mirage." She nuzzled her face into the crook of his neck, inhaling his woodsy scent. She could have stayed in this spot forever.

Several clicks popped nearby, and she lurched back at the familiar sound. Callan swiveled around, protectively pulling her behind him. They saw Camera Guy at the same time.

"You've got ten seconds to get off my property," Callan growled.

Camera Guy waved a hand. "No need to get hostile. I'm just doing my job."

"Maybe you should find another job." Callan stepped forward and Camera Guy's eyes widened.

"Got it. I'm leaving." He scurried off jogging down the driveway and disappearing into the night.

Callan turned toward Hannah. "Are you all right?"

"I'm fine. I'm sorry, Callan. Those jerks won't leave me alone."

She squeezed her arms tight around her chest preparing for him to push her away once again. When he pulled her back into his grasp, she bit her bottom lip, restraining an audible gasp of relief.

"It's not your fault. Come on. Let's get you back to the bungalow." He opened the passenger door for her, and she slipped inside grateful for his understanding.

"Let me know if that guy shows up at the bungalow. I don't like the way he follows you around."

His protective side made her swoon. "It's okay. I can handle him. He'll eventually leave me alone."

"Eventually isn't soon enough. I have a friend at the

sheriff's station. I know he'd send a cruiser over to keep watch if I asked him."

She could sense the wheels spinning in his mind, his take-charge attitude shifting into gear ready to put Camera Guy on notice. Callan was a kind soul, but he was protective of his world and everyone in it. Realizing she was a part too, however small, sent a glimmer of hope through her chest. What if there was a part two to their love story?

When he pulled up at the bungalow, she grabbed her purse and tugged on the handle of the door, pushing it ajar.

"Wait." He raised his palm and peered out the windshield. "That guy is persistent. He might be lurking around waiting for you."

"I didn't see any cars in front of the winery or parked along the road."

"Hmph," he snorted. "That doesn't mean he's not hiding somewhere ready to jump out and take more pictures."

"It's getting late. I think the coast is clear. For now."

What she didn't say was that she knew he got the snaps he wanted. Pictures of her kissing Callan were a goldmine to guys like him. Her only hope was that it'd been too dark for him to get a good shot.

"I'm walking you all the way inside to make sure." He got out of the truck and walked around to her side, then closed her door after she stepped out.

He searched every room, every closet, until he was satisfied no one was waiting to pounce on her with a telephoto lens.

"Those guys don't normally break into people's houses," she assured him.

"Normally isn't good enough for me," he grumbled.

She slid her arms around his waist and snuggled in close. "While I like your protective side, I can handle myself.

I'm used to those guys, and as annoying as it all is, I know that eventually they'll go away."

She was trying to convince herself as much as him. Her rational side told her she was right, but living in the thick of it with the media frenzy over her divorce from Luke made it hard to see the light at the end of the tunnel.

More than anything, she wanted it to all go away so she could focus on the next chapter of her life. One that might include Callan.

"I know you're capable." He flashed her a sheepish grin. "But I'm going to call my buddy anyway."

She shook her head, smirking. "Fine. Thank you for a wonderful evening."

She kissed him on the cheek before sliding out of his grasp.

He walked over to the front door and opened it. "Lock your door."

She held up three fingers in a scout's honor gesture. "Promise."

After he left, she waited to hear his truck roar to life, the crunch of gravel splaying as he drove off. She made sure the door was locked and then headed to the bedroom to change. When her head hit the pillow, she drifted into a peaceful sleep with images of her and Callan floating in and out of her mind. Dreams of Callan Locke were the sweetest.

HANNAH BUZZED around the winery prepping for the special tasting event. Lizzy had her hands full with two tours and tastings on the books for the day, plus she spent some time with Jen going over their social media marketing plan for the rest of the month and into the holiday season. That left

Hannah on her own, although not for long. Summer showed up with Connie and Hank, and she made a beeline for Hannah.

"Need any help today?" Her enthusiasm was infectious.

"I can always use your help," Hannah responded with a grin.

Summer bounced up and down ready to go.

"She's been itching to get here to see if you and Lizzy need any help." Hank chuckled and Hannah could see the pride dancing across his features over his granddaughter's interest in being a part of their business.

"She's a great helper." Hannah flashed Summer a wink and the little girl giggled.

"Well, then, I'll leave her in your capable hands." Hank patted her shoulder and took off toward the office with his wife in tow.

"Let's get to work," Hannah said to an eager Summer.

Eight guests would be attending the event and Hannah wanted to make sure she created an inviting space for them. The tasting would take place in the tasting room, as all tastings did, but she wanted to bring in extra decorations highlighting the wines, the history of the vineyard, and the family who brought it to life.

Luckily, Lizzy already had a collection of photos on her phone from when they first opened, to different tastings and tours, to shots of the vineyard and each building.

She shared them with Hannah who turned them into black and white photos that she sent to a local printer in Austin to create poster boards in various shapes and sizes to place around the room. She also ordered balloons and flowers from the local florist in town, Belle's Blossoms.

Summer followed Hannah around, glued to her side, eager to pitch in with any task she threw her way. From gathering name cards Hannah could write on to choosing the items for the charcuterie board, Summer dove in happy to be a part of it. Her work ethic was another trait reminiscent of her dad.

By the end of the afternoon, they had everything in order for the event. Hannah had poured them each a glass of lemonade from Connie's stash and taken them outside to the picnic table where they could enjoy a satisfied break.

"You've been such a big help today. Thank you, Summer."

The little girl beamed with pride. "I like working with you. It's fun."

Hannah's chest swelled at the compliment. While she enjoyed putting together such fun gatherings, she didn't expect an eight-year-old to experience the same level of enjoyment. She was falling for Summer as hard as she was falling for Callan. The little girl effused sweetness, whimsy, and a bundle of energy Hannah wished she could bottle.

"I like working with you, too." Hannah tapped her finger on the tip of Summer's nose in a playful gesture.

"Looks like you two are having fun." Callan walked up from the vat room where he'd spent most of the day. "Did you save me a sip?"

He reached for Summer's glass, and she moved it to the side away from his grasp.

"This is mine. Bitty has more inside." She wrapped her small fingers around the glass as if it were a prized possession.

Hannah chuckled. "You better hurry. There wasn't much left when I poured these glasses."

He acted like he was going to reach for hers and she moved it to the side emulating Summer with a firm grip. The little girl giggled in amusement.

"Wow. I've never seen two people so protective of their lemonade." He plopped his hands on his hips, glancing between them.

Hannah and Summer shrugged their shoulders at the same time.

"Fine. I'll get my own." He relented. "Five minutes, squirt, and then we've gotta head home. Tomorrow's a busy day."

"Everything okay?" Hannah asked.

"Yeah, I need to help Brian with deliveries. He has midterms coming up, so he's working fewer hours this week."

"If you need any help, let me know," Hannah offered.

To be honest, spending another afternoon riding around with him, dropping off deliveries, sounded more like fun than work.

"I would, but Lizzy's already told me she has two more tours and tastings tomorrow as well as an appointment in the afternoon. She plans on asking you to cover while she's out."

"Can do."

She was going to miss her days at the winery whenever Roberta returned, but it was time to sink her teeth into her own business plan. Starting a business from scratch was no easy feat. All the things she'd been doing lately helped fuel her creativity, which was just what she needed to spur her on. She envisioned long yet fulfilling days in her future. Something she hadn't imagined in a while. It felt good.

The next couple of days blurred by. When the day of the special wine tasting arrived, Hannah arose with a jitter of excited nerves. She decided to ditch her usual jeans and sweater and wear a dress instead. Something cute and casual.

She chose a fitted sleeveless number in mustard yellow

that she topped with a cropped cardigan in the same color. Fall was her favorite season. Diving into this part of her wardrobe always made her happy.

As the time for the event approached, Hannah cut out from the shop and made her way to the tasting room. She and Lizzy had already set everything up, but she wanted to walk through one more time for a final check. When she entered, she found Callan circling the table.

"What do you think?" She ambled up to him curious to hear his thoughts.

"It looks great."

She smiled as she glanced over the table taking in the fresh wildflowers from Belle's Blossoms that she'd arranged in tin milk jugs. Three cans bursting with fall colors that set the tone of the event. She left enough space between them to set up two charcuterie boards for guests to snack on after the tasting concluded.

"People should be arriving soon. I'm curious to see which infusion wins."

"I think it's going to be the mint." He folded his arms across his chest, confident.

"That's because that one is your favorite," she teased.

"It's also the perfect complement to such a crisp wine."

"But the chamomile adds a warmth and sweetness that rounds out the wine with a full flavor."

"Look who's the wine pro now." He nudged her arm, and a surge of heat flushed her cheeks.

She never imagined she'd be standing here flirting with Callan Locke, yet here she was.

Lizzy popped her head into the room. "Our tasters have arrived. Ready for me to bring them in?"

"Yes," Hannah and Callan said in unison.

"I'm going to get the wine while you seat everyone."

"I'm on it." She snapped her fingers and pointed at him in a playful manner.

He snuck a quick peck on her cheek before he left the room, and she had to remind herself to keep breathing. It would take all her focus to get through the tasting without daydreaming about their kiss the other night.

~

"LAVENDER? I never would have guessed that one." Callan scratched his head making Hannah chuckle.

The tasting had been a success. Laughter, conversation, and wine flowed while the guests enjoyed trying the different infusions. They had been eight strangers when they'd entered the room who had left as new friends. Such a successful event made Hannah giddy.

The wine choice perplexed Callan. He really believed the mint infusion would have been the top choice, yet lavender had won in a unanimous vote.

"The important thing is that everyone had a great time, and no one left emptyhanded. You got a nice little bump in sales this afternoon."

"I'm happy about that," he agreed.

"Me too."

She folded her arms, satisfied with the outcome. Seeing Callan upbeat again made her happy.

"Now, I need to package a sample to send to the festival with my entry."

"Guess I'll leave you to it."

"Thanks again for all your help."

On that note, she turned to leave.

"You know, I'm ready to take you up on that dinner invitation whenever you want. If you still feel up to cooking for Summer and me. It doesn't have to be tacos."

He shoved his hands in his pockets, shy and flirty all at once.

She bit her bottom lip, thrilled at the chance to spend more time with him. "How about tomorrow night?"

"Perfect. Does six o'clock work for you?"

"Works for me. Tell Summer I'll make dessert, too. Something chocolatey."

He grinned. "She'll be ecstatic."

With that, Hannah exited the tasting room on a cloud of cozy dreams. A second time around with Callan would be even sweeter than the first.

24

———

Wandering down Main Street with extra pep in her step, Hannah gathered the ingredients she needed to cook dinner for Callan and Summer. At the farmer's market, she'd chosen fresh squash and zucchini to sauté with onions and garlic for a healthy and robust side dish. For the main course, she'd decided on baked chicken topped with a creamy mushroom sauce. A side of mashed potatoes would round out the meal.

Dessert was trickier. She went back and forth between chocolate chip cookies and brownies before finally settling on homemade brownies made with chocolate chunks. Summer wouldn't be able to resist so much rich, chocolatey goodness.

To be fair, neither would she.

Back at the bungalow, she spread all her ingredients out and set up a workstation on the kitchen peninsula. It was a tight space, but it still felt good to be cooking for others again.

Her phone buzzed and she answered on the first ring.

"Hi, Mom."

"Hey, honey. How are you?"

The level of concern in her mom's voice triggered a wave of queasiness in her belly. Something was up.

"I'm fine. What's going on."

When her mom didn't readily respond, she braced herself.

"Mom? Is everything okay?"

If something had happened to one of her parents, she wouldn't know how to handle it. Growing up as an only child, they were like the three Musketeers. They did everything together.

"Well, I was flipping through channels earlier and one of those celebrity gossip news shows was on and they were showing pictures of you. And Callan. Together."

Mom paused, and Hannah grasped the counter, gripping it until her knuckles turned white. Camera Guy had published the pictures he got of her and Callan at his place.

"What did the photos show?"

"Um, you were in Callan's arms and y'all appeared to be kissing. The pictures are kind of dark."

"Oh, my gosh." She rubbed her fingers across her forehead, mentally assessing the damage such shots would cause.

"Like I said, the pictures aren't clear since they were taken at night, but I knew I had to tell you about it."

"Yeah, I definitely need to know. Thank you, Mom."

"I'm sorry, honey. I know you're tired of dealing with all this attention."

"I am, but this is even worse. Now Callan is caught in the middle of it. What was said about the pictures?"

She didn't want to know, not really, but she knew she

needed to have all the details before she reached out to her attorney.

"The headlines claim that maybe you were unfaithful to Luke."

Hannah gasped. "That's so not true."

"I know that, but those trashy gossipmongers live for this kind of stuff. They don't care about the truth."

Mom's fierce, protective side came out, and while the gesture comforted Hannah, she knew a lot of people would feed on whatever salacious lies they were fed.

"I need to reach out to Sheila. Can I call you back later?" She hated to cut her mom off, but she needed to move into damage control mode, and Sheila would be the one to lead the charge.

"Of course. Call me when you can. I love you."

"Love you, too. Bye, Mom."

Hannah ended the call and allowed herself to take three cleansing breaths before she called Sheila. She was surprised her attorney hadn't been blowing up her phone already. Normally, she knew about things before Hannah did.

After three rings, the call went to voicemail. Hannah left Sheila a frantic message. She'd probably have to listen to it a couple of times to make heads or tails of it.

Warily, she pulled up Instagram and scrolled. Her feed was filled with shots of her and Callan next to his truck. Dark or not, they still painted a questionable, if untrue, picture. As bad as the pictures were, the comments were even worse. Judgment leaned in the direction that people believed the salacious lies the tabloids were selling. She tapped out of the screen, frustrated.

She reached for her phone again to call Callan. He

needed to know what was going on. As she held her phone in her hand for a few seconds, she decided this would be better as an in-person conversation. A phone call seemed like the wrong choice.

After she put away all the ingredients for the dinner she had been so excited to cook, she took off the cute little cotton apron she'd picked up in town and hung it on the pantry door. If she hurried, she'd catch Callan at the winery before he left for the day. While she'd cut out early to prepare for tonight, he'd stayed to finish working and send off his sample for the wine festival in Fredericksburg.

She headed straight to the vat room and found him hanging up his clipboard.

"Hey. I'm glad I caught you."

A broad smile spread across his lips, and she dreaded being the one who was about to wipe it off.

"Couldn't find anything chocolatey enough for tonight?" He sauntered over with a mischievous twinkle in his eye.

"I have something to tell you." Her voice was hoarse with concern. "Camera Guy published those pictures of us he got the other night. It's all over social media, those gossip shows, you name it."

She pressed her hand against her brow, worry dripping from every pore.

"Slow down." He reached for her hands and pulled her closer attempting to steady her with his gentle touch.

"I'm so sorry, Callan. I never meant to pull you into this mess."

"It's not your fault. Those guys are going to do what they do no matter what."

"Yeah, but you didn't ask for this." She fought to keep her voice from quivering, but she was too rattled to speak calmly.

"Neither did you."

He squeezed her hands and then let go, giving her space but not backing away.

All she wanted to do was curl into his chest, close her eyes, and make all this craziness disappear, but hiding from it wouldn't make it go away.

Summer burst into the room, breathless, a tiny sob escaping her lips. She ran up to Callan, wrapped her arms around his legs, and buried her face into his waist.

"A boy at school was teasing me about pictures of you and Miss Hannah. He said he heard his mom talking about it with his aunt and that y'all were kissing. He called you mean names and made fun of me."

She heaved a breath, trying to control her tears.

Callan squatted down to face her. He placed his hands on either side of her cheeks.

"It's okay. Take a breath and tell me what happened."

Her little chest surged up and down while she tried to catch her breath. The sight broke Hannah's heart. Kids could be cruel, but Hannah knew she was the reason for it, and that was the cruelest part.

There was nothing she could do to stop it. No amount of pleading or playing nice or even going along with the paparazzi would make them leave her alone. Until her divorce was final and there was nothing left to print, they'd be hounding her.

"I'm so sorry, Summer." The little girl wouldn't even turn her way. Callan seemed to be struggling with how to react, too.

She knew what she had to do.

"I'm going to give y'all some privacy. Let's reschedule for another day."

And by reschedule she meant stop everything. No

dinner, no getting back together, no more Callan and Hannah. Her divorce could drag out for months, maybe longer. Sheila had said so herself. She couldn't put Callan and Summer through that kind of scrutiny.

Summer swiped the back of her hand across her eyes, wiping away the tears streaming down her cheeks. She could barely look at Hannah.

Callan stood, one arm still wrapped around his daughter. His grim features said everything.

"Why don't you run inside and ask Bitty to fix you a glass of lemonade? I'll join you in a minute."

He stroked a stray tear from Summer's cheek with his thumb.

She nodded and quickly walked past Hannah without looking up. Once she was gone, Callan slid his hands in his pockets.

"I think maybe it's best if we hit pause," Hannah said, the lump in her throat threatening to choke her.

Seeing Summer so distraught distressed her beyond words. She also had her divorce to consider. There was no telling how this coverage would affect the proceedings. Even though Luke left her for someone else—a widely known fact—she knew his wealth and influence could sway the outcome.

"I think you're right." His bright eyes dimmed and the sight of it nearly tore Hannah in two. His readiness to agree sealed the deal. It was over before it began.

One by one she felt the doors of the vault she'd once erected around her heart swing shut, the locks slamming into place with a heavy thud. Leaving Callan the first time was hard, but the second time around promised to rip her in half.

No matter how short-lived the notoriety surrounding

her might be, the constant glare it presented would put a wedge between her and Callan. He was a private person with a young daughter to protect.

It would seem there was no happy ending in store for her.

25

—————

Hazy morning sunshine cast a muted glow over the hills. Hannah was up early, taking a quiet walk, when she noticed a patch of raspberries not far from the bungalow. While it was late in the season, there were still enough to fill a basket. It was more than enough to make preserves. Something she hadn't done in a while.

In all fairness, she needed something to keep her mind off her last conversation with Callan. The one where a rekindling between them ended before it had a chance to get started.

Lizzy had told her to take the day off to do what she needed to do about the latest batch of pictures plaguing her. She appreciated Lizzy's understanding. Too bad it wasn't enough to roll over to Callan, but Hannah couldn't fault him no matter how much the emptiness in her chest ached. He had a daughter to protect, a life he'd built that he didn't need disturbed.

Right now, Hannah was a big disturbance.

After a quick trip into town to get supplies, she

hunkered down in the tiny bungalow kitchen and prepped the raspberries, cleaning then smashing some for a varied texture. Digging into something kept her thoughts from running amok.

It didn't take long for the sweet scent of raspberries to fill the kitchen. The fruity aroma soothed her. After lining up mason jars, she stirred the bubbling pot of raspberries, keeping a watchful eye on the mixture. Once they hit the right temperature, she turned the heat down to medium-low and let them simmer.

When the preserves were ready, she let them cool and then filled the jars, sealed them tight, and put them away in the refrigerator. The process eased the tension in her neck, so she decided to jump into another project.

This time, she decided to play around with different bath salt mixtures. With four ideas top of mind, she decided to create one for a calming, relaxing bath, one for an energizing soak, one for a luxurious and therapeutic bath, and one to soothe sore muscles. Each with different essential oils for a different aromatic sensation.

There was nothing like getting lost in creating something with one's hands. The way Hannah's mind settled with the soothing repetition of measuring, mixing, and layering the large glass jars she'd purchased with Epsom salt and sea salt, adding in dried flowers and leaves, along with drops of essential oil.

In the end, she made a calendula and chamomile blend, a rose and Himalayan pink salt bath, a eucalyptus and rosemary soak, and an energizing bath with grapefruit essential oil, which was probably her new favorite.

A surge of pride coated in joy filled her up as she stood back and admired her handiwork. Day by day she was beginning to believe her dream of creating a lifestyle brand wasn't so far-fetched. She had plenty of ideas she wanted to try. Plus, the sky was the limit on which products she wanted to create for her line. She could pick and choose whatever she wanted. Backed with her drive to find her footing again, her spirit soared. She could do this.

Her phone rang right as she finished cleaning up after putting away the bath salts. One peek showed it was her attorney.

"Hi, Sheila," she said as she tossed the dish towel over her shoulder. "Sorry for the rambling message yesterday, but I guess you've seen the news by now."

"Oh yeah. I've seen it, heard it, read it. It's all over."

Hannah leaned back against the kitchen counter, defeated once more. "I've seen enough. I can't bring myself to look at it anymore. How bad is it?"

"Bad enough for Luke's attorney to contact me to let me know they're going to court with allegations that you cheated first, causing the breakdown of your marriage and forcing Luke into the arms of someone else."

Hannah's knees locked as she straightened up. "That's not true. They can't make up lies like that."

"They can use any angle they want. It's on us to prove them wrong."

"I hadn't seen Callan in seventeen years until I ran into him after I got here. How can Luke's attorney prove something that couldn't have physically happened? I was in California until a couple of weeks ago."

"You might have been living in California, but who's to say you and this Callan weren't already speaking by phone, planning your exit and return to your hometown?"

"Sheila, you know that's not true. Luke cheated on *me*. Not the other way around."

She fumed at the notion that she was the one who had

been unfaithful. Luke had blindsided her with his admission. How could he even consider trying to pin such a thing on her?

"I'm not the one you have to convince, Hannah. It's the judge. He'll review all the documents and every piece of evidence presented to him, including the pictures of you and Callan together."

Hannah gritted her teeth until her head hurt. At first, she'd been portrayed as the oblivious, unsuspecting wife. Then she'd been blamed for not being attentive enough to Luke and his career because she was too wrapped up in playing hostess to the who's who in their wealthy circle of associates. Now, she was being called resentful for giving up her own career and lashing out with someone new.

She couldn't win. Worse, it was all lies. Huge, blatant, hurtful lies that not only affected her, but Callan and Summer as well.

Knowing that image played a big part in these types of proceedings, and her public image was tainted to say the least, she decided to make a bold move. A tug of war over he said, she said in the press would be exhausting. Plus, the narrative and what the judge perceived to be true would affect the final outcome of the divorce settlement.

"You know what? I'm done."

"Hannah, wait—" Sheila interrupted, her tone softening to that of a concerned friend.

"It's not you, Sheila. You've been supportive and so helpful since the beginning, but I don't want to fight anymore. If this is who Luke is now, then I want to get this divorce over with as soon as possible. Let's accept the divorce agreement as-is without fighting for any additional assets I believe are owed to me. I'd rather walk away and be done with it all than to drag people I care about through such contentious court proceedings, including myself."

Hannah heard tapping on Sheila's end and figured she was absentmindedly bouncing her pen on her desk. Something she did often when she was deep in thought.

"I understand your frustration, Hannah, but maybe think about it first before making any rash decisions. Once I file a motion to accept the agreement as-is, the wheels will move quickly."

"I know. I'm just ready to move on."

Hannah slumped down on one of the chairs around the dining table. This whole ordeal had taken its toll on her and more than anything, she wanted to put it behind her and make a fresh start. Whatever had been blossoming between her and Callan came to a screeching stop yesterday when Summer experienced firsthand the harshness of someone's cruel words. She couldn't bear anymore.

"Okay. I'll prepare the motion and let you know when it's ready to file."

"Thanks, Sheila. I really do appreciate all you've done for me."

"I'm happy to fight for more because I know the truth, but I respect your decision. We'll talk soon."

Sheila ended the call, and Hannah propped her chin on her hand, her mind mulling over the last couple of months and how she ended up in such a predicament. She knew she held some responsibility over the breakup of her marriage, even with Luke's infidelity. Rarely was it solely one person's fault for a relationship to end.

Maybe her attention had drifted. With Luke's busy schedule, she grew accustomed to doing things on her own. In the beginning, she'd missed him a lot when he was out of town, but as time wore on, she found ways to fill her days and to be honest, she'd begun to notice his absence less and less.

Relationships change, people evolve, and sometimes couples drift apart. Had a lack of connection driven him away? Whether or not that was true, it still didn't justify what he did. He should have talked to her.

Tired of thinking about all her troubles, she brushed her hair from her face and rose. Tomorrow was a new day, and she was done with stressing over this one.

HANNAH ARRIVED EARLY at the winery at Lizzy's request. Lizzy had told her she could take as long as she needed to handle whatever she needed to with the onslaught of tabloid photos affecting her divorce proceedings, but Hannah confided all the latest details in her and Lizzy encouraged her to come back and help out instead of hiding out at the bungalow alone.

She worried about how Callan would react seeing her there after what happened to Summer. Facing his rejection in person was worse than replaying it over and over in her mind away from his awkward glances.

But Lizzy insisted things would find a way of working themselves out. Ever hopeful, Hannah decided to trust Lizzy knew her brother better than she did. They had been apart seventeen years, after all.

It didn't take long for her to run into Callan. Gloomy-faced and hunched over at his desk, he looked about as approachable as an angry bear. She thought about breezing in and out to put away her purse without saying anything, but then she figured that would be rude.

"Morning," she said as she left her purse on the shelf and turned to sweep out of the room.

"It's too late to enter the festival," he muttered.

"What?"

She wasn't sure if she heard him right. He had been so jazzed about entering their lavender infusion into the Fredericksburg Wine Festival, she couldn't imagine he'd misread the dates.

"The deadline changed this year. Something I failed to notice." He ran his fingers through his rumpled hair.

"There's no option for a late entry?"

"Nope. We missed the deadline by less than a week."

"Oh, Callan. I'm so sorry."

The urge to reach out and place a comforting hand on his shoulder overwhelmed her. Fighting to restrain the urge took all her strength.

"It's not your fault."

"I know, but it's still a shame." She approached the desk with caution, an awkward line settling between them.

"Guess there's always next year," he said with forced enthusiasm.

"And there's not enough time to put together any type of festival with you and other local businesses like we talked about?"

She knew the answer, but she wanted to put it back out there in case there was any possibility.

"Nah. Not if we want to do it right."

"Well, Lizzy and Jen have increased marketing planned out for the next couple of months. That'll help. Plus, the special tasting created buzz for your new lavender infusion. I believe Hillcrest Vines Family Vineyards is going in the right direction."

"Yeah, I just wish it were faster. But enough about that. How are you doing?"

She was surprised he asked. Given the way he'd readily agreed to taking a break—an indefinite break—she figured he wouldn't be interested in hearing any more about her troubles.

"I'm fine. I decided to accept the divorce agreement as-is so I can get this whole mess over with. My attorney is preparing the motion now."

"I'm sure that wasn't an easy decision, but I get it. Sometimes it's best to move on."

She wondered if he meant more about that last statement than just her divorce. Maybe he'd told himself the same thing. The reality gutted her.

Any sliver of hope she held dimmed.

"That's what I think. Especially with the way I'm being portrayed in the media, which is unfair and untrue."

"What do you mean?"

She'd forgotten his lack of social media presence or any interest in the celebrity world.

"I've pretty much been called everything from an oblivious wife to resentful for not having my own career to cheating on Luke first and forcing him into another woman's arms."

"Are you kidding me?" His voice rose with indignation.

"Sensationalized news sells, whether it's true or not. Luke's attorney is ready to use that to their advantage with the proceedings. You know what they say: all's fair in love and war."

"Lies aren't fair." He rose from his desk and walked around to her side, his hands buried in his pockets.

"No, but life isn't fair. And I'm tired of dealing with this. I'm ready to move on with my life."

Her eyes darted side to side, unable to hold eye contact with him. Those chocolate eyes of his turned her insides to mush.

"I think you should fight to clear your name and image."

She opened her mouth to respond, but he kept talking.

"Tell your ex if he agrees to withdraw his claims, you'll sign off on the papers. If you're not going to fight him on additional assets, he can at least concede the character defamation."

His idea was valid. Surely Luke would be reasonable and withdraw any false claims against her if she was willing to give up her rights to any joint assets gained after the post-nuptial agreement was signed. It was worth a try.

"That's not a bad suggestion."

"You're giving him what he wants." His nose wrinkled in disgust.

When she looked at it from that angle it bothered her, not because she was giving in to someone's demands but that her whole marriage to Luke had dissolved into something ugly and petty and not at all what it was in the beginning. The love she had for Luke might not have been the same as what she felt for Callan, yet she had loved him. They were two people who had chosen to commit to each other, for better or for worse.

Mistake or not, those vows should have been untangled in a better way. One without cheating or sides or a reckless display of he said, she said blasting across all media.

Today was a new day. She could change the narrative of their public separation. Agree to a compromise with Luke, bow out gracefully, and allow each other to walk away and live the life they were intended to.

Purpose and passion. That would be her new motto.

Walk the path God put before her, embrace those he set in her lane, and make every choice, every action count.

26

Sheila answered on the first ring as if she were expecting Hannah's call. It was no surprise given their last conversation. Clients didn't usually concede everything in a high-profile divorce.

"Hi, Hannah." Sheila's greeting sounded more like a question than a statement.

"Hi, Sheila. Do you have a minute?"

"Of course. What can I do for you?" The eagerness in her voice was palatable.

Hannah pictured her sitting in her fancy leather chair, phone pressed to her ear while she typed on her laptop. Sheila made multitasking look easy.

"I want to make a change to the motion. Have you filed it yet?"

She held her breath, praying her ever-efficient attorney had not already checked that off her to-do list. If there was one time Hannah needed her to put something on the back burner, this was it.

"I thought you might have a change of heart, so I put it to the side. Are you ready to fight for what's due to you?"

"Yes, but it's not what you're thinking. I want my name cleared."

Saying it out loud boosted her confidence, making her believe more than ever that this was the right choice. The truth was more important than money.

"Come again?" The image of Sheila in Hannah's mind changed from doing three things at once to shifting to laser-focused attention on every word coming out of Hannah's mouth.

"I don't want to drag this out any further by fighting Luke for more assets. I signed that document, whether I knew what I was signing or not, and what's more important to me is making sure the truth is known about both Callan and me. Our reputations are more important than any amount of money."

Hannah waited out Sheila's silence. She knew her attorney was one of the best in the industry, and walking away without fighting for what she honestly believed was due to her client wasn't in her DNA. But she also knew Sheila cared about her clients. If this was what was important to Hannah, she'd abide by it.

"Anything else?"

Hannah had considered this, and while she didn't care about pressing for a part of Luke's millions, she knew she deserved half of what their house was worth. She'd helped turn that house into a home. She'd played hostess to his many colleagues and helped build him up into the success he became. Her supportive role to his career shouldn't be dismissed.

If Luke were being fair, he'd understand. That money could go a long way in helping her get her own business started so she could move on with her life.

She shared her desire with an attentive Sheila.

"Understood. I can rewrite the motion and have it ready to be sent out today. I want whatever is best for you, Hannah." Her calm tone soothed Hannah.

"Thank you, Sheila. I know I've said it before, but I appreciate you so much."

"We'll talk soon. Take care, Hannah."

With that, the tension balled up in her neck eased. Letting go could be just as empowering as fighting. It was the only way to move forward.

At the winery the next day, she found out Roberta was finally well enough to come back to work. Today would be her last day. She didn't know how to feel about that.

Realizing her time around Callan was coming to an end was bittersweet. They'd bridged the seventeen years they'd spent apart, experienced closure on the past, and even forged a new friendship of sorts, but any potential future between them had dulled with the onslaught of tabloid photos published of them, ruining a chance at a new beginning.

Even once her divorce was well past her and the media coverage faded, would he be comfortable in taking a chance with her? Her notoriety as Luke Miller's ex-wife would never go away. At least not completely. Her heart ached at what could have been.

Late that afternoon as she was putting her touch on one last display near the front counter, Summer came dashing in all smiles.

It was the first time Hannah had seen her since the incident.

"Hi, Miss Hannah," she said as if the recent teasing she'd taken at school had never happened.

Her jovial behavior was a welcome sign that all was fine between them.

"Hi, Summer. Ready for the weekend?"

She finished arranging the display and focused her attention on Summer, the little girl's cheeks rosy from running. Hannah was thankful to see her smiling again.

"I'm having a sleepover tonight and guess what I made for my friends?"

"What?"

"A sleepover basket!"

She clasped her fingers together, excitement oozing from every pore.

"A sleepover basket?"

"Yeah, wanna see it?"

Summer zipped behind the front counter and pulled out a round basket filled with three pairs of fuzzy socks, snack bags of miniature chocolate chip cookies, apple juice boxes, and tiny princess dolls from every Disney movie imaginable arranged in separate piles by their movies.

Hannah was in awe at the detail she'd put into it. Her heart squeezed all over again. She'd grown fond of Summer and would have loved to spend more time around the little girl, but there was no future for her and Callan. She couldn't allow herself to get attached.

"This is incredible, Summer." She bent down and looked over the entire basket with glee. "Your friends are going to love this."

"I even set up blankets and pillows in the living room so we can watch movies, too." The little girl's enthusiasm was contagious.

"You might have a bright future as an event planner." Hannah rose.

"When we go to my friend Britney's house for her birthday next weekend, I'm making nail baskets so her mom can do all our nails. That's what she does for work."

She spoke so matter-of-factly as if she were eight going on thirty.

"That's a brilliant idea," Hannah enthused. She loved seeing Summer so excited, and she especially loved seeing her back to herself again, the classmate's teasing long forgotten. Having Summer receptive to her again was a big plus. Even if she had to keep her distance, at least all was good between them.

"Will you help me put them together?" Summer asked, doe-eyed.

Caught off guard, she didn't know how to respond. On one hand, she'd love to help Summer prepare her baskets. Spending time with the little girl was a joy. On the other hand, there was Callan to deal with. His readiness to hit pause on a relationship between them had not left her mind.

"I'd love to, but today is my last day at the winery, so I'll have to check my schedule. Can I let you know?"

It was the best she could come up with. And it nearly killed her to say.

"Okay." Her answer didn't seem to bother Summer.

"Hey, squirt. Don't you have a sleepover to get ready for?" Callan strode over, his presence surprising Hannah. She hadn't seen him enter the winery.

"Yep! Are you ready to go?" She clutched her basket in one hand with her backpack slung over her shoulder.

"Why don't you go tell Bitty and Pop bye first?"

She handed her basket and backpack off to her dad and took off for the back office.

"You see what you started." He waved the basket in front of Hannah.

Fighting a slew of emotions over their un-ignorable

connection, she pulled together every ounce of resolve she could muster.

"She's a natural." Her words were soft, resigned.

"Guess she'll be dragging me all over to buy stuff to make gift baskets now." He rolled his eyes in a teasing manner.

"Some kids play sports, others like to make things. Everyone has their thing."

She waved her palms up and down mimicking a scale.

He smirked, then shifted into a more solemn expression. "About the other day—"

"You don't have to explain." She raised her hand. "What I'm going through is a lot for anyone to handle, especially someone as young as Summer. For what it's worth, I took your advice and reached out to my attorney to make a change to the motion, requesting Luke and his attorney to set the record straight and for me to get half of our home's value. If they do that, I'll accept the divorce agreement."

"That's great, but—"

She had to get this out. If she didn't, she'd turn into a puddle all over the floor.

"I want to leave here on a positive note, Callan. Upsetting you and Summer was never my intention. Taking a break to let everything cool down was my idea, and you agreed, and all I want is for us to part as friends this time."

Each word burned her tongue. Parting as friends was the last thing she wanted, but he made it clear he wasn't ready for anything more like he'd thought. He was happy to push stop before anything more brewed between them, and she needed to respect that.

He raised his hand, ready to respond, when a voice called out to her.

"Hannah. We need to talk." The familiar sharp West coast accent wound through the air almost knocking her over.

"Luke. What are you doing here?"

He stood inside the front door dressed in his usual tailored, white button-down shirt, top button undone, no tie, with charcoal grey slacks over his favorite loafers. His standard work attire. What was new was the leggy blonde, up-and-coming actress clinging to his arm.

The sight made her bones rattle.

"I was on my way to Houston when my attorney called me about your latest demands. I decided to make a detour." The way his girlfriend cradled her not-yet-showing baby bump lit a fire inside Hannah.

"Demands?" Her jaw tightened in response.

When she realized numerous eyes from customers wandering around the shop were glued to the scene unfolding, she took a quick breath and said, "We should talk outside."

She stepped forward toward the door, but Luke didn't budge.

"You need to let this go, Hannah. Just sign the papers and move on."

His jaw worked from side to side, his stance rigid.

Fire coursed through her veins, yet it was nothing compared to the heat she sensed rolling off Callan.

When he took a step, both Luke and his girlfriend shot him a wary glance.

"I believe she asked you to take this conversation outside. Shall we?"

Callan reached around Luke to grab the door handle. He pushed it open and with a sweeping motion of his hand, he pointed them outside.

Fortunately, they had the good sense to listen. Hannah followed them out into the parking lot expecting Callan to close the door behind them, but he stayed right behind her. He probably wanted to make sure they didn't cause a big scene outside the winery. That wouldn't be good for business.

It certainly couldn't have anything to do with her.

The brisk autumn breeze did nothing to calm her escalating nerves. A rumble of thunder roared underneath her skin, and she forced herself to count to five in her head before she whirled on Luke and let loose. A rational mind was the only one that would prevail.

"I'm not asking for half of the assets we built up during our marriage, Luke. I gave that away when you tricked me into signing that document."

As levelheaded as she tried to be, she refused to not say anything about what he did.

"I didn't trick you, Hannah. I told you the document was to protect our assets, all of which I earned. I made sure you got half of everything I'd done by that point, and I didn't touch anything of yours—at that point in time or anytime in the future."

His new significant other wrapped her hand tighter around his arm and scooted closer to him in some sort of protective stance. The move set Hannah off.

"And this?" She flung her hand toward Luke's girlfriend. "*You* cheated on *me*. I was never unfaithful, yet you're more than happy to allow my name to be dragged through the mud along with other innocent people like Callan." She flicked her thumb in Callan's direction. "All I'm asking for is for you to set the record straight."

"And half of our home's value," he replied with a huff.

His eyes darted toward his new significant other and back in a quick flash. She remained glued to his side.

Clingy meant insecure. Hannah was starting to piece the puzzle together.

"A home I helped build and sustain. While you devoted your time to your work, I made sure our house was well-maintained. I entertained all your colleagues. I turned that house into a home so you could come home, relax and enjoy without worrying about anything. I managed our whole personal life so you didn't have to lift a finger. It's a fair request and you know it."

A glimmer of understanding washed across his face, but it disappeared in a blink when his girlfriend gave him a slight nudge.

"Everything's been handled fairly. I'm not going to be shaken down for more money when I did all the work."

A sea of noise raged in Hannah's ears, her pulse racing as blood pumped through her veins. Before she could respond, Callan stepped up beside her.

"It sounds to me like she did a heck of a lot of work to make sure you could pursue your career without a care in the world. Just because someone doesn't go to a job in a corporate building somewhere doesn't mean they don't work, and if you were half as smart as the world makes you out to be, you'd know that."

Callan balled his hands into fists at his sides, his chest rising and falling with each heavy breath.

"And I'm supposed to believe there's nothing going on with you two?" Luke smirked at Hannah with a shake of his head.

"You know as well as I do that I had no contact with Callan until I came back here. The paparazzi are following me because of who *you* are, creating false narratives to sell a story. And you're okay with that. You're not the same guy I married, Luke." Her voice softened at the admission, yet his gaze held nothing.

"My attorney will be in touch. This isn't over, Hannah."

She sensed Callan leaning forward and she placed a gentle hand over his. The last thing any of them needed was for this to escalate further.

At least Luke and his girlfriend took the cue and left.

Her whole body trembled with rage. How could Luke accuse of her of anything with Callan? He knew better. And to show up here with his *girlfriend?* Unbelievable.

She closed her eyes and counted to three, forcing her breaths to slow, her fingers to unclench from the fists gripped at her sides.

When she felt a semblance of composure, she opened her eyes and turned to Callan. "Thank you for standing up for me."

She flashed him a sweet smile, grateful for his gesture. It showed a level of compassion and friendship that would remain no matter where she ended up. That alone was an improvement from where they were when she'd first arrived.

It was better than nothing.

"He's got some nerve showing up here with his new girlfriend, acting like he's all that matters. You deserve better. I'd be happy to talk to his attorney and set the record straight. Whatever you need."

"I appreciate that, but I need to handle this on my own."

He set his jaw in a hard line. She knew it wasn't easy for him not to jump in and fight for what he believed was fair. He always stood up for the people he cared about. At least she was one of those again.

"You know I'll respect your wishes. Now, back to what I was trying to say earlier."

She waved her hands in the air, ready to let him off the hook from explaining why they could only be friends. She knew that but hearing it from his lips stung. She'd rather walk away with an understanding that didn't require words.

He grabbed both of her hands in one of his, gently holding them as he moved closer. When she opened her mouth to speak, he placed a timid finger on her lips. His touch sent a wave of electricity that could take out a small town.

"Let me finish. Please."

She nodded, her gaze lost in his.

"What happened to Summer the other day was upsetting, but it wasn't your fault. Kids can be cruel. It stinks, but it's also a part of life. She adores you and she understands that you had no control over Camera Guy."

"But—" she managed to mumble before he interrupted.

"This will all pass, Hannah. It might not feel like it right now because you're in the thick of it, but it will go away eventually. And when it does, you'll see I'm still here. I adore you, too. The last thing I want is to lose you a second time."

The entire world except for Callan disappeared. All she could see was him, all she could hear was him, all she could *feel* was him, his finger slipping from her lips to the bottom of her chin where he tipped her head up.

"Being just friends with you is impossible, Hannah Whitmore."

His lips pressed against hers, moving slowly in gentle strokes that held the promise of two souls coming together as one.

She fell into the kiss, letting it take over every thought, every doubt that had surfaced in recent days.

He wanted her.

He *loved* her.

Every ounce of her filled with overwhelming joy.

Callan Locke was the only man she ever wanted to kiss.

When they finally pulled apart, she snuggled into his chest. Her favorite place to be. She still had a fight in front of her where Luke was concerned, but she had an idea. One that might appeal to both of them.

27

———————

At first, she was going to call Luke, but doubting he'd answer if he saw her name she decided to text him instead. That way he'd get the message whether he wanted to or not.

When he didn't respond right away, she grew concerned. She had one chance to get this right. Luke had a private jet at his disposal. He might have already left town. If so, then any hope she'd had the day before would vanish in an instant.

After what seemed like an eternity but was more like ten minutes, he answered.

I'll meet you in an hour.

She bounced on her toes. Maybe she'd finally reached through to the man she'd first met all those years ago. She responded with *Thank you. See you in an hour.* Short and polite. It was all that needed to be said.

HANNAH ENTERED CAFÉ DES AMIS, the lunch crowd winding down in the charming café with mid-afternoon approaching. The aroma of fresh-baked cookies wafted through the air, making her mouth water. She made a mental note to order a half dozen before she left.

After the young guy at the front counter welcomed her, she found her way to a table for two by the front window. Luke hadn't arrived yet. To be fair, she was early. She'd requested this meeting, and more so she wanted to show him a level of respect could exist between them even with them going their separate ways.

Both wanted to move on with their lives. That much was obvious. There was no need for their divorce to continue down a nasty, hateful path. That kind of behavior served no one.

The bell over the door jingled and Hannah glanced up to see Luke enter. Alone. He'd respected her wishes, which was a good sign. A compromise could only happen if both parties were willing.

He gave her a curt nod as he took a seat across from her. "Your text sounded urgent. I hope you're finally ready to sign off on everything and be done with all this."

She kept her hands folded on the table, a way to steady herself. A level head and friendly tone would go a long way in keeping control of this conversation.

"I am, but I wanted to talk to you first."

Skepticism was clear in the tilt of his brow. However, she didn't waver.

"Luke, I know things changed between us over the years. We drifted apart in some ways. I see that now. I'm still trying to figure out my part in it, but one thing I do know is that this whole thing has gotten out of hand."

He ran his hand over the top of his short-cropped hair, clearly frustrated.

She leaned in, her eyes focused on his.

"I want you to be happy. You're about to be a dad. That's huge. All this fighting and name-calling isn't getting either of us anywhere. I have no interest in taking all your money or making life difficult for you. All I want is what's fair so I can start over."

He massaged his temples, then propped his elbows on the table, his chin resting on his folded hands.

"I never meant for any of this to happen, Hannah." His usual clipped tone was quieter, reserved. "Not with Claire. Not with our divorce. Not with any of it."

He sat back with a sigh.

Hearing his girlfriend's name roll off his lips didn't upset her like it used to. Maybe she was getting over the heavy crush of it all. Healing was a process. It took time and dedication and a person willing to let go of past hurt.

Since arriving in Falls Hollow, the comfort of this tiny town she once called home had wrapped her in a snug embrace, the promise of a better tomorrow only a breath away. She'd changed, made tiny steps in a new direction. The weight of the unknown had started to lift.

"Remember when we first met?" he asked.

"I do. It was at my friend's birthday party, and you told me if I gave you a chance, you'd show me the world. And you did."

It was the first time in a long time that the memory bubbled to the surface on a cloud of fondness. Luke had been all sharp wit and ambitious charm with a killer smile she couldn't resist. He was that guy you had to get to know. From there, everything unfolded at a rapid pace—relationship, marriage, buying their dream house. She realized now it was a relationship that was meant to happen. It just wasn't meant to last forever.

In a lot of ways, she became the person she was destined to be because of him. In their time together she discovered her love of creating beautiful things, of cooking and gardening and entertaining, of growing into the woman who appreciated the beauty in simplicity, in the extra touch to make someone's day.

"We had some good times, didn't we?" A genuine smile graced his lips and the sight of it gave her hope.

"Yeah, we did."

He leaned forward, his arms folded on the table. "I'm sorry, Hannah. That's something I should have said a long time ago."

"You're saying it now. That counts." She reached across the table and put her hand on his forearm, giving it a little squeeze.

He responded, placing his hand on top of hers and doing the same.

"I should have talked to you when things started feeling off. Instead, I buried myself in my work and the lifestyle that went with it. That wasn't fair to you."

"Thank you for telling me now. I know things changed, although I can't say whose feelings started to shift first. Maybe it all happened at the same time."

"Maybe. But that was no excuse for my behavior. Please believe me when I say I never meant to get involved with Claire. It just sort of happened. My fault. I let it."

He raised his hand accepting responsibility for his actions. The first and only time he'd done so.

It was enough. Forgiveness wasn't an easy task, but when one truly cared about others as well as themself, they found a way to dig deep and offer someone grace.

A bolt unlocked in her chest and relief poured through.

"The last thing I wanted to do was hurt you, yet I couldn't bring myself to tell you what was going on with me. Maybe because I didn't fully understand it myself. I mean how do you articulate that something's changed, that a whole relationship is no longer what it used to be? It's an ambiguous feeling, a change in dynamics. I don't know."

It was odd to see him struggling to find the right words. Luke was never at a loss for what to say.

"I get it. We fell in love, but our trajectory from meeting to marriage was fast. Once the dust cleared and we settled into our life together, I believe we grew along different paths.

"We were also young. I don't think either one of us fully understood who we were yet, and by the time we figured it out we'd been living different lives in a way. I'm just as guilty for not speaking up. It was easier to go along with the status quo than to face something uncomfortable."

Months of stress rolled away the more they talked. Things were clearer in hindsight. They were two people who'd had a whirlwind of a relationship, and neither had known when to draw the line. Life wasn't perfect, but if you looked closely enough you could always find good with the bad. And she and Luke had experienced good times, too.

"You deserve half of the house, and I'll personally put a stop to all the awful things that were said about you. We both have a second chance in front of us. Let's not waste it."

He put out his hand, palm up, and she placed hers in his.

"I want you to be happy, too. This life suits you, you know." He glanced around the café acknowledging their surroundings.

"It does, doesn't it?" She slid her hand from his and folded it in her lap.

She'd reached the man she'd first known, her whole reason for asking him to meet her in person, just the two of them. A fragment of the connection she'd believed forever lost was still there. Relief over finding common ground with Luke soared through her. A new day was dawning, a new path unfurling beneath her anxious feet.

"I'll tell my attorney to cite irreconcilable differences and make sure you get half of our home's value, and then I'll reach out to the press myself and fix this mess."

"Thank you, Luke. I'm going to reach out and do the same. If we let the world know we're parting as friends, the press will disappear."

"Yes, it will."

"For what it's worth, I think you'll make a great dad if you allow yourself the chance."

Luke was driven, but he was also hard on himself. A not so unusual trait for such an ambitious person. Discipline started from within, and he expected a lot from himself. Being a good parent meant time and patience, and accepting the fact that you wouldn't always get it right.

"I plan on embracing this next chapter full force." He flashed her a hearty grin before sobering. "If you ever need anything, don't hesitate to reach out. I want the best for you, Hannah."

An idea bloomed. One that required a special touch, and Luke held the golden hand.

"I want the same for you. And on that note, I do have one request."

28

D awn broke across the early autumn sky in bands of muted gold. Hannah reclined in one of the chairs on the front porch, feet propped up on the railing while she sipped her coffee. Rich notes of hazelnut rose to the surface of the bold blend. Her favorite.

Her last day at the winery, although bittersweet, had opened a door between her and Callan she'd feared was forever closed. Thinking back to their kiss, the way he'd stood up for her to Luke, settled into her bones with a comforting caress.

A second chance with the boy she'd loved long ago was real. That made today's sunrise even sweeter.

Pulling on her jeans and a silky navy-blue blouse, she decided to drop by the winery to show Lizzy her bath salt creations. A bevy of new ideas sat in the notes on her phone. From bath salt mixtures to fruit spreads to a variety of dishes to try, she'd jotted them all down with fervor, ready to dig her hands into creating the perfect items to add to her brand.

On the business side, she had a lot to do. She'd yet to

come up with the perfect name for her company. That would set the tone, so it needed to convey the right message. Even if she used her own name in the title, it would have to be in a way that made sense. After that, she'd need to set up an LLC, get a tax ID number, open a bank account—the list was long. It would be a lot of work, but the thrill of building something of her own from the ground up consumed her. This was her moment.

The winery buzzed with customers when she arrived. More than usual. She waved at Jen who was behind the counter taking care of the line snaking its way toward her. Callan would be pleased to see all the activity—wherever he was.

"Hannah! I was hoping you'd come by." Lizzy approached and pulled her in for one of her big bear hugs, reaching around the large basket Hannah held in her hands.

"Hey! I have something I want to show you." Hannah pulled one of the jars of bath salts out of the basket. "Smell this and tell me what you think."

She handed the jar to Lizzy, curious to see her reaction.

Lizzy opened the top and took a whiff of the contents. Her eyes rounded. "This smells amazing. What is it?"

"That's my rose petal bath salt. Think luxury meets summertime in a hot bath soak."

"I could swim in this," Lizzy enthused.

Hannah lit up. "I'm so glad you like it. I have three other blends in here and I'd love to get your opinion on them."

"Does this mean what I think it means?"

"If you think I've decided to start my own lifestyle brand, then yes. It's what you think it means." Hannah laughed, joy emanating from every inch of her.

Saying it out loud somehow made it more real.

"That's wonderful!" Lizzy's enthusiasm buoyed Hannah's spirit.

Having someone so supportive and encouraging rejuvenated her soul in a million ways. A real friendship was growing between her and Lizzy. Something she hadn't experienced in a long time.

"Want to come over later for some cheese and crackers and a glass of wine?"

Hannah hadn't invited anyone over, one on one, in ages. Outside of hosting large gatherings, she hadn't cultivated a true friendship with any one person since graduating from college. There were neighbors and colleagues, acquaintances and circles of friends she and Luke interacted with, but her last real friends had been her college friends, and they'd grown apart over the years, life taking them in different directions.

Her post-college life had been big and beautiful, but it had lacked intimacy. Something she hadn't realized how much she craved until now.

It was easy for life to feel full when you stayed busy, but it was in those quiet moments when you had time to reflect and ponder if the fullness was real, or if it was merely a schedule littered with appointments and activities. In retrospect, she knew the answer.

"I'd love to. Maybe I can convince you to stick around a while, maybe even help out here on occasion. Our marketing efforts are starting to pay off. Bookings for tours and tastings have increased."

Lizzy bit her bottom lip, a sparkle of hope spreading across her features.

"That's awesome!" Hannah was thrilled to hear they were experiencing an uptick in business. Hillcrest Vines Family Vineyards was a special place. She hoped many more people would discover it. "My time here has been exactly what I needed, so thank you for that. But Roberta is back. You don't need me anymore."

Lizzy swiveled to peer at a woman fussing over a display several feet away. "Roberta loved what you did while she was out."

Roberta glanced their way and waved. Curly hair framed her round face, a broad toothy grin gracing her cheeks.

Hannah waved back, glad to finally put a face with the name. "I think you're in good hands."

"We're fortunate. We have an amazing team."

"So, tonight? Around seven?"

Lizzy reached for another jar of Hannah's bath salt. "That sounds perfect. And whenever you get your line up and running, I'd love to carry your products here."

She waggled the jar from side to side.

Hannah bounced on her toes, giddy. "Absolutely! I'd love that."

"Cool. See you tonight." With that, Lizzy turned and headed toward Roberta, holding up the two jars of bath salts to show her employee.

As Hannah turned to approach the front counter where Jen was busy bagging up customers' purchases, Callan entered from the back entrance. He appeared lost in thought, eyes cast down, not noticing her as he headed toward the counter. When he finally looked up, he caught sight of her and a mischievous glint took over his gaze.

"Fancy seeing you here. I figured you'd enjoy sleeping in this morning now that Roberta's back."

"I'm not exactly the sleeping-in type." She chuckled.

His demeanor turned serious. "Have you heard any more from Luke?"

He leaned one hand on the counter while sliding the other in his front pocket.

"About that." She faced Jen. "Can I stick this behind the counter for a minute?"

"Sure." Jen took the basket from her and placed it underneath the counter.

"Thanks," Hannah said before turning back toward Callan.

His phone rang. When he looked at the screen, curiosity took hold.

"Hold that thought. I need to answer this."

She nodded as he stepped away to take the call. It didn't take long for him to wrap up the conversation, but he appeared dazed when he walked back over.

"That was the festival director. He said I can submit a late admission if I send all the details of my entry by tomorrow. Something about a friend calling in a favor."

She bit her bottom lip, fighting back a smile.

"As I was about to say, I need to catch you up to speed."

He suggested they take their conversation outside to the picnic table behind the building. Sitting across from one another, Hannah propped her forearms on the table ready to share all that happened between her and Luke's compromise.

"I'm happy y'all found some middle ground, but I don't know how comfortable I am having a favor called in by him."

He didn't look as enthused as she'd hoped he'd be.

She reached for his hands, cupping them in hers. "When I found out who the festival director was and that I knew him and his wife through Luke, I had to ask. Your wine deserves a chance to be showcased as soon as possible."

He shifted in his seat, shoulders tense.

"This whole divorce nightmare is finally settling down. Luke and I are both moving on. Amicably. Honestly, we both realized we were growing apart for a long time, even if we didn't understand it in the moment."

"I'm happy for you, Hannah." He squeezed her hands, relief spreading across his features like the rays of early morning light.

His demeanor shifted, relaxed.

"It would be great to get our wine into this festival."

"Send in your entry. Let people rediscover your wine and this place."

She soaked in the beauty of the winery, of the vineyard spread across the rolling fields in trellises wrapped in luscious grapes. Callan's family's vineyard was special. Spreading the word about Hillcrest Vines Family Vineyards had become important to her, not just because of Callan and his family, although reconnecting with all of them had been the best surprise of all, but their vineyard was a part of this community she once called home. A place she grew more attached to by the day.

"I think this calls for a celebration." He tugged her up from the bench and encircled his taut arms around her waist, pulling her close.

Plenty of yesterdays sat in his gaze, but the tomorrows were dawning in visions of love and home in ways Hannah hadn't dreamed of in a long time.

"What do you have in mind?" she asked as she nuzzled in closer.

"I'm thinking a picnic by the lake in our special spot with some take-out and a bottle of wine. Maybe a couple of lemon lavender cupcakes from Café des Amis for dessert."

"Mm, that sounds perfect." She tilted her head up inviting him with one look.

He leaned in to answer when a voice rang out.

"Ooh, are y'all going to kiss?"

Both jerked back at the jest in Summer's voice.

"Aren't you supposed to be helping Bitty with inventory?"

Summer giggled at her dad's question, unable to contain herself. Connie walked up behind her.

"Sorry, you two. This one got away from me." She placed a protective arm around her granddaughter and gently nudged her toward the back entryway.

"It's okay, Mom. We were just talking about having a picnic. What do you think, squirt?"

Summer gasped. "I love picnics!"

She pulled away from her grandmother and rushed over to Callan, dimples blazing.

"My Aunt Lizzy said you're starting your own business. Are you going to open a store in Falls Hollow?" Summer looked up at Hannah with a gleam in her eyes.

Fondness for the little girl rose in Hannah. While she hadn't voiced out loud her desire to stay in this tiny town, the thought of finding somewhere new to settle down no longer felt right.

"I don't know about a store, but I suppose I'll need office space. Maybe somewhere in town. You could help me check out a few places."

Summer clenched her fists together in excitement. "Okay."

"Come on, sweetheart. Let's go finish the inventory." Connie reached out her hand and Summer clasped it, content to run along now that she had time with her dad and Hannah on the calendar.

"I'll be back when we're finished." She assured them.

Both chuckled at her eagerness. Hannah especially liked the fact that Summer had welcomed her into her life like Callan had. Reuniting with the boy she'd left behind meant more now that he was a single dad, and Hannah thrilled at the chance to join their world.

Alone again, she wrapped her arms around Callan's neck. "I believe we were planning a picnic."

"Actually, we were done talking."

He closed the gap between them and pressed his lips on hers. Starry nights and fireflies and days packed with the sweetest contentment filled his kisses. Hannah's mind buzzed with days of busy work building her business from the ground up, and nights of sweet bliss spending time with Callan and Summer, finding their groove as they moved down this new path laid before them. One she couldn't have dreamed into existence any better.

Sometimes falling in love was sweeter the second time around.

EPILOGUE

NOVEMBER – ONE MONTH LATER

Tourists and townsfolk alike spread out around the field where the Fredericksburg Wine Festival was being held. Tents with wine tastings, food, and all kinds of local vendors displaying their wares dotted the perimeter.

Hannah helped man the tent where Lizzy and Roberta had set up Hillcrest Vines Family Vineyards' display and tasting. She mingled with curious festivalgoers who were eager to learn more. Fielding questions, offering small cups to taste the wine, even starting a waiting list for those wanting to schedule a tour and tasting at the winery filled the time.

She was happy to help. Mostly, she was thrilled to see the lavender infused sauvignon blanc she and Callan had created earn top honors. Watching pride swell in his chest over the accomplishment gave her such joy.

His family's wine was delicious. It deserved the recognition and the chance to grow.

With the lavender fusion going on the market next to their original sauvignon blanc, Callan had reached out to a distributor to increase their reach across the state. He'd even mapped out a long-term plan of taking their wine to the regional level and beyond. It was a long road of work in front of him, but he was jazzed to take the business to the next level.

"I can't believe I've had to get Brian to restock the table twice. Good thing I had him pack extra bottles just in case." Lizzy stacked another column of tasting cups on the back corner of the table, her energy buzzing with her fast movements.

"This festival brings in a larger crowd than I expected. It's great!" Hannah took a few cups from the stack and placed them in a row in front of the bottles of wine.

On one side of the table there were bottles of the regular wine and on the other side were bottles of the lavender infusion. In the middle was a wooden stand with a framed picture of the vineyard. It was one of the shots Hannah had taken. Informational brochures were stacked in front.

"Next year you can set up a tent of your own." Lizzy nudged Hannah's arm with a friendly wink.

The idea that her business would be launched by then, ready for customers, dizzied her thoughts. She'd spent the last month setting up the infrastructure for her business, such as the name, LLC, tax ID, and bank account. She'd also decided on which products she'd start with and how she'd ramp up over the next several months to add additional items.

The longer part was figuring out packaging, especially since she still hadn't decided on a logo or brand look for her products yet. Ordering ingredients, finding office space to lease that would accommodate an area to create her products, and securing a long-term rental where she could live were on her laundry list of things to do. Although that last item had been recently checked off. Callan offered the bungalow as a place for her to stay until she found what she wanted.

How could she refuse?

"I'm so glad business has picked up for y'all," Hannah said.

"Girl, our bookings for tastings and tours have almost doubled. I've bumped Jen up to more hours each week, which she wanted, and I've hired another full-time employee. I'm so glad I listened to you and increased our marketing efforts. I should have done that a long time ago."

"Better late than never," Hannah joked.

But in all seriousness, she was glad she'd been able to help in some small way. Callan's family was amazing. The way they'd welcomed her back to Falls Hollow, and back to them, reminded her of the importance of community, of friends and connection and surrounding oneself with the people that mattered the most. Even her parents were excited to come visit and cheered her on with her new venture.

"Can I steal you for a break, Miss Whitmore?" Callan walked up to the tent, a teasing twinkle in his eye.

Summer was right beside him. Sporting a cute red dress with cowboy boots and her own personalized Hillcrest Vines Family Vineyards' apron over her outfit, she played the part of a mini-Callan with a clipboard clutched in her hands.

"You can have her for five minutes. No more. We're

busy." Lizzy pointed an accusing finger at her brother, a playful smirk spreading across her face.

Without hesitating, Callan grabbed Hannah's hand and whisked her away, leading her along until they ended up in the parking lot by his truck.

"What's going on? Hannah asked, unsure why both Callan and Summer looked like they were hiding a secret.

"We have something to show you," Callan said as he let down the tailgate of his truck. He picked Summer up and placed her in the bed of the truck. "Whenever you're ready, squirt."

Summer cleared her throat, then squared her shoulders. Hannah marveled at the resemblance between the little girl and her dad. Not just physically, but the way she carried herself in bold, confident strokes was so much like Callan. It was adorable.

"My dad and I have been working on a special project. We wanted to help you the way you've helped us, and since you decided on a name for your business, we came up with an idea for a logo and labels you can use. If you want."

The way Summer spoke so thoughtfully, so grown-up, tickled Hannah. However, when she pulled out the papers from her clipboard and held them out for her to see, Hannah choked back a sniffle at the images gracing the sheet.

Her initials *HW* connected diagonally, sprawled out in an elegant cursive flourish in a deep shade of plum. The logo captured the simplicity of using her initials as the name of the company, paired with a graceful style. It evoked opulence without being over the top. Printed on ivory parchment paper added the perfect touch. All the elements came together to create something more beautiful than Hannah herself had dreamed.

She covered her mouth with her hands, overwhelmed by their gesture. "I can't believe y'all did all this."

"We can't take all the credit. We had help. I hired a graphic designer, who was really good at taking our ideas and mixing them with her own suggestions."

He wrapped his arm around her shoulders. "What do you think? We can tweak the style and color, or anything you want to change to make it how you want."

Shaking her head, she lowered her hands. "It's perfect."

"The *HW* brand is born." He high-fived his daughter.

Hannah reached in and wrapped Summer into a hug. "Thank you, Summer. I love it."

She picked the little girl up and tucked her on her hip. Happy tears spilled down her cheeks and she didn't bother to wipe them away.

Callan embraced them both in his arms. "I think this calls for a celebration. How about I cook dinner for everyone tonight?"

Hannah's gaze darted toward Summer whose eyes rounded.

"What? I can cook," Callan huffed.

"You can," Hannah agreed. "But maybe we can try something new tonight."

Summer nodded vigorously. "Yes, please."

Callan told Hannah early on that he kept five meals on rotation. In the last month they'd spent together, she'd enjoyed those same meals on repeat. They were good, but burnout had crept in. Given how Summer grew up on those meals, she could only imagine her desire to try some new dishes.

"How about I make a new dish I've been wanting to try? Summer, you can be my sous chef." Hannah put Summer down but kept her little hand snug in hers.

Over the past several weeks, she'd grown closer to Callan's daughter, much to his and her joy.

Summer was a kindhearted young girl with a big personality. Hannah might not have had a child of her own yet, but Summer was fast becoming like a daughter to her.

"What's a sous chef?" Summer scrunched her nose in confusion.

"It means you get to help Hannah cook, squirt." Callan ruffled her hair.

"Yay! I'm going to go tell Bitty and Pop."

She whirled around and took off back toward the festival entrance.

"Finally. I get you all to myself." He pulled Hannah into a tight embrace, his forehead bent down touching hers.

Hannah giggled. "There's nowhere else I'd rather be."

"Good, because I'm never letting you go." His lips crushed hers and she melted underneath his touch.

Coming back to Falls Hollow had been unplanned. Reconnecting with Callan was unexpected. So much had changed since she'd arrived almost two months ago. Challenges and changes, questions and hard-won answers filled her days. But she'd discovered peace and happiness that soothed her soul.

The empty ache was gone, replaced with a fullness words couldn't describe, and finding love again with the boy she'd lost so many years ago was a gift from above.

With the aftermath of her divorce behind her and an unwritten future in front of her, the whole world had opened in ways she'd never seen coming. This detour had become the greatest adventure of all.

A NOTE FROM COLLETTE

Hi!

Thank you so much for picking up my novel, *Falling with You.* I hope it whisked you away to picturesque Texas Hill Country and wrapped you up in a cozy hug. Mostly, I hope it reminded you of the power of true love.

If you'd like to know when my next book is coming out, you can sign up for my newsletter on my website:

www.jcollettesmith.com

It's the best way to keep up with my latest releases, bonus content, and giveaways, and I won't share your information with anyone.

If you enjoyed *Falling with You,* please consider posting a review online. Getting feedback from readers helps others discover my books, and it would mean the world to me.

Happy reading!
Collette

ACKNOWLEDGMENTS

First and foremost, I want to thank my family. For my husband, who supports my writing ventures, and my two sons, who make my life so full and happy, I'm eternally grateful to call you mine. You're the ones who keep me going and keep me inspired every day. And a special thank you to my granddaughter, AKA Hotshot, for being the most amazing little human on the planet.

I want to give a big shoutout to my amazing beta reader and writing friend: Laura Luna. Thank you for taking the time to read my work, share your thoughts, offer suggestions, and encourage me to dig deeper. Your feedback is always on point and has helped my writing grow.

I'd also like to say thank you to my editor, Cortney Pearson. Your attention to detail, thoughtful notes, and kind words helped make my story stronger. Thank you!

To my amazing cover designer, Evelyne Labelle (Carpe Librum Book Design), thank you for creating another gorgeous cover and bringing this next book in the Falls Hollow series to life.

To the place I once called home. The place that inspired this series: Austin, Texas. A city with an eclectic vibe and neighborly love where sunsets streak the sky in buttery gold. A place where keeping it weird is the highest compliment. Stay true to your roots, Austin.

And to you, my dear readers, none of this would be

possible without you. Thank you for reading and sharing and loving my stories. There's nothing like putting your words out there and having someone connect with them. It's the best feeling! Thank you for taking a chance on me. My gratitude runs deep.

ABOUT THE AUTHOR

Collette is a romance and fantasy author who grew up reading fantastical tales filled with happily-ever-afters. She turned her love of reading into a love of writing and now spends her time creating stories of her own.

When she's not writing, you can find her hanging out with her family, dreaming of travel destinations to add to her must-see list, or curled up with a good book.

ALSO BY J. COLLETTE SMITH

Also by J. Collette Smith

Romance novels

Falls Hollow series:

Summer of Sunsets

Standalone YA Fantasy novels

Ruin of Gods

A Knot of Lies and Rebellion

www.ingramcontent.com/pod-product-compliance
Lightning Source LLC
Chambersburg PA
CBHW020333180726
47991CB00020B/1561